WICKED FIRE

ANGEL FIRE, BOOK 2

MARIE JOHNSTON

Jagger Hancock is a fearsome warrior for the angelic realm, slaying demons left and right on Earth and protecting the human race. But when a powerful senator is murdered, he's reduced to acting as a bodyguard for the grieving daughter. Too bad she's the same female who ruined his one and only chance at happiness.

Felicia Montclaire looks as angelic as the rest of her kind, but she hides her scars well. Yet the male who gave them to her is not just after her again, but seeking conquest over the entire realm too. While her life goes up in flames once more, the last thing she needs is a cranky bodyguard…even if he's the only one who can keep her alive.

Jagger and Felicia might not survive each other, much less the constant attacks from their enemies. But when danger drives them back to the angelic realm, they'll discover their past is waiting for them—and it's far more dangerous than anything on Earth.

CHAPTER 1

"The team needs me." Julian Hancock, or Jagger to everyone but his mother, managed not to sound pleading as he addressed his former team leader. Bryant Vale was the warrior director now and less interested in hearing his arguments. "With you off the team and no replacement yet, my place is here."

Jagger should be in his typical uniform of black tactical pants and a long-sleeved black shirt specially designed to fit around his wings. It seemed sacrilegious to sit in his boss's office wearing a blue T-shirt and a pair of black athletic shorts. But it was necessary for his latest assignment.

He couldn't take another day shadowing Felicia fucking Montclaire. She was in some danger he only knew vague details about and she'd demanded him as her bodyguard. *Demanded.* Like the spoiled priss she was.

Spoiled and superficial and haughty...and strong and gorgeous and willowy. Her legs went for miles and haunted his dreams.

He clenched his jaw and steadied his gaze on his new director. Felicia Montclaire was only an obstacle to what he really wanted. Someday, he'd have his own team to lead and he couldn't do that stuck among humans, babysitting the aimless daughter of a senator.

A flash of guilt flared. Felicia was still technically a senator's daughter, but her father had been murdered a couple of months ago. She'd weathered the news well, but then he hadn't expected her to get weepy or be derailed by her grief. He hadn't expected her to show any feeling at all. And he'd been right.

His director, Bryant Vale, was as expressionless as a wall. A dark, glaring wall. "I understand your complications with Ms. Montclaire—"

"Forget our history," Jagger gritted out.

He hated that anyone knew the story between him and the vexing angel he was protecting. Or rather, the lack of a story, the result of *Ms. Montclaire* not setting the record straight and letting everyone think he was a cheating asshole.

"The team needs me." He said it as much for himself as to make a point. "If Felicia truly requires protection, then she should stay in the realm, in a designated home, with a designated guard."

Director Vale's demeanor had hardened as soon as Jagger had cut him off. Damn. Jagger had meant to use a lighter touch, not charge in like a bull at his first sight of red. "Sit down."

Jagger took his time selecting the backless seat across from the obnoxiously large mahogany desk. He draped his wings over the edge but couldn't force them to relax. "Director Vale—"

"Shut it." You could take the warrior off the team, but you couldn't soften his personality. Director Vale leaned across the desk, his eyes blazing. "I can't believe you're dense enough to think that Felicia is safer here. She can help identify her attacker and lead us to the people behind the conspiracy against this realm. The ones who could tell us just what this conspiracy entails. Have a think on it."

Jagger refused to drop his gaze, and that was a harder challenge than most when Director Vale was pissed. The scars encompassing half the male's face didn't make him easy to look at on most days.

The director wasn't finished. "Her family's mansion was burned to the ground by angel fire while over half our team was inside. While *my mate* was inside. Director Richter—" His gaze cut away. Leo Richter was no longer the director. He'd lost both legs at the knee thanks to the fire and was still recovering. "Felicia can hide among the humans better than in our realm. Numen isn't safe for her. And do I need to go into the main reason why you shouldn't be tied to the investigation, why you're too close to the case?"

Jagger's teeth should've cracked under the pressure of his jaw. His father, James Hancock.

His good-for-nothing, cheating father, who'd risked their entire race by spilling the news of their existence to his human side piece. His father, who'd had several human side pieces, and probably a few angelic ones, while he'd had a committed mate.

His father, who'd had his wings taken, been declared a fallen, and tossed out of the realm forever.

His father, who was working with the creatures of Daemon to take over Numen, the realm where his own son resided. If he were a weaker male, he'd feel like his father had chosen the demons of Daemon not only over the angels of Numen, but over him too. Now the man would work with anyone or anything if it served his agenda. Archmasters, symasters, sylphs—the new "Jameson Haddock" didn't seem to discriminate.

But then if Jagger had ever meant a damn thing to his

father, then perhaps Jameson would still be an esteemed senator of Numen.

Not that his father's multilayered betrayal affected him.

He kept his voice even. "Our team is two short. Dionna took over as leader, but we no longer have you, and with me tied up…" Literally, if Felicia had her way.

His team was everything to him. Having lost his father so young, and his mother… Well, Chanel Hancock wasn't known for her nurturing nature. She'd turned twice as cold and ten times harder than marble after what she referred to as "your father's unfortunate choices."

"I understand." Director Vale sat back. "But they aren't functioning as a traditional warrior team, not until this is over. They—*you*—are under my personal direction. You're the only ones I completely trust now."

The director's unwavering trust mollified him. For now. He'd grown up getting side-eyed by his peers, as if they wondered when he'd follow in his father's footsteps. And then he'd weathered the Felicia storm, which had broken the trust of the one most dear to him. Without those experiences, Director Vale's words wouldn't have meant as much.

To still have Bryant Vale in his corner after they'd learned his own exiled father was the one behind the trouble in the realm was humbling.

And he needed to make sure he continued to earn it.

Even if he had to deal with the fallout of the maelstrom that Felicia Montclaire brought to his life.

"HE's in there right now, asking to be rid of me." Felicia sipped her sparkling water from a crystal goblet. She wasn't allowed to go anywhere by herself, but at least she had a few moments with her sister.

She'd rather have this conversation in private, but Bryant had hired an administrative assistant. Odessa had kept bugging him to get help so he wouldn't be so cranky after a day of penning scrolls for the senate to review.

The new girl—Tina? Tera? Tenley, that was it—sat at a large desk surrounded by stacks of scrolls and training charts. Bryant had redesigned his office to make room for an assistant, giving himself a smaller and more secluded office with Tenley acting as gatekeeper. Felicia sat with Odessa in chairs placed as far across the room from Tenley's desk and as physically close to the door to the hallway as possible. Bryant wasn't the only one who liked his solitude.

"He is not asking to be rid of you." Odessa chewed her lip. "No, you're probably right. But in all fairness, you haven't told him the reason why you're in this position. None of it is your fault."

"I know." Felicia lowered her voice so only Odessa could hear. "But I shouldn't need to suffer all over again while a noble warrior treats me like a hussy who can't restrain herself."

Odessa's mouth twisted as she tried to hold back a smile. "In all fairness," she repeated, "you go out of your way to make him think you're a hussy who can't restrain herself."

"And he buys into it so easily," Felicia hissed. "Ass."

"What would you do if he didn't?"

Felicia huffed but had to look away. What would she do if the sexiest male she'd ever met looked at her with less disdain and more respect? What would she do if that male thought she might be worth more than the lint that collected under his wings?

On the subject of wings, she involuntarily stiffened. Odessa, bless her golden heart, thought it meant that she'd crossed the line.

Her sister laid a hand on her arm. "Sorry. He shouldn't treat you like he does, regardless."

Felicia patted Odessa's hand and stood to pace. Restless energy had filled her ever since she could remember. Add in her traumatic past and that made lying down to sleep troublesome.

"No, I agree with you on both accounts. As for your question, he'll never treat me like an equal, so it's not something I have to ponder."

She still remembered the words he'd hurled at her when she'd refused to shout from the rooftops that she hadn't slept with him.

It's ridiculous, all this. As if someone like me could ever be interested in someone like you. You're so deceitful, you won't even unfurl your wings. Too afraid we'll see that they're as black as your heart?

A lump formed in her throat.

No, she'd never confessed that they hadn't slept together. Because she'd never claimed that they had. Someone else had spread the word that she'd messed around with him. And since she had a reputation, the lie had been accepted without doubt.

Her kind might not be divine angels, but they liked to pretend that they were—unless gossip was involved.

She hated this whole realm. Almost as much as she missed it.

Bryant's office door flung open behind her. Felicia forced herself to turn around, her brow raised in polite question. And Jagger would damn well know that she was mocking him. He hadn't made it a secret that he'd come here to be rid of her.

And she couldn't blame him. Half the time, she didn't want to be around herself either.

Her right shoulder blade tinged. She flexed the muscles

and prevented the pain from showing on her face. Her kind could morph their wings, unfurling them at will or furling them into their backs and hiding them from view. The morph used to take nothing more than a thought. Now it took so much concentration—and was extremely painful. She should be accustomed to this routine by now, but keeping her wings hidden in public for long stretches of time was still uncomfortable eleven years later.

Angels had to do it when they were working among humans, and since she lived in the same realm as humans, most didn't question it the few times she came back home. The constant morph of her wings added to her aloofness and fueled the lies about her.

He bowed his head to Odessa, probably wondering why Felicia couldn't be more like her sister. Kind. Considerate. Serene. Odessa in the long, traditional white robe, with her perfect downy wings and her admirable job as an analyst for the realm.

Felicia was wearing shorts that rode so high, her ass cheeks were almost hanging out. Almost. Because this brand was excellent at concealing her privates while allowing for maximum height on her kicks. The krav maga gym she worked at didn't care that she showed more than a little leg. They were more worried about self-defense and mastering self-control. The gym owner had once told her that she should be able to walk in nude and still be safe in his domain.

At least she'd thrown a white tank top on over her neon pink sports bra before coming to this meeting with Bryant.

She had no trouble thinking of Bryant as her brother. He was Odessa's mate and one of the few beings alive who knew of her past. He was also one of the few of her kind who treated her like she was worthy of his respect. So, dammit, she'd make sure she was. Of Bryant's, anyway. Jagger could kiss his own ass.

To get her mind off her own problems, she looked at the studious new assistant. "How are you liking the new job?"

Tenley smiled. She looked young, like the rest of the realm, but her luminous brown eyes were more world-weary than innocent. "It's such a nice change from my work at the archives." Her smile was warm. "I rather like creating the records instead of sorting them."

Odessa sent the young female a fond smile. "She's even excited about hunting a box of missing vials."

Tenley's head bobbed, her eyes lighting up. "A real-life mystery. An entire shipment. But I'll find it and get the warriors their ration of angel fire as soon as possible."

A pang of envy came and went. It must be nice to be useful. But Felicia would keep creating her own usefulness, even if wasn't in this realm.

"Let's go," Jagger said curtly, whipping open the door to the hallway. His surfer-blond hair hung over one eye. When it wasn't slicked back it reached down to his chin. Why did he have to look so fine? He gave her an expectant stare.

Right. That meant she would take her time. "Odessa, when are you coming to visit next?"

Odessa wasn't stupid, but she was discreet. After shooting Felicia a droll look, her expression turned thoughtful. "I'm not sure. They offered me Cal's position and I'm thinking of taking it, since Millie is shunning all my offers of help with Director Richter—I mean, Leo."

Bryant came out of the office, shuttering a hard stare toward Jagger. Felicia didn't bother to look at her guardian even though his impatience would be so satisfying.

Bryant crossed to Odessa's side and another pang of envy hit. The two were so stupid in love—and newly mated. At the thought of mating, a wave of panic rolled through her, leaving her feeling itchy. Syncing to another being only meant heartbreak worse than one could imagine. She'd seen it too often.

"Not referring to Leo as Director is a hard task," Bryant said. "And I rather like how Odessa being offered a supervisory position is making certain members of the realm nervous."

Odessa grinned. "And he likes how it'd give me unfettered access to Numen's surveillance records."

Apparently today was the afternoon for feeling jealous. Theme of the day: green. Odessa's job was admirable. Only highly intelligent angels could be analysts. They sifted and combed through the records watchers made of human activity, looking for patterns and trends that indicated Daemon influence. Who was being toyed with by demons, who was possessed, where the demons were hiding. It was Odessa's work that had uncovered a fallen angel's conspiracy to overthrow the senate, and she'd almost died because of it. Her previous supervisor *had* died because of it, in fact.

And then there was Felicia. Aimless. Irresponsible. Deceitful. Jagger was correct about that. She was a walking lie as she pretended she was unaffected by anything and everything.

She was a senator's daughter, yet she'd done nothing in her twenty-six years. Her kind might be immortal, but they settled into their careers after schooling. Yet she wasn't smart enough to be an analyst. Nor was she quiet enough or stealthy enough to follow humans all day, taking notes like a watcher.

God forbid she had to watch humans die and guide them to the light like chaperones. She almost shuddered. With her skills, she should be a warrior fighting demon influence in the human realm, but with her history in Numen, they wouldn't take her seriously. Neither would the police force of Numen, the enforcers. Though it seemed they had a bit of a corruption issue going on.

A senator's daughter. One would think she'd follow in her daddy's footsteps. But no. She'd get laughed out of the senate coliseum by half the senators and propositioned for favors by the other half. Many of her father's "friends" had already offered to let her service their needs.

No, thank you.

A girl should be able to have sex when she wanted to and move on, but this was the wrong realm to do that in. She'd learned that the hard way.

So, maybe it was a good time to leave Numen and go back to where everyone didn't know her name.

"I guess. My bodyguard is waiting." She hugged Odessa goodbye, ignoring the burst of agony in her back when Odessa returned the embrace. "Goodbye, Tenley."

The female gave her a brief smile and went right back to work.

Jagger was out in the corridor. Hearing her, he started for the exit. They had to be outside to to transcend to another realm and she couldn't wait to descend back to the human realm. Warriors passed them, averting their gaze and inspecting corners. A refreshing change. A few months ago, some angels wouldn't have hesitated to snicker at her or toss Jagger looks full of innuendo. But now that she was basically the sister of their new director, she was dutifully ignored.

Outside, Jagger cocked his elbow. While they'd both been to the secret nook used when descending to her home, as her protector, he insisted they travel together, and that included transcending at the same time. The man was honorable, if nothing else. Given who his father was, his honor was a prickly topic.

He followed her lead for the descent. An odd thing for him to do, considering his behavior, but she knew the layout of the city better. If they sensed they might get spotted by a human, she could cart them immediately to another place.

The vibrant smells of the city surrounded her. Car exhaust, dirty concrete, a splash of sunshine, and the faint smell of urine. Home sweet Atlanta. If she strolled a few blocks in either direction, she'd get a whiff of the magnolia trees. But her section of town grew only concrete.

Numen always smelled nice. Powered by its own energy, the realm was an elegant copy of what humans probably envisioned utopia to be. Numen wasn't heaven, but it never smelled foul. Even when angel fire, the divine plasmic eternal flame, had burned her sister's home down, there hadn't been smoking remnants. Just ashen rubble.

Her kind could grow grass and flowers and trees with little effort, so if ever there was a smell in Numen, it was floral. Pleasant. Cheery. And that was probably why she stayed in Atlanta. It was large enough to get lost in, and when the magnolia trees bloomed, she could pretend she was home.

They each listened for a moment before Jagger gave the all clear by walking away from her.

"Couldn't get out of my detail, huh?" She tried to keep her tone light, but it wasn't fun being someone's worst job ever.

"Nope."

He punched in the code for her apartment and held the door open for her. His gentlemanly act was just that, an act. He opened the door to look, listen, and feel for trouble, then she entered and he followed so he could check for a tail.

She jogged up the stairs. The same process was repeated with her apartment door.

Feeling the need to punch a few things, she was heading to her practice room when her phone buzzed. She'd left it here while they were in Numen. The thing was for emergencies only.

Jagger narrowed his eyes on it and she realized she hadn't made a move toward it. It buzzed again. A foreboding sound. That it had happened as soon as they walked in the door was concerning.

Jagger started for it the same time she did, but she beat him to it, curiosity propelling her.

"It's probably just Ode. Bryant probably forgot to mention something." Which totally wasn't like him.

Felicia glanced at the message, blinked, and held it closer, as if reading it was the problem.

It came from an unknown number.

Tell my son I want to talk to him. –J

CHAPTER 2

Jagger snatched the phone out of her hand. "It says what?"

His heart thrummed in his ears.

He didn't have a phone. They were a liability, a way for a tricky demon in a computer-savvy host to track him.

So who else with the initial J would send Felicia a text telling her they wanted to talk to their son?

Fuck.

He tapped on the screen. Nothing happened. "What the… Who's it from?" The force of his taps was increasing.

Felicia caught his wrist in a surprisingly strong grip and snapped up the phone with her other hand. "It's an unknown number. I can try to call it."

He hovered over her as she concentrated on the screen. The mind fuck that his father might be trying to reach him was the only thing keeping his gaze off the way her tank top gaped to reveal impressive cleavage. Or how her hair glimmered like hammered gold in the sunlight streaming through the sliding doors in her main room.

She held the phone to her ear and met his gaze. He was inches from her but he didn't back away.

A ringtone vibrated on the air between them. The message had come just as they'd returned. He should be shutting blinds, spying out the windows, updating Dionna. But he couldn't pry himself away from Felicia and the possibility that his dad might be on the other end of the phone.

The ringing stopped. His lungs seized. Someone had answered.

"Ms. Montclaire."

Jagger sucked in an icy breath. That voice. He hadn't heard it for years. How long had Father been fallen?

Felicia's eyes widened when she got a load of his expression. He had no idea what he looked like, but his skin was probably as pale as his hair.

She stepped back just as he was reaching for the phone. "That's me. I'd ask your name, but I don't care to end up fallen for associating with one. So let me ask this instead—there's a guy standing next to me. Is he the one you want to talk to?"

Jagger dropped his hand. He'd forgotten all the instructions drilled into him the day he'd lost Father. No contact. No checking up on him. No aid whatsoever. It was as if his loved one had died and there was no place to pay respects. His loved one had vanished and was gone. Forever.

Jagger could lose his own wings for talking to Father. But at the moment, it didn't seem to matter. He'd reverted to the sixteen-year-old kid who could hardly comprehend what was going on.

The rumble of a smooth chuckle was clear on the other end. "Ms. Montclaire, you surprise me."

"Do I?" she asked innocently. "You chose me to contact, after all. So why would you want to talk to him?"

"Put my son on the line."

Jagger's hand twitched to grab the phone.

"Wrong answer," Felicia replied. "See, the guy next to me, his dad hasn't talked to him in a while. Years. And he's had good reason not to. And I would think that if my friend's dad cared about him, he'd know the trouble he'd be bringing down on him just by contacting him."

Jagger had never been so grateful for Felicia's presence and her calm, collected demeanor. Part of him feared that she'd never give him the phone, but she was right not to. And as the warrior, he should be disconnecting the call and apprising his boss of what was happening.

But he couldn't. He leaned closer to hear Father's response.

"Hand the phone over, Ms. Montclaire." The charm was gone, the demand clear.

Felicia didn't immediately hand the phone over. She held it away from her ear and regarded him. The unspoken question was in her eyes. *Are you going to risk it?*

She'd already risked herself. For him, no less. He wasn't going to think deeper about it, wasn't going to consider that there was more to Felicia than her beauty and privileged upbringing. And he could pass off this conversation as part of the investigation. He was still a warrior.

He accepted the device. Unsure what to say, he went with a gruff "What do you want?"

"Julian." Relief and satisfaction poured from his father's voice.

He wanted to point out that no one called him that anymore, and that Father would know that if he were around. Father would know if hadn't chosen to fall in love with some human and place her feelings over his family's safety. But Jagger stayed silent.

Father waited a heartbeat before he spoke. "It came to my

attention that you may have gotten mixed up in some of my affairs."

"The whole realm is mixed up in your affairs."

"Yes, well. It wasn't my intention for your safety to be in question."

"My job is to put myself in harm's way to keep the realm safe," he said tightly. "From people like you, apparently."

"There is no one like me. It's why they're scared, and they'll use you to get to me."

There is no one like me. What an understatement. And disturbing for a kid who'd grown up being reminded how much like his father he was. "Who will use me?"

"Those aligned with me who seek to control me, and those who aren't and seek to stop me. Watch yourself, Julian."

He hated how much he craved hearing his name spoken in that voice. "You could just bow out and get an honest job and leave the realm alone. Boom. You're out of danger. I'm out of danger."

"You know that can't happen."

"Can't it? Or you don't want it to? I guess you wouldn't have risked everything if you'd thought about more than yourself sometimes."

"Fair enough, son."

"Don't call me that." Instant regret coursed through him. His deepest fantasy was talking to Father again, and he wanted to take back his demand. But he wasn't that sixteen-year-old boy anymore. He was a warrior raised by a single mother.

Jameson, because that was what Jagger would have to start thinking of him as, didn't reply for a moment and when he did, his voice had dropped low, like he knew Felicia was trying to listen in. "Again, that's fair. Watch your back. To do that, you'll have to keep protecting that pretty little angel. It's seems my associates have secrets of their own."

"Like what?"

"If I knew, they'd be dead already. I won't risk us both by speaking to you again. Goodbye, Julian." The call was disconnected as Jagger was opening his mouth to protest. *Don't hang up. Keeping talking. Just...don't go.*

The silence on the other end of the line stretched on. He was staring at the floor.

Felicia's soft skin brushed his as she took the phone and shut it off. "Are you going to tell Bryant?"

He nodded numbly. He hadn't reached out to a fallen, and talking to him was part of the investigation, part of catching him. So Father could be properly executed.

God almighty, the man had murdered a watcher. Watchers were tasked with monitoring humans. They were a threat to no one. But the poor female had deduced what Jameson was up to, and when she'd reported it through the proper channels, she'd gotten killed for it.

That was just one they knew about. The frequency of warriors' deaths had increased in recent years. Was he behind any of those?

Why hadn't Jameson Haddock faded into obscurity like the rest of the fallen? It would've been the last decent thing he could've done as a father.

Jagger couldn't look at Felicia. The sympathy in her eyes would remind him too much of how others had looked at him years ago.

That poor child. The son of a fallen senator. How humiliating.

Energy swirled inside of him, coiling and uncoiling. He wasn't so dense that he didn't know it was his emotions.

He glanced at Felicia. She didn't wear those sexy clothes to taunt him. It was the way she normally dressed; it wasn't for his benefit. And didn't that ruffle his feathers?

But he'd been around her long enough to know that she

beat the shit out of her punching bag when something was bothering her. Lately, that something had been him.

She might be onto something.

He turned away and stormed to her workout room. "I'll call Bryant. First, I need to use your bag."

Felicia perched on her couch. Rhythmic thumping came from the back of her apartment. Good thing this place had solid insulation, but even better—tenants she got along with and talked to regularly. The rooms above and below the workout room were guest rooms. The renters always let her know when someone was staying with them so she could take her workouts elsewhere.

She tapped her fingers along the cushion. She'd heard most of the conversation. Jameson Haddock was a fallen, but he'd only gotten worse after losing his wings. But that wasn't why she was worried.

Jagger's reaction. The yearning in his eyes. The hopefulness he'd tried to hide. The hurt and anger of a kid toward a parent.

She knew that one all too well.

But this was Julian Hancock. He was untouchable, unflappable, nearly as stone cold as his mother. To see him vulnerable and hurting…

A twinge in her back took her mind off him. Her shoulders ached. For years, she could pretend to forget what had happened to her and the agony of the days after. Recent events had brought it all back, making it harder than usual to ignore the constant throb in her shoulder blades and back muscles.

Her wings were morphed, and more comfortable than they would be if she were forced to extend the damaged scar tissue. When she was alone, she would let them hang out, gut through the agony, but with Jagger around constantly, she'd held them in more than usual. It was like keeping her leg bent twenty-four/seven. First the limb itself ached, then soon after the surrounding joints.

Going to the medicine cupboard in the kitchen, she pulled out a couple bottles. She threw back a few ibuprofen and an acetaminophen and turned around, and almost yelped.

A scowling, sweaty Jagger was frowning at her, his mint-green gaze flitting from the pill bottles to her. Sweat dripped down his forehead and he'd pulled his hair back into a stubby queue at the base of his head, muting the surfer look and playing up the killing-machine vibe. His shirt was off.

"What the fuck are those?"

The accusation in those words wiped out her sympathy for him. She shoved the medicine back into the cabinet. Snarky comments almost left her mouth, so she slowed and drank a glass of water. "They're my drugs."

"What kind?"

"You know, opiates. Laced with fentanyl."

"The problem, Felicia, is that you could be telling the truth."

She slammed her glass down, a crack renting the base to the rim. "When you get tired of lashing out at me because of your daddy issues, let me know."

She pushed past him, wishing her kitchen entrance were wider so she didn't have to brush up against his hard muscle. He grabbed her arm and she wanted to strain against him, to lengthen her cramped muscles, to use him as her own personal stretcher.

"Don't you dare minimize that. My father betrayed us at every level and continues to do so." He released her. "Can't you take anything seriously?"

Her patience had hit its limit. This was why she hadn't explained any of her actions to him. He didn't deserve an explanation, but she didn't deserve his insulting treatment of her.

"I'll tell you what I take seriously." She crossed her arms. Instead of punching her bag, she might take a long soak and loosen up her joints. "My father's murder. We weren't close for a reason, but it wasn't always that way. Maybe someday I'll have the luxury of mourning him, but I'm kind of trying to stay alive right now."

Jagger's jaw flexed and he had the grace to look ashamed.

"Another thing I take seriously? My mom walking into the fire."

He blanched, but she couldn't be smug. The pain of her mother killing herself was too raw. Her kind were immortal, but they had an out. Angel fire. The bane of her own existence. The underlying cause of her constant pain.

A fountain of the deadly substance erupted from the center of the realm. And Mother had taken a long walk off a short pier right into it. As if that weren't bad enough, Father had shut down that day, and every day of his life thereafter. Felicia had been little more than a nuisance to them.

She cocked her head. "What? Did you think my father was so hateful that Mother was hiding out in a spa for the rest of her days?" It had always bugged her how rarely anyone asked after Mother.

"I didn't know."

"Yeah. Not many want to know."

He went tense, his eyes hardening. Always defensive. "Why the drugs?"

She rolled her eyes. "I reveal two of the three worst days of my life and you're still on the drugs? They're over-the-counter painkillers, asshole. As for the why, I'll let you wonder. I've already explained myself far too much to a guy who's set on hating me. Now I'm gonna go take a bath. Try not talking to me for as long as you can possibly manage."

CHANEL HANCOCK STARED across the desk at Director Vale. She'd gone to the warrior compound and that act alone had shocked him, not that anyone would know from his admirable poker face. She looked him in the eye. His scars scared weaker angels, but not her. She was in awe of them, and if she didn't think it'd belittle the nightmare he'd gone through, she'd think harder about how she must resemble him on the inside.

Scorched. Shredded. Healed, but never like before.

And like the director, she was facing that which had inflicted all the harm. Her mate. What did he call himself now? Jameson Haddock.

With that name, he mocked them all, just like he had as James Hancock. Fucking his way through the realm and then plowing through human women left and right. He hadn't even changed his initials, the seedy bastard. No wonder he worked so well with the creatures from Daemon.

He hadn't deserved his downy, light gray wings. They should've been as black as cinder and as leathery as old cowhide.

The director was giving her the latest report on a missing batch of vials used to store angel fire. Apparently betraying her mate and then raising a son who shunned his father's existence so much he took up arms had been enough to earn the director's trust.

It was flattering, actually. Quite refreshing for once to not have to deal with insecure personalities who thought she didn't know how they demeaned her behind her back, yet cowered in front of her.

She interrupted his tale of woe. "Have you located Senator Kenton yet?"

Director Vale clenched his jaw, but she didn't apologize for talking over him. "We have not. Once his traitor status was revealed and he fled the senate auditorium to descend, we found no clues as to where he went. But since Enforcer Stede went missing, too, we assume they are working together in the human realm as they did here."

When the director paused, she caught the heaviness weighing on him. There was more. "Do proceed." She didn't even bite his head off. That was how much she respected him.

Resolve filled his face. "It's only a suspicion, but the rise of angelic deaths in the earthly realm continues." Yes, she was concerned about that as well. Lingering guilt was stoked by the thought she was somehow responsible for those deaths. She'd unleashed her mate on the world, and he'd had nowhere to go and lacked the grace to die. "I would have expected a decrease. Our people know there's danger and our warriors are prepared for it, especially those in or serving around the Las Vegas area."

She immediately caught his drift. "He's changed tactics. Any idea what his advantage is?"

"First, it's only speculation that Jameson is behind it."

She refrained from rolling her eyes.

"But I think it's a solid assumption. If it's not him personally, it's one of his people. Director Richter—Leo—is adamant that after he was nicked with the blade, before the fire, that he couldn't descend."

It was on the tip of her tongue to ask why Vale's predecessor would flee to the human realm when he was burning alive with angel fire, but then rational thought during that situation had likely been hard to come by.

The director continued. "We suspect there's a substance that's inhibiting our ability to transcend."

She blinked. How could such a thing be possible? A few select senators granted those from Numen the ability to ascend or descend. Transcension wasn't tangible. The ability was more akin to a divine gift, and while too many of them used it for fun and relaxation, they still earned it throughout their long life. A century goofing off was nothing compared to two spent serving humans or their own realm.

"Like a chemical?" she asked.

He shrugged. That was never a good sign. His tidbit was almost as shocking as finding out her mate was behind an uprising and she hadn't had a clue. "I have very few I trust to brainstorm this with."

Ah. Her respect rose a few more notches. She'd been around much longer than him, so long that she'd forgotten her own age. After James's—Jameson's—betrayal, the years had bled into themselves. She didn't care how old she was, only putting one foot in front of the other. Only recently had she taken a lover, though she disdained that word. She'd loved James Hancock with all her heart and soul. She'd waited centuries for a mate and he'd swept her off her feet. For a while, he might've even loved her in return. But not more than himself.

Thankfully, Director Vale yanked her out of those thoughts. "In the human realm, he'd have access to any chemical he wanted. He has the money."

She waved it off. "Nothing that could affect us. We are separate beings and our immortality spares us. It'd have to be from Daemon." She relaxed enough to let her expression slide into pensive, rather than aloof. "But they'd likely have figured something like that out by now. No, it's something about James. *Jameson.*" Argh! Others had adapted to calling him Jameson easily enough, but to her he was the same male that had torn her apart. She couldn't separate them into before and after. "Jameson. It has to be something unique Jameson brings to the table."

"We are sadly deficient in information regarding fallen."

She fully agreed. Once they lost their wings, it was like they had never existed, and that had never felt…fair. Her mating had been real. Her broken heart had almost killed her. But she had to admit, militantly pretending James Hancock had never existed for her son's sake had been oddly therapeutic. She'd pushed her boy to defy the expectations of their people. To be everything his father wasn't.

"Do you think his blood would be enough?" The director cleared his throat and rushed on like he was afraid she'd scoff at him. "As a fallen, he's lost all ability to move through the realms. Do you think the act of falling is so powerful that his blood alone could inhibit others' transcension?"

She gave an indelicate snort and ignored the shocked expression Vale tried to cover. "If anyone's blood would be cursed enough, it'd be his. He's already proved capable of mutating a horrible situation to his benefit. If his blood can affect us by association, then yes, he's discovered it."

Bryant's nod was grim.

She had no idea what propelled her to say her next words. "Trust me, I'm questioning why I didn't just hire a thug to kill him right after he fell." She'd been angry enough.

The heartbeat of silence should've been awkward.

"You had a son," he said, though his tone also made it clear he was of a like mind.

And I was hopelessly in love and so tragically hurt. She had hired someone to spy on him after he'd lost his wings. Once. And she'd regretted it. The report had been crushing. He'd been selling himself for whatever could make a buck. Her strong, charming mate reduced to a product.

She'd looked away and never looked back. A mistake, obviously. "Speaking of Julian. How is he?"

An unreadable emotion rippled across Vale's face. "He remains on his protection detail."

"But?"

He blew out a breath like he wished he could bullshit her at least this once. "Jameson made contact with him."

The tidal wave of rage that followed should've lifted her off her seat. How *dare* he? That male had never changed a wet nappy or soothed nightmares. He'd been out "working," work that she'd later learned included a lot of time spent between women's thighs.

After what he'd done, falling for that human with the son. When the watcher had approached her and confessed to seeing him play ball with his mistress's son, it had been the final straw. That was when she had tattled. Petty? Absolutely not.

The director's hands were folded but his knuckles were white. She must look like a nuclear warhead ready to detonate. Inhaling slowly, she said, "I'm surprised he's chosen now to take interest."

"It could be accessibility. Jagger has been in the same place for months."

Jagger. Her boy's nickname. She approved of it. It distanced him even farther from his father.

"Jameson passed along a warning," Director Vale said. "He seemed worried that Jagger would be targeted because of him."

She cocked a brow. It took more mental effort to keep the rest of her face from revealing her rage. Curse James and curse the Jameson he'd turned into. "Indeed."

Perhaps she could use this information. Her pride for Julian had its limits. Constant worry gnawed at her and it was worse now that she knew what her son was tasked with. Before, he'd never visited, much less discussed his work.

Not for the first time, she wondered if she'd sheltered him a bit too much from emotions that made a person weak. He'd been sixteen and, she had assumed, less affected by her brutal emotional shutdown.

"Jagger's a good warrior," the director said like he could tell she was also concerned. Or he'd deduced that if one parent was worried, the other would be too. "He may be in more danger than initially understood, but both he and Ms. Montclaire are highly capable."

Ah yes. Ms. Montclaire. The troubled young daughter of the recently deceased Kreger Montclaire. Chanel hadn't known the mother well, but considering what Kreger had been willing to do for her safety and the safety of his children, she had more than a few concerns. Would Julian cast off all good sense? Did he have enough training to keep a pretty young female from affecting his decisions?

He couldn't escape being his father's son, after all.

"We'll keep monitoring the situation, of course," Director Vale said.

Yes, she would as well. And she'd use her not inconsiderable power to interfere if she had to.

"I'll do some discreet checking with those responsible for granting transcension." She rose and fluttered her wings. "You know where to find me." She swept out of the office, dutifully ignored the new assistant, and continued out of headquarters. The bodyguard she'd appointed for herself fell in step next to her from where he'd been posted outside of the office.

Mateo was young, obedient, and good in bed. Young enough to not get attached. One could hope.

CHAPTER 3

igure it out. The way Felicia had said it, so flippantly, like if he thought he was so smart, he could. If he knew her well enough.

He knew as much as he needed to about Felicia Montclaire.

Two days had gone by since his father's phone call. He'd dragged Felicia back to Numen to meet with Director Vale. Tattling on Jameson was his duty. Didn't mean he'd felt right about it.

The male had called to warn him. He shouldn't look further into it, but how could he not? Even if Jameson Haddock cared about him at all, he was still working with Daemon. He wasn't backing off because it could get Jagger caught in the crossfire. He hadn't even backed off when he'd realized Jagger was on the front lines. Or as close as he could get while acting as Felicia's bodyguard.

Jameson was watching Felicia's. He'd known when they arrived. Had he been in Atlanta personally, or was paying one of his demons to watch the place?

Jagger might hate his assignment, he might be harboring

a ton of resentment about it, but he didn't slack on his job. He hadn't sensed anyone watching them. And they varied their routine as much as they could while being sequestered in a two-bedroom apartment. They never grabbed groceries on the same day each week, never at the same time.

He paced the apartment. The blinds were drawn. Felicia bitched about the lack of sunlight, but she'd helped lower them. Then she'd gone about ignoring him.

Figure it out. He hadn't known her mother had walked into the fire. A senator's wife offing herself should've been bigger news.

Did that mean her death wasn't well known? Had Senator Montclaire concealed the real reason his mate wasn't around? Numen angels with no official position often lived in the human realm, doing good deeds and aiding the needy. It was their calling to help humans. He was stunned to realize he hadn't wondered about her mother's whereabouts until now.

There were a lot of reasons why Felicia's father might've hidden the truth, or at least hadn't been forthcoming about it. Shame. It certainly didn't reflect well on him that his mate couldn't spend eternity with him. Angels weren't as advanced in mental health issues as humans were, though Jagger suspected they weathered the same disorders. Their natural healing might help, and of course mating was supposed to accelerate the healing process. Mates could share energy to repair tissue, and he doubted the nervous system was exempt. But that didn't mean they were shining beacons of functionality at all times.

Felicia's father had been murdered, but she'd claimed to be estranged from him. And now she admitted her mother had walked into the fire.

What would tear them apart? And what would give an angel chronic pain? That was a foreign concept. Though he often wondered if Director Vale still suffered from the pain of his injuries. Angel fire was the only thing capable of causing lasting scars—

Had Felicia had a run-in with angel fire?

Was it connected to her mother's death?

When she and Odessa were together, they acted as if they had once been a loving family.

Jagger couldn't relate to that part. Had his parents ever liked each other? Growing up, his home had been...cold. Like his mother. But she'd mated his father.

He'd never had the guts to ask her if she and Father were a natural match. His kind either found a mate at some point in their long lives or were granted a mate when one was needed most. Warriors like him were often gifted a mate when they were critically injured, though they could also choose their own.

Jagger was alone, and that was fine with him. He'd rather linger at death's door than take a mate he'd never met only to heal himself. An unfeeling, frigid life spent paired with someone from eternity was hell on—well, not on Earth, but in his realm.

A door down the hallway squeaked open. Felicia's bedroom. He'd memorized the sounds of her moving around.

She appeared in the hall dressed in her typical fitness gear. Short shorts and a tank top with a dark sports bra underneath.

Not for the first time, he wished she lived somewhere other than Hot-lanta. Somewhere cold, where she'd have to cover up.

Like every other day, he had to force his gaze to her face and away from her long, golden legs. The way the muscles flexed and bunched were mesmerizing.

Her expression was pinched, and he was starting to think

it wasn't from living with him. He'd heard the pill bottles rattle like clockwork every four to six hours. He'd read the instructions and verified the ingredients.

Why the fuck did she need painkillers?

"So, Ted needs some help at the gym." She stuffed her feet into her athletic shoes, then tortured him by bending over to lace them. He ripped his gaze away before his dick decided it liked the view.

Scratch that—his dick had decided long ago it loved any view with her in it.

Traitor.

"And you told Good in Bed Ted no, right?" He knew the answer, but dammit. Sitting in the apartment with her was mind-numbing torture, but protecting her in public, and doing it while keeping his kind secret? He'd rather waste away on this stupid couch-slash-bed. Add in the fact she'd slept with the gym owner, and well, didn't his mood sour.

"Funny story. I told him that I had an old friend in town who was kind of a loner and I felt bad leaving him. I promised you'd sit in a corner and glare at everyone because you had trust issues."

He surged to his feet to cover how frustratingly accurate she was with her description. "Don't you think about anything before you act?"

She straightened and planted her hands on her hips. "I know you're going crazy in here. I am too. The thing is, unlike you, I can't just go back to Numen when this is over. I built a life here. A good job with good people and my own money. I'm not ruining it. I already quit my main job. My hiatus is up, my rent money is burned. So unless you're going to kick in for bills for the next who knows how long, I need to work."

Rent? Bills? He...hadn't thought about any of that. He'd assumed she was floating by with her family's money. Part of the senate's job was to fund their people's work in the human realm.

So how did she make a living?

~

FELICIA DELIVERED a slow-motion kick to the middle of a white rectangular pad. Her partner didn't even grunt since she'd dialed down the force of the blow to negligible levels.

She turned to her captive audience of ten-year-olds. "Ready?"

Out of the five, Bristol shot up his hand first and skirted to the front of the line. "Ready, Felicia."

The other four fell in behind him. Leyvonna, Theo, Kraig, and Claudia in that order. Claudia. Always last. Her mother had to drag her in each evening, but the girl had proved herself proficient time and time again. It had been weeks since Felicia had helped out at the gym, but concern had already settled in about Claudia. Her shoulders hung and she looked a few nights short of a good night's sleep.

As Felicia talked her pupils through the next round of practice kicks, she remained way too attuned to the man leaning against the wall.

Jagger's hair was brushed off his face but some strands fell forward like they were compelled to frame his strong jaw. She knew the feeling.

As always, ignoring him proved impossible. The lick of his gaze traced her back, oddly a brief reprieve for her aching muscles. If only she could bottle the effect into her own version of Icy Hot, she wouldn't have to worry about money. Add his face to the packaging and watch the cash roll in.

She wished it were cool enough for him to wear jeans, but in the Atlanta heat and humidity, the running shorts clinging to his thick thighs were a better choice. Not for her. He could've found a looser T-shirt. And maybe in a color that didn't highlight his unusual eyes. The dark green technical fabric did his eyes as much justice as his abs.

He was a long way from the robes of their realm, and he fit in here way too well. Except for the massive scowl on his face.

She straightened her own T-shirt. It had the gym logo emblazoned on it. She'd chosen krav maga because this gym wore street clothing to train in. The white linen pants and white tunic other martial arts used reminded her too much of home. In this building, respect was earned. Money and station had nothing to do with it. She got more respect when she stepped into the gym than any other day at home.

So it sucked that she missed her realm so much.

Class wrapped up.

"Felicia." Ted crossed to her side, giving his back to Jagger. "Is everything okay?"

"You mean other than the beach boy I can't seem to shake?"

"You know I don't blame him." His lips twitched. Ted had a girlfriend now, but he never pretended they hadn't killed time in bed together. "It's none of my business, but you've missed a lot of work and then you show up with this guy. I can't have parents questioning the dude hanging out in the back glaring at you."

"My family is..." She got a twinge in her back just thinking about them. But living here, she'd crafted her story long ago. "They got into some trouble and they're afraid that it'll come back on me. Jagger is an old friend of the family." She lifted a shoulder in a way that massaged her scar tissue more than strained it. "They want him to look after me. Do you mind if he tags along?"

That was the best explanation she could give. She didn't want to lie and say that he was her boyfriend, and bringing her guy with her for every shift would be even weirder anyway. Ted Benson would call bullshit faster on that than on the mafia-laced story she'd just given him.

"Humph." Ted's grunt was more of *that's too ludicrous to even be false* than all-out disbelief.

"This job means a lot to me." And she didn't want to lose it, even if she was only an on-call instructor. Then she'd have nothing. She'd have to live on the streets or move back home, and since her home had been demolished, that left the streets. She'd die before she was homeless in her own realm, giving those of Numen even more reason to look at her with disdain. They would just wonder why she wasn't whoring her way through life, not why she'd rather be alone in the pristine alleys of her realm.

But she wasn't bitter.

"It means a lot to me too." His lips flattened and he peered over his shoulder. "But if you're bringing him around, then he'll need to work."

"He'd be glad to." He'd have to, and she'd relish every ounce of angst it would squeeze out of him.

"How's Sasha?"

His smile warmed her heart. Humans had such short lives —to them, mating for life didn't mean eternity. Happily ever after was easier to attain for fifty years than it was for five hundred.

"Good. And you know I'm gonna mention Crabby Pants over there." Ted lifted his fist. Jagger's arms were crossed over his broad chest, and his forearms flexed as if he planned to fly off the wall and tackle Ted. Her bodyguard would be in for more of a fight than usual if he did.

"Tell her I said hi." She tapped her fist against Benson's. "See you tomorrow."

Lifting a cool brow at Jagger, she crossed toward him. Her back ached. The years were adding up. She was beginning to doubt that she could do this for as long as it took to capture Jameson and the angels responsible for trying to overthrow the realm. Without the reprieve of being in her own place and letting her shattered wings change position once in a while, she might destroy her range of motion altogether.

Tonight. The door would be locked, blocked, and the window fully covered, but she'd have to let it all hang out. Didn't mean the idea of being at her most vulnerable around Jagger didn't chafe.

CHAPTER 4

"He wants me to do what?" Jagger shook his head like he was getting water out of his ears. He was walking back to Felicia's place, his body primed for conflict, but there were no people or cars out of place. Was his father still in town or back in Vegas? Was he using surveillance of the two-legged or electrical variety?

"Laundry. Clean pads. Sweep." The vexing female was taking ample pleasure in the details.

"Is he jealous?"

She rolled her eyes so hard her ponytail swung. "You can do anything that's not leaning against the wall, looking like a predator around a bunch of kittens."

The kids. Right. He had worries about one kid in particular. "The quiet one. What's her name?"

Felicia's full lips scrunched at his one-eighty in the conversation. The pause was oh so satisfying. "Claudia?"

"It's her mother."

He waited to say more until they were in her building and safely ensconced in her apartment. She must've sensed from his tone that it wasn't a subject that could be discussed in public.

He flipped the dead bolts on her door. One was native to the door, the others were additions. She'd never answered him when he'd asked if she'd installed them. She was filling a glass of water when he finished. "She's dogged by sylphs."

Her head whipped around, eyes flaring. "Claudia's mom?"

He dipped his head. She was back on those painkillers again. Throwing them back, she put the glass to her mouth and drained it in one gulp. He couldn't rip his gaze away from the flex of her neck muscles. His last long-term relationship, the one Felicia had ruined, had been with a petite female. She'd been an entirely different kind of feminine. Soft curves thanks to extra padding and the lack of hard muscle, and a pouty countenance that had bordered on annoying. She had wielded her attributes like a weapon.

The *thunk* of the glass preceded her "We need to do something." She wiped the corners of her mouth, another move he had a difficult time looking away from.

"I can let Director Vale know."

She shook her head. "I can't wait for it to get worse. Claudia was quieter than normal today. Sad. Those little bastards are affecting her mom's behavior. It could be any second before she's weak enough for an archmaster to possess her." She pressed her fingertips to her forehead. "How did I not know?"

"Have you been trained to stop demons in this realm?"

Her flat look was less than complimentary.

"I'm serious." He hadn't meant to be insulting and that surprised even him. "Angels come and go from this realm, thinking that just because of their place of birth, they'll sense when a demon is nearby. As if Daemon's creatures haven't been concealing themselves for centuries. They're getting harder to hunt."

Interest reflected in her eyes. After what he'd seen this afternoon, he had no doubt she'd make a good warrior. His feathers would be ruffled if they were out. Why'd she have to be good at...everything? But then he recalled her innate resistance to following orders, a trait that would exclude her from making a squad.

"Harder how?" Her curiosity was intoxicating. Not only that, but there was no animosity for once.

"There's a special technique to seeing them. Basically a thousand-yard stare, and when they're visible, it's like a 3-D hologram. Look one way, you can see them; look another, and they're gone. The archmasters are getting stronger, submerging into the human more completely."

"So, they're, like, having the sylphs do more of their dirty work to prep the host?"

"No, they're just getting that strong."

"Well...aren't *we*?"

He'd never imagined talking shop with Felicia—and enjoying it. He couldn't let her get to him. He leaked arrogance into his voice. "Of course. Now back to Claudia's mom. We can ascend and inform the warriors."

Her expression clouded and she shifted her shoulders. "I'll call Ode. Or better yet, you can."

"Talk to your sister? Why?"

"To ask her to hand the phone to Bryant, who is probably in bed next to her." She snorted. "Or on top of her."

"I do not need that image of my boss in my head."

"Whatever. But if he doesn't prioritize Mrs. Washington, I'm going to." She sauntered to her room. How could such a powerful woman sway her hips like that? "I'm not going anywhere else tonight, FYI."

"Oh, good. Because I'm only on the third season of *Game of Thrones*," he called after her. Wasn't she going to have dinner?

"They all die," she said as she disappeared into her room.

He glared down the hall at her closed door. The next best thing was to pace the room. Boredom was going to kill him before any demon got a good shot with angel fire.

As he was flopping onto the couch, a moan propelled him back to his feet. Balancing on the balls of his feet, he listened hard. Where had that come from?

A sharp gasp was next. Was that from Felicia's room?

He crept closer. A soft hitch in her breath came through the door, the next moan louder still.

He pounded on the door. "Felicia, are you okay?"

"Leave me alone" was her strained reply, pain lacing every word.

He tested the doorknob. Locked. "What's going on?"

"What makes you think something's"—her voice caught —"wrong?"

"Damn it, Felicia. What the hell are you up to?" His imagination went haywire. Was she digging out her weapons to go after Mrs. Washington? Had someone gotten in and was holding her hostage?

"Nothing." Now there was anger.

"Those moans weren't nothing." He hated the door blocking him.

"Moans. Wanting to be alone." A small grunt. "Figure it out."

A flush swept through his body like he'd been doused in angel fire. She was...pleasuring herself? The picture of her baggy shirt ridden up past her breasts while her legs splayed open, her elegant hand inching down her belly... A tent erupted in his shorts. Good thing he had a door between them.

She let out a tiny yelp.

He blinked. None of her noises were like any his partners had ever made. "You sound like you're hurting."

"That's me. A real masochist. L-leave me alone."

He tried the knob again. Rattled it. Dropping his hand, he glared at the plank of wood. He could break it down to ensure she was well. But if she was— He couldn't risk it. Seeing her bare legs and keeping the same level of antagonism toward her was difficult enough. "Swear to me you're all right."

"Jagger." Damnation, she sounded on the verge of tears.

"Swear it or I'll break this door down."

"I'm all right," she said in a ragged whisper. "I'm no worse than I've ever been."

His exhale whooshed out of him. *Game of Thrones* it was then. He adjusted himself in his shorts and tried not to question why he was satisfied with only Felicia's word.

FELICIA AWOKE WITH A START, her heart pounding. The echo of a sinister voice grating next to her ear died away. *"Don't make a sound..."*

Those fucking nightmares. She scrubbed her face.

A hard rap on the door startled her into jumping out of bed. The sudden weight on her wings took her breath away and she hit her knees with a gasp.

"Felicia!"

Jagger. Always him. He couldn't leave her alone. Cool relief poured through her back with the weight off her wings. She usually took getting out of bed slowly, letting her ravaged back adjust to gravity.

"I'm fine!" Pressing her hands into the floor, she rose in increments. She was naked. Another reason she was grateful he hadn't beaten the door down.

"What the fuck is going on? And don't say you're..." An

angry huff came through the door. "Don't say you're masturbating."

She choked on a laugh. Almost made last night's agony worth it. "Maybe I'm just stiff from a shift at a job I've been away from too long."

She'd have to wait until he was in the shower before she morphed her wings in. It wouldn't be as bad as unleashing them after weeks of being confined, but it would hurt.

"I can tell a not-truth when I hear it."

She sighed and looked heavenward. Old habit. The belief that there was a higher power watching out for her had faded long ago. "Look, sometimes a girl just aches and needs a little privacy."

"And painkillers."

"Yep."

"Fine. I'll be in the shower."

The bathroom door clicked shut. She stayed put until the shower kicked on, then gave him another minute.

Biting her lip, she concentrated on morphing. Something she used to play at with her sister had become an excruciating mental exercise. Not only was the skin and muscle around her wing joints permanently damaged, but the bones sheered by an angel-fire-covered blade had never healed properly, making the folding required for morphing the wings a painful challenge.

Sucking in a breath and puffing it out, she completed the transition. Her misshapen wings were again invisible and her back looked perfectly human.

"Fuck me," she muttered. She tossed on a baggy shirt and went to the kitchen for breakfast.

She opened the fridge, then leaned back to look around. Was she seeing things?

Inside, a plate covered in plastic wrap sat on a shelf. Piled on it were spaghetti and meatballs. Six, like she always took. Two full servings of noodles and her carby reward for hitting the bags for hours. A glass of chocolate milk was next to it.

"I thought you'd come out for dinner."

She whipped around and immediately wished she hadn't. Slicked-back, damp hair made his sharp features more savage. His chest was bare and *dude*, he was ripped. Those low-slung shorts of his didn't help prevent her staring. The fridge door shut behind her and she jumped.

Spinning back around, she opened the door again and gathered the plate and the glass. "Thanks."

"Don't mention it." He was right behind her. Her ass was sticking out in the air and if she was on her game, she'd wiggle the hell out of it. But her "restful" night hadn't exactly been that. She needed another week of wings-out shut-eye.

She kicked the door closed with her heel. Yep. He'd been watching her.

Did he realize she taunted him so mercilessly because he was unable to hide his reactions?

He followed her to the counter. She drained her milk while warming up her food. He took a bowl out and prepared himself cereal. The smell of her shampoo rolling off him did nothing for her nerves.

Good thing she was better at hiding how he made her feel.

Maybe in another lifetime they would've been the star couple of Numen. The children of senators, her with her big aspirations—whatever those would've been—and the handsome warrior.

But his father had fallen and his mother was as cold as an Antarctic winter. Her own father had been murdered and her mother had killed herself.

And Jagger despised her and thought she was worthless.

Now they were just two firsthand witnessed to why mating for life didn't work.

"Yeah." Jagger answered his phone while wiping a drop of milk from his chin. "No. I understand. I can handle it." He paused, his jaw going tight. "No, ma'am. I understand, but it's a few sylphs. I can take care of them and her." His gaze flicked up at her. "Besides, she has her own skills. It'd be good training. They may send more after her."

That was a turn of events she hadn't seen coming. She didn't know who was on the other line, but Jagger wasn't running her down. Not only that, he sounded like he was going to be proactive in his duty to protect her.

Her heart rate kicked up. She could learn how to fight demons. Right now, she could only fight the host an archmaster possessed. But the actual demon? Yes, please.

He clicked off. "That was Dionna. I notified her instead of the director since they were just sylphs."

She carried her plate to the table. "Don't you wonder why we weren't given a better way to communicate with each other? Like, telepathy or something?"

"Probably because we were created several millennia before mobile phones were invented." Then he surprised her again by agreeing. "But some mental connection would've made this job easier."

She rolled noodles onto her fork. "I guess for balance, then the demons would also be able to communicate telepathically."

He cocked a brow but nodded. "Why aren't you a warrior?"

She paused with her fork stabbed into the middle of the plate. Her trust in Jagger only went so far. Only three people alive knew what had happened to her. Odessa, Bryant, and the bastard who'd mutilated her. There had been a fourth, but the intruder's partner, the one who'd held Odessa down, was dead, thanks to Bryant. If Felicia were a whole angel, she'd hunt down the knife-wielding male who had hurt her, but she wasn't there yet.

"As you know, just because we're born in privilege and grow up in gilded mansions doesn't mean our lives turns out perfectly."

He pushed his bowl away. "Well, we all know what happened to me. What about you?"

She couldn't casually turn the conversation about, so she was blatant about the topic change. "What did Dionna say?" She shoved a forkful of noodles into her mouth to punctuate her point.

He watched her. There was so much of his mother in him. Felicia was old enough to remember going to the senate with her father. Chanel Hancock had frightened her. Frigid, golden eyes. Bony countenance. Frosty demeanor. She was never hostile, but never warm or welcoming either. The longer Felicia was around Jagger, the more she thought the same of him.

It'd explain a lot.

But not this plate of leftovers and that glass of milk he'd left for her. Those had nothing to do with protection.

"She said she passed the information on to the director, but a team wouldn't get to Mrs. Washington as soon as she'd like. The warriors are short staffed." And, he didn't have to say, their realm was in a state of alarm after the attack on her sister and the death of her father.

"But she okayed you taking me?"

He nodded and he picked up his bowl, twisting in his chair to face her. His expression was serious, his gaze knowing. "And, Felicia, with something like this, you will listen to me and do as I say. I won't ever train you in the ways of Daemon if you don't follow my lead."

"Yessir." Oops. Her usual flippancy escaped, but she meant it. She wasn't stupid about fighting, or about demons.

His eyes narrowed, but he didn't challenge her. Maybe he was starting to see the pool of bullshit she swam in.

*I*f this male didn't feast on her like she was the finest dining in the realm, she would've gotten rid of him long ago.

Chanel clamped her hands around Mateo's head, burying her fingers in his crown of rich, brown hair. She was about to come, but if he moved one millimeter, she'd slip away from the precipice.

"Just like that," she gasped. She hated the noises she made during sex. *In the throes of passion* they called it, but this was only a release. She hated sounding needy.

Mateo grunted but she didn't loosen her grip until she blew apart. Her body tightened, nearing a painful point since she was always wound as tight as a winch, then release blew through her.

She ground against his face, shouting into the silence of the room. Only when she'd toppled over the crest and milked out every drop of pleasure did she release her hold on the young male between her legs.

He crawled up her body. "You called out his name again."

She shot her lover a dirty look, hating the reminder. That

was all Mateo ever mentioned of it. *You called out his name.* It must hurt his feelings. "Then make sure you fuck me hard enough that I can't remember it."

He came closer, lifting her legs over his shoulders and pounding into her wet sex so hard and fast she had no choice but to come again. This time, she made sure to keep her cries to herself. Her little gift to Mateo.

Because what he didn't understand was that he lacked what her late mate had excelled at. James had used charm in spades to get his way and she'd fallen for all of his false words.

His betrayal had left her a shattered shell of what she'd once been. And after the unloving home she'd been raised in, that was saying a lot. Watching his wings get carved out of him hadn't filled her with satisfaction. The whole messy process had been more like tying off a garbage bag and tossing it out. Necessary to keep her environment clean. Both the garbage and his wings had met the same fate: disintegration by angel fire.

Thanks to his fallen status, she could even mate again. Their bond had been severed with his wings. She wished the process had taken her memories of him as well.

Mateo pushed off her with a grunt. He went to the guest bathroom to clean up, after which he'd return to his duty as sentry outside of the senate coliseum gates. She rolled off the bed and, ignoring every mirror she passed, went into the master bath.

A quick shower later, she toweled her short, bobbed hair off and donned a long, pristine, white robe. The after-sex glow had left her body and she was back to being Chanel Hancock, senator.

Mateo would be waiting for her. They always determined their next rendezvous before he left. It was easier than passing notes among the nosy senators. Prying bastards.

How could she still cry his name? Thankfully, only Mateo could coax a climax out of her and she hadn't humiliated herself in front of anyone else.

Another sin she wished James could pay for. She hated him all over again for upsetting the realm and creeping back into her thoughts.

Spritzing herself with rose water, she finally looked at herself in the mirror.

When had she gotten so old? To humans she'd look like a rocking fortysomething. But when she'd been synced, she'd looked fresh out of college even at centuries old.

Breezing out, she trailed down the stairs as light as a dove, her sandaled feet quiet on the white marble floors. She might be broken and battered, but she moved gracefully. Never let them see the cracks.

Thank you, Mother.

Mateo was posed at the window. He was back in his short robe, wearing sandals that wound up his shins. The Greeks had copied them at some point in history, but none of them had looked as good as Mateo.

He was peering out around the thick maroon velvet drapes. She'd special ordered them from a store in the human realm during the days she used to venture down there. Once she'd become a senator, her life had been dedicated to the job.

He glanced back and put his hand up. She stopped at the base of the stairs. He never commanded her. She was in control, always. That he did now? Something was wrong.

He reached to his waist, but the long dirk he carried when he was working was gone. He never came to her house armed. His dark brows closed together as he looked around.

Damnation. She didn't have weapons either. But her kitchen had the next best thing. She pivoted and scurried away from the window.

"Chanel," Mateo hissed.

Her sandals whispered over the floor. A shadow moved in the corner. An intruder was using her damn drapes to hide. With a cry, she dove toward the butcher block.

The strange male charged her. She pushed as much speed as she could through her body until her hand closed around a handle. A butcher knife whistled free.

She spun, bringing the knife down in an arc and slicing the intruder across the chest. His eyes went wide and he jumped back. She didn't recognize him, but his wings were morphed and he wore all black. Numen wasn't a shadowy realm, but night was falling. He'd planned this.

There was a vial in his hand, the cap off. The substance inside hadn't registered when Mateo barreled into him from behind. Chanel jumped onto the island and scurried over the other side. A wild scream erupted from one of the males.

What the hell was going on?

Grunts and muffled thuds came from the other side. The male was still yelling, his voice at an agonizing pitch. She gulped and crawled back onto the counter. Creeping to peer over the other side, it was all she could do not to run screaming herself.

Mateo had the male pinned under him. His hands had tendrils of clean smoke coming from them. But the intruder. He was worse. Much worse.

When Mateo had tackled him, the vial of angel fire had spilled over his neck. All Mateo had to do was hold him down until it ate through the flesh.

The male's screams were cut off as he lost his vocal cords. The fire burned deeper and the light winked out of the male's eyes.

"Oh. My God." She didn't dare drop down. Were there others? The knife was clenched in her white-knuckled fist. She'd probably start sleeping with it.

"He's gone." Mateo pried his fingers off of the man's chest and raised them. Tiny dots of blistering red spattered his shaking hands. He sucked in a wobbly breath.

"Mateo. You're hurt."

He nodded grimly. "But you're alive." He caught her gaze. In his she saw what she'd been denying for the months they'd been sleeping together. He cared for her.

The fool.

She gathered all the regal composure she could muster, calling on skills learned over her entire life. Both her parents had been senators, after all. After a couple of centuries, they had walked into the fire, weary of life and unwilling to find purpose in the human realm doing humanitarian aid.

"Come. I may have some ointment for that." All she could do was make him feel better. Angel-fire wounds were permanent. Their natural healing tendencies wouldn't prevent scarring.

"Later, Chanel. I must report this trash to the enforcers."

She nodded, feeling like those odd bobbleheads she'd once seen during a foray in the human realm. Her gaze kept straying to the garish red droplets on the floor. Quit looking! "Yes, of course. He attacked a senator. He must be reported."

All of her years at the highest station in Numen and that was all she could say.

Mateo scowled at his hands, his body tight. His shaken but steady gaze met hers. "The burn is complete. You should accompany me. There could be more after you."

She would ask if he was sure the male had been after her, but she was the ex-mate of the fallen who was plotting against the realm. She was never one to get lost in wishful thinking.

"Of course." Put her on repeat. She was always the most levelheaded one in the room. After what she'd seen in her life, she would scoff if anyone suggested otherwise.

Mateo hefted the male, his dusky gray wings twitching with the effort. He motioned for Chanel to stay behind him. Kicking the door open, he peered outside. "I only sensed one."

She nodded though he couldn't see her. Putting one hand on her heart, she willed it to steady itself.

Through the rest of the evening, she layered her icy facade back into place. At the enforcers' headquarters, her embarrassment at being caught having a fling with a sentry faded with Mateo's respectful explanation. One would think they were contemplating a sync with the way he talked about her. Protective. Considerate. Adamant. He cared for her and he'd known better than to show it.

She was going to have to break it off. Never would she make herself that vulnerable to a male again.

She brought a trembling hand to her forehead. But she had been. Her life had been at stake and he'd risked life and limb to save her.

Leaving the white marble structure was the first time she'd taken stock of the building. It was the first time in her long career that she'd set foot inside. For such a large, square structure, it was nothing more than a cubicle farm broken up by larger offices and meeting rooms. She hated the place.

One thing she'd determined as they outlined the sudden attack: her ex was involved. It was too much of a coincidence that she'd done some light questioning regarding transcension and then a couple of days later someone tried to kill her.

Julian. The danger to him was only increasing, and she didn't give a gutter rat's ass how well he was trained. Mateo was trained, too, and it'd only been luck that the vial had landed on the other male.

Mateo stopped beside her. Not once had he taken her hand, nor had he put his hand on the small of her back. He gave her space, perhaps sensing she would suffocate from proximity and touch. It was not unlike the way he read her in the bedroom. No kissing. No small talk. No cuddles.

"Would you like me to spend the night?" he asked.

Her muscles went rigid and she lifted her chin to make it seem like she wasn't unstable. Going back to her home? Where a male had just died?

Atrocious.

But where else would she go? The enforcers had offered a guard detail and she'd shut it down with nothing more than a look. She hadn't thought beyond that.

Yes, she'd need Mateo under the same roof, if not in the same room. The same bed was up for debate. She hadn't slept with anyone since she'd learned of her mate's many betrayals.

But there was one thing she had to do first.

Her only child was off in another realm doing his job while males in black might be hunting him.

That was unacceptable.

Anger built inside of her, stronger than she'd ever known. She would not let her son fall victim to his father's machinations, no matter what Jagger's position was. Going against his father would tear him apart.

It was a hell of a risk, but her dormant motherly side roared to life.

"Yes, Mateo. If you could stay with me, I would greatly appreciate it. However, I have one stop to make first. Oh, and pack your weapons."

"THIS ISN'T A GOOD IDEA." Mateo pulled at the collar of his plain white T-shirt as he climbed out of their rental car.

The club her ex supposedly ran was a block away from where they'd parked. She didn't know how to drive, but that was another talent of Mateo's, she'd learned. Her toes were pinched in her shoes, but she used the pain to fuel her aggression.

Humans swarmed the streets, all lost in their own thoughts. To think, the previous night, she'd been attacked in her own home, and now she was in Las Vegas in the middle of the night where she could be attacked anytime.

Chanel agreed with Mateo. This wasn't a good idea. The price of this excursion could be her wings. And Mateo's. Yet he was still here. She trusted him on that basis alone. "Only I can get my point across. He gave Julian one warning already. Perhaps hearing the danger is real will spur a reaction."

"Julian was competent all the way through school and I've heard he's a skilled warrior."

Chanel wanted to groan. Mateo was the same age as her son? What did the humans call females like her? Cougars?

"Yes. But he's not usually facing off with his father." And a true father would do all he could to protect his children, even if that included dropping his ridiculous notion of taking over Numen.

The street they were on smelled like exhaust and garbage, and a cloud of marijuana smoke blew across her face. She wrinkled her nose. Why anyone would smoke something that smelled like a smoldering pair of dirty socks, she would never know.

Back in the day, she'd never minded puffing on a quality Cuban, but the smoke had rolled over her tongue like evaporated caramel—rich, potent, and full of status.

She glanced down at her own charcoal pantsuit. A fuchsia scarf draped over her baby-pink shirt and she wore pointed kitten heels. It was her only armor against seeing her ex again. Her clothing and Mateo.

They'd descended to Earth and stayed in a hotel overnight. She'd ordered clothing, but he'd insisted on garments he could move in. From his dubious expression at the suit she'd pulled up on the hotel's computer screen, he must not think he could fight in a tux. He'd picked a T-shirt and jeans. The ball cap pulled down low to conceal his face wouldn't have gone with a proper suit anyway.

Oddly enough, they both blended in Las Vegas, though the closer to the club they got, the more they stood out. Too little skin showing, and they were both missing any goth appeal. However, the street around the club was pristine. And it smelled better.

She eyed the place. Fall From Grace. *Bold, James. Bold.* A three-story building that must've been a warehouse at some point in its seedy life was now a trendy club that didn't look like it'd normally attract the clientele heading inside.

She glanced at Mateo again. Looking at him too often had been a problem all evening. He was just so…different than her ex.

Perhaps that'd get to James. That she was with a rugged male, not one who hid behind expensive threads, perfectly coiffed hair, and false promises. Mateo hastily hand combed his hair. She knew him enough to understand that his pristine appearance on duty was not the same as off duty.

"I've read the reports." She hadn't told Mateo about her obsession with the latest news regarding Jameson Haddock. She'd read all the analysts' notes. It paid to have power. "He arrives before the club closes—after lurking somewhere else doing God knows what." Though James was her problem, not God's.

"We should have done surveillance for a few days." Mateo didn't like her being exposed.

She didn't bother to reply. He understood it wasn't possible to spend the next three days watching this tasteless club and its wretched humans willing to sell their soul for a connection.

Get a puppy.

She kept her chin in the air as she strutted along the street. Time was running short. They'd watched this place all evening. Mateo had noted where all the surveillance cameras were positioned, pinpointing where they could make their presence known while avoiding photographic evidence of violating Numen law.

There were demons present. Filthy creatures, but they preferred to roam closer to the entrance. People crowded the front, but the back was quiet, as if they all knew Jameson preferred the privacy and were too scared to disobey. An empty alley held no appeal for interfering sylphs.

Mateo had suggested she wear a disguise, but she refused to face her ex-mate while cowering from her own kind. No. He needed to know how deadly serious she was about the danger to their son.

"They should be arriving soon if they're coming straight here."

How would she have possibly done this without his help? He might be younger but was apparently quite experienced in the human world. Finding the social sites James's followers used, he'd learned when and where James and his latest plaything were dining.

The alley was one way, and his three-story club took up an entire side with a distillery or some such bordering the other side. The backdoor was closer to this end of the street, which was the exit. Perfect.

An engine rumbled from the alley. The driver must've entered from the other side.

Mateo turned the corner and she walked behind him. Over his broad shoulder, she squinted around the headlights of the audacious vehicle. The driver had opened the back door and was now holding open the entrance to the club.

A familiar figure stood next to him and ushered in a

woman teetering on impossibly high heels. The heels had more length than her skirt.

Just what James liked. The male had never been one to work for anything in his life; why would female's clothing be any different?

"Mr. Haddock, we need to talk to you," Mateo called, his voice calm but authoritative. Her pulse jumped. There was no going back.

James didn't give them so much as a nod. The driver's hand slipped under the lapel of his jacket. She wasn't naïve. He was reaching for a weapon. No wonder James liked it on Earth better. He wielded more power here than he ever had in Numen as James Hancock.

She spoke, her own voice surprisingly strong. "Tell him to give us a moment, *James*."

His head cut to the side and he stared over his shoulder. His narrowed stare passed over Mateo. Her companion didn't move, and he wouldn't until all other witnesses were inside.

Her mate murmured to the driver. The man stiffened as if to argue, then thought better and followed in the direction the woman went. The three of them were alone in the alley.

Mateo didn't move forward. This was the area the cameras didn't reach well.

"Come out of hiding, my dear." The taunt dripped from James's tone.

She stepped to Mateo's side. Strong and silent, she'd never felt more protected. She faced her mate. Ex-mate, though with the way he haunted her, she had to remind herself of the "ex" part. He looked well. Dashing. Handsome as ever, but with more...confidence. Swagger. Refinement. His dark brown hair was stylishly long, giving him an air of seductive mystery. The eyes that made it hard to look at her son directly were keen and clear. His suit was more expensive than any she would've ordered Mateo, and his shoes were probably imported from another country. Whatever his journey as a fallen had been, he was thriving now.

She despised him.

Seeing no reason to spend more time on this errand than necessary, she was blunt. "You're endangering the life of our son."

Even in the shadows of the alley, the flex of his strong jaw was visible. "Is that why you're here, Chanel? Did you bring the muscle to rough me up?"

"No. I wanted to know if you were too stupid to have realized that your ridiculous notion of using demons to gain control of Numen could get your son killed. I wondered if you were too selfish to have thought of him or his well-being at all."

Mateo quit breathing next to her. He was worried she'd laid it on too thick, that James would react with volatility. That wasn't James's way and she wished she had all night to rail at him.

Displeasure rippled through James. "Chanel, you're as tiring now as you ever were. I can see the years have not melted the ice off you." He tilted his head. "Did you come all this way just to tell me that you fear our son, who is a warrior trained to fight and kill all manner of demons, might be in danger?"

"You at least know he's a warrior." She said it as snidely as possible.

"My dear, I was never as stupid as you treated me."

"Yet you're missing a set of wings."

His sharp inhale echoed across the distance and his upper lip curled. "You're a frigid bitch."

A low rumble emanated from Mateo. James's regard shifted, interest lighting his cunning gaze. She wanted to step in front of Mateo and block him from view. But one thing she'd learned in her career was to show no emotion, only evoke it.

"Are you with her?" Jameson's tone lightened. He dropped his head back and laughed. "Oh Chanel, get them young when they don't know any better, correct? I guess that's what you did to me."

"We were sync mates. I had no choice in the matter." Gifting her with an existential crisis. What horrible thing had she done to deserve him? She folded her hands in front of her, like she had all the time in the world. "I was attacked yesterday, in my home." She'd almost said "our."

Jameson's smile faded. He hadn't known. "Indeed." He was trying to play it off, but she could see his mind spinning. "It must've been scary for you."

He sounded like she'd done nothing more than trip over a pebble and skin a knee. His attempt at intimidation was obvious. He sought to use the information to his advantage, make her think she should be terrified of him.

She knew him. He knew her, and that was the only reason they were still in this foul-smelling alley. He sensed she had something important.

"James, our souls were once linked. Don't try to play it off. You didn't know about the attack on me, and I doubt you know how entrenched Julian is in this situation. I honestly don't care about your petty attempt to overthrow Numen. I don't believe you can do it, and I trust you will be stopped." She took a step forward. Mateo put a hand on her arm and she barely restrained herself from jerking out of his grasp. "I'm here to inform you that you need to clean up your mess. Send a message to anyone who thinks they can hurt Julian that they will be obliterated. Then follow up. You failed me. You failed at your job. You failed your realm. Don't you dare fail him."

James winced. Mateo's grip softened. He might've feared

her motivation for coming was to indulge in some female drama over a male she once used to love with all her being.

No, she was, above all, a mother. "You destroyed us, James. Julian is all I have left and he's *good*. Noble and honorable. You've put him in the atrocious position of defending the realm against his fallen father who doesn't have the grace to stay down."

James's mouth worked, chewing on words he had yet to utter. Finally, he spoke. "I've already sent word that he should be cautious."

She sneered, an unladylike sound ripping out of her. James's eyes flared. Mateo's gaze jerked toward her. Yes, it was unlike her and she didn't care. "*Sending word* isn't going to protect against angel fire. It isn't going to keep his wings attached if he gets framed like Director Vale was, nor will it provide a miracle for getting them back. I want you to send your people a message: fuck with your son and die."

Her ex watched her as he took his time inhaling and exhaling. "Point made, Chanel. I can't help but wonder... If you'd shown this much emotion during our time together, perhaps things would've been different."

She'd had many years to ponder these questions. She'd gone through all the stages of grief more times than she could count and had a few realizations along the way. "Don't you dare blame me for your fragile masculinity. So I was cold. I didn't smile enough. We had eternity to work on us. You gave up on me."

There went the muscle in his jaw. "Ah, but as I recall, you were the one who got the ball rolling. There was no talk of reconciliation. Who gave up on whom?"

She cocked her head, giving him an appraising look that was meant to strip his delicate ego further. "It really is all about you, isn't it? You didn't think of our son and how he was getting old enough to follow you to this realm? Or how he was curious about what his father was up to?" She straightened her gaze. "Or how those people you colluded with might try to sway him? All scenarios that could've cost him his own wings?"

His nostrils flared. No, he hadn't thought about all that. He really was as selfish as she remembered. Probably more so.

"I may not be *warm*, James. I didn't fetch your slippers or rub your back. I wasn't playing hide and seek with Julian or building gingerbread houses. No, I wasn't the warm and fuzzy matron you and others thought I should be, but one thing was and still is my priority—Julian's safety, and it doesn't matter if he's the fiercest fighter in the realm. Because I'm a *parent*." She hooked her hand around Mateo's arm. This conversation was nearing its end. "Do you have the balls to be one?"

She tugged her companion away. There was no resistance. He was stunned by her comments, but not nearly as much as her ex.

But that was the thing about James, or Jameson—it didn't matter the name. He underestimated those closest to him.

ight was falling in Atlanta. Jagger hunkered down in a sedan he'd rented just for tonight. The quaint, two-story house had a new paint job that was at odds with the overgrown grass and untrimmed hedges.

According to Felicia, Mrs. Washington and Claudia were often alone. Her husband was a truck driver. Was Mrs. Washington normally so unaffected by how her yard looked, or was she distracted due to the demon presence in her life? Were there more than sylphs tampering with her? He spotted a familiar statue in the garden.

"A fucking gnome," he murmured.

Felicia shifted next to him. They were parked half a block away in front of a house with a for-sale sign. Her hair was bound behind her neck and she was dressed in a black T-shirt and black leggings. He'd done the same to blend better.

She'd balked at slitting her top in the back, but depending on what they were up against, they might need their wings to fight. *Now's not the time to think about fashion, princess.* The statement had felt wrong when he'd said it, and so had the beat of alarm in her eyes when he'd handed her the scissors.

Felicia was a lot of things, but the more he was around her, the more inadequate "princess" was for a description.

"What's with the gnome?" She squinted and tilted her head from left to right.

The harder she tried, the less she'd see. "Relax enough to lose focus. Remember what I said: thousand-yard stare."

He'd already studied the surrounding houses and found no similar garden decor. Good. This was an isolated demon infestation.

"But it's a gnome. What does a demon need with an inanimate—oh." She slumped in her chair, her eyes wide, her mouth open. "I see it."

Those full lips. He dragged his gaze back to the garden. "They prefer gnomes. The face confuses the eye. Most angels roaming the realm wouldn't think to look at them, and if they do a double take, they're looking harder and won't see the gargoyle hiding inside."

"I had no idea they could possess statues."

"Not possess. Hide in. They can't move or command the statue like an archmaster does with a human."

"I see. What's the point, though? I thought they ate human flesh, and biting the ankles of a human weeding the garden seems counterproductive."

She'd likely come up with the answer, but their time was limited. The gargoyles would alert the sylphs inside the house to their presence. And while he enjoyed far too much seeing how quickly she problem solved issues that'd cause most people to give up, she had a lot to learn.

"They're the carrions of the demon world. Scavengers."

"Ah. No need to hide bodies when gargoyles can eat them." Her gaze flicked from the garden to the house. "They aren't planning to kill Claudia's mom, are they?"

"Maybe. Maybe not. Has she alluded to having you over?"

Felicia shook her head and froze. "Wait. She mentioned a

party to celebrate the class achieving a new level. She said the instructors were invited as well."

"When?" The invite had to be more than a coincidence.

Her brow crinkled as she thought. "It was before all this started."

"Right before? Like when Odessa was going through the records of the watcher Jameson murdered?"

Felicia's expression turned troubled. "About the same time."

He wasn't getting a good feeling.

"But I wasn't there, so they didn't test." Her eyelids drifted shut. "The class insisted on waiting until I got back. Dammit. No one was supposed to know where I lived."

"Did your father?"

She answered gravely, "He wouldn't have told anyone."

"But if he'd had the information recorded somewhere…"

She watched the house. Heartbreak rippled over her strong features. "I have to quit my job."

He followed her gaze. It was on the tip of his tongue to deny what she'd said, but her students—kids—were being used to spy on her. "I'm sorry."

There were no tears, just grim acceptance. He couldn't take his eyes off her. There was more going on behind those pretty eyes of hers than sorrow for walking away from a job she loved.

She chewed on her bottom lip and he had to switch his attention to the house. "I can't afford to move."

"Where did your father's wealth go?"

Her tone was flatter than the tires on the bicycle dumped in the Washingtons' yard. "Holy shit, I'm rich." She rolled her eyes toward him. "I'm not touching his money. He was nothing more than a puppet for some very bad people."

All senators were rich. It was the nature of their station—

the angels working in their households made money for them. Most angels had no need for currency. Their realm ran on the exchange of goods and services, and if gold was transferred, it was only because money would be needed in the human world.

"No one would fault you for using it to take care of yourself." He would've, once, but he'd seen how little she cared to touch it. He'd been living how she lived. Making his own breakfast, lunch, and dinner, and cleaning the bathroom once a week.

It…sucked.

"I would. He was a crook and people got hurt because of it."

"Like Director Vale." His director's burn scars were from a doomed mission Felicia's father had sent him on.

"And so many others." The incident was before Jagger had trained to be a warrior, but there were a few openings on Bryant's team afterward, so no, it hadn't turned out well for those warriors.

"It's almost dark enough. We go in after sundown." It hadn't been necessary to stake out Claudia's house, but once he'd gotten the go-ahead from Dionna, he couldn't have stayed in that small, square apartment any longer.

They waited in silence as night fell. Felicia fingered the edge of the blade he'd loaned her. He didn't care to go in with half his gear, but he also wasn't going to tell Felicia to stand back and watch. One, she wouldn't. And two, she'd still need to be armed.

Even though this was a simple in and out with minor demons that didn't concern Jagger, he was as nervous as his first battle, and not for himself. Felicia sparred. She'd never been in a life-or-death fight. He didn't have to ask to know.

The way she weighed and studied his blades told him

enough. In her beautiful face was too much curiosity and more innocence than she'd have if she'd battled for her life.

Yet there was a hardness there he couldn't explain. She'd grown up as privileged as him. His father was a fallen and his mother could make granite cry. He used to think he'd won the award for shittiest upbringing, but Felicia's mother had killed herself and her father had dabbled in treason.

Then there was her reputation, and he had to admit it didn't bother him like it once had. After the attack, she'd started living life on her own terms, and that had included sleeping with whomever she chose. Those who gossiped about her were trying to control her by shame, or make themselves feel more righteous. Either way, it was about them and not her, and he'd done the same. All the while, she'd had her flings. She remained friendly with some, but respectful about them all.

And as far as being respectful, she hadn't offered herself to anyone since he'd been guarding her. She didn't complain about needing to get laid or boast of her past conquests—yet she was savvy enough to know that would get to him. So either she didn't care to rile him in that way or…she slept around when she wanted to but she didn't want to right now. Because of him? That was obvious, but his mind churned over the why.

She was a puzzle. He only had pieces and no clue how to put them together.

Thank God it was finally dark out. He was driving himself crazy. "Ready?"

"Let's go save Mrs. Washington."

THIS WAS the closest to being a warrior she'd ever get. Without functional wings, there was no way Bryant would sign off. Not that she'd try. Or that she'd thought about it. Much.

What was she going to do? She couldn't work around humans if it brought demons to their door. She couldn't go back to Numen and twiddle her thumbs while living off Father's money. And no to sleeping in the pristine alleys of the realm. Two of those scenarios would only make her people nod sagely and say, "I knew it."

She walked casually next to Jagger. When he darted into a neighboring yard, she followed. But when he pried out two landscape bricks, she didn't know what to do.

He handed them to her. "I'll go in the back. Take out the gnomes before they can sound an alert."

Her first foray into the world of demons and it was going to be smashing cute garden statues. "The gargoyles will go back to Daemon, just like that?"

Jagger nodded and held up three fingers and counted down. Once he made a fist, they each swept into motion. She gripped the heavy landscaping bricks and smashed the gnomes just as Jagger set off the car alarm. The snarls of the gargoyles faded into the night with the alarm. He pocketed the key.

They waited in tense silence. No windows opened. Had the occupants heard? Were they going to come out and check? Sylphs were like ghosts, and if they popped out and saw the gnomes shattered, they'd know they'd been discovered.

Nothing happened.

"There," Jagger said. "That mess is done. Now we wait again."

"Claudia should be in bed."

"If there's one thing I've learned hunting possessed parents, it's that just because kids are in bed doesn't mean they're asleep."

The nights she and Ode had stayed up whispering and giggling sprang to mind. "Oh."

"And the more awake they are, the harder the sylphs will try to either rouse them and bust our cover so we're in danger of exposing ourselves, or use them against us."

The gravity in his tone made her wonder if he'd learned the hard way. His job was harder than she'd thought. Truthfully, she hadn't given it much consideration. Warriors muttered some incantation that booted the demon out of the host's body and disappeared into the Mist. Sylphs were even easier because they weren't inhabiting an earthly creature. They just got booted to the Mist and terminated. Harrowing complications like witnesses, children, and discovery hadn't occurred to her.

An hour ticked by. Her knees were getting as tender as her back, but Jagger hadn't moved or grunted so she wouldn't either.

A light flicked on behind a small square window she guessed was the upstairs bathroom. She lifted her gaze and gasped.

"No," she breathed.

Mrs. Washington peered out between the blinds, but it wasn't just her. Overlaid over her features was a gnarly face with horns. The woman was possessed.

"Hold still," Jagger murmured. They both crouched in their hiding spot as Mrs. Washington glowered at the street before ducking back. "Remember the plan?"

She nodded. He'd discussed this scenario with her before leaving the apartment.

"Follow my lead."

Trailing behind him and his tight ass was no hardship. *Keep your head in the game, girl.* This was her first demon fight. Maybe. She was only here as backup, but she had to be ready.

He withdrew a pick kit from his pocket. The door was wired to an electronic security system and she was about to whisper what the hell was he thinking when he used his free hand to send a pulse of energy to short the system.

Her jaw dropped. She'd never used her natural Numen energy on Earth. Would've never thought of it. In her realm, she could power minor devices that needed electricity. But on Earth, there was, well, electricity. If she used her own mojo, she risked raising questions that could risk her wings.

She'd resumed her composure by the time he freed the lock. Tiptoeing in behind him, she ran through the plan. They were going to jump as many sylphs as they could while Mrs. Washington was in the bathroom. That was it.

It sounded easy, but Jagger was in stealth mode. He didn't make a sound and he moved swiftly though the back entry into the kitchen and glided up the stairs, hugging the wall.

She mimicked everything and grimaced each time her back brushed the wall, the whisper of fabric against the wallpaper as loud as the shout of a bullhorn. They reached the top and he peered down the hallway.

He pointed to the far side of the bathroom door. That was where she was to go. He would stay on the side Mrs. Washington was most likely to turn when exiting and she would be there for backup, just in case.

Once positioned, he caught her eye and tipped his head toward the far end of the hall. Claudia's room. And the damn door was open.

No big deal.

But it could be. She didn't want to be spotted by her former student doing this nasty business. Once she and Jagger disappeared into the Mist, then Mrs. Washington would be left behind, confused and reeling. But they had to get to that point without being detected.

Words drifted out of the bathroom. Manic rumblings.

She glanced at Jagger.

He mouthed, "Sylphs."

How had she never heard them before? Was it just a case of not paying attention? No, just as this realm wasn't overrun with angels, it also wasn't spilling over with demons.

Why were the sylphs still around if the archmaster had gotten ahold of Mrs. Washington's soul?

She made out growled orders. "Scare the kid. Scare the kid."

More than one sylph and they were exiting before Mrs. Washington. Those little bastards were hers and he'd dive in to get the archmaster out.

Balancing the knives in her hand, she dropped into a ready position.

The handle jiggled. Poor Mrs. Washington. She was trapped in her own body, no longer the driver of her brain. From what Jagger had taught her, most humans had no recollection of what happened while they were possessed. The few that did had allowed the possession in the first place.

The door swung open and two sylphs arguing with each other spilled out. Neither one noticed her or Jagger at first.

Her hands tightened around the blade as her breath caught in her throat. She'd expected them to be small, but reality stalled her initial pounce. Somewhere between bipedal and four legged, they also had features reminiscent of an ogre. Tiny ogres. The mix gave them a familiar look. All those horror movies must derive their inspiration from somewhere, even if the creators didn't realize how close to reality they'd come.

When Jagger slipped behind them into the bathroom, she broke into action. Her one shot at surprise would take out at least one of them. Jagger had said they could still be killed in this realm. She was going to test that now.

Swinging her arm down, she buried the blade in the skull of the first sylph, using the follow-through momentum she'd learned in the gym. The knife sank through the skull just like Jagger had said it would.

Our steel isn't ordinary steel.

The second sylph cried out at the same time Jagger's words drifted to her. Thunks and grunts came from inside the bathroom. Jagger was still here.

She was jerking her weapon free as the demon disintegrated around it.

Damn.

It threw her off. The second sylph screamed and darted down the hall toward the stairs. She charged for it, Jagger's instructions streaming through her head.

Her arms wrapped around the creature and she pictured the hazy, cool environment of the Mist.

Wet droplets surrounded her as she rolled onto fluffy wet grass. The sylph didn't waste time while she was down. It jumped on her, yellow fangs flashing in her face.

She'd lost her knives in the transition. Punching out, she caught its jaw and flung it back. Rolling up, she did exactly as it had done and jumped it while it was down.

The creature brandished an impressive set of claws on its hands—paws?

Blocking its attempts to slash her, she stayed in a crouch and landed every hit she could. This wasn't a form of fighting she'd learned, battling a demon that stood less than three feet tall.

Her brain registered a fight behind her. Snarls and grunts lingered in the Mist, and the metallic tang of sour blood hit the air. Jagger must be making progress.

A silver gleam caught her eye. One of the knives.

The creature spotted it. She dove for it at the same time it did.

Claws jabbed the back of her hand, but she got the blade, spinning her body at the same time. Her knee clipped the beast's head. It toppled back and before it could right itself, she hammered down. The blade embedded into the skull.

Kill two. Done.

The knife wasn't as easy to free this time. The sylph didn't disintegrate. She didn't have time to recall what Jagger had said about bodies in the Mist. She wiped the steaming blood off on the grass as she evaluated Jagger.

As soon as we get into the Mist, let your wings go. You'll need them for protection.

He wasn't going to take her disobedience lightly. He might even use it to refuse additional training. She'd have to deal.

Readjusting her grip on the knife, she approached the dueling males. The archmaster wasn't what she'd expected. Just as tall as Jagger, the male was packed with muscle. Powerful frame, thick thighs, and lightning-fast moves. His wings were a leathery, inky black and he used them as ruthlessly as his fangs and claws.

Jagger's moves were as fast, his hits as lethal. They were locked in a gruesome dance. The archmaster's wings had claws as sharp as razors. One bop to the head and she'd be reeling, trying to stay conscious.

She'd have to make sure she stayed far enough away.

But they shuffled closer, their wings locked together, grunts dying in the Mist.

She weighed the blade in her hands. All she needed was an opening and she could bury it in the demon's back, just under the wings, where he'd be nice and tender.

Balancing on the balls of her feet, she slipped closer.

"Felicia," Jagger's warning growl hit her ears before the whoosh of a wing.

The demon had spun, shoving away Jagger and whipping

a dark wing down on her head. She'd been so focused on her own stealth, she'd miscalculated the boldness of the underworld. And she had no wings out to block the move. Her arm wasn't strong enough for his momentum.

A solid thump to the head preceded total darkness.

CHAPTER 7

A warrior had lost his legs because of her.

Sierra stared at the winged statue outside of an old Catholic church. An angel. Cold. Unfeeling. Covered in bird shit.

She could be that statue.

Her entire life, she'd had a single-minded mission. Get close to the sister who knew nothing about her, then eventually reveal their connection.

I know your secret.

Because she shared it.

If anyone knew about them, they'd be killed. The senate would go apoplectic before going after them with such zeal they'd foam at the mouth.

Two girls who shouldn't exist, yet here they were. Warriors for their people.

Except, was she?

The male who'd blackmailed her for information was the real villain. But she was an accomplice, a sad excuse for someone who'd vowed to put the safety of the realm over her own life.

She hadn't been able to put the safety of the realm over her sister's, though. Not before the female knew about her, before she knew she wasn't alone.

Her gaze lingered on that marble statue, on the melancholy expression as it watched over the cemetery. Sadness, caring, servitude.

What was she? A lying, weak, poor excuse for a warrior. She should confess and lose her wings, but call her a coward, she didn't want that fate.

Though sometimes she wondered… Her gaze swept from the statue to the cemetery plots. Watched over after death. In her efforts to find the one responsible for the plot against the realm, she'd tracked down one of the fallen here. Most of her team's search had led to similar places. Cemeteries and nondescript headstones.

Not Jameson Haddock. He'd proved that falling did not mean certain death.

She sighed, the sound lost in the gentle breeze blowing over the plots. A human stepped out of the church, an older woman with salt-and-pepper hair tied down with a scarf. She was wearing floral-print work gloves and sturdy blue jeans and carrying a small trowel.

Sierra was about to turn and go, but the woman waved, her smile wide. It'd be rude to turn and run. Half of her screamed to do it, to wait until the woman was a few feet away, then flounce off. At least her dark side no longer demanded violence. Her work as a warrior helped with that.

"Can I help you find something?" The woman's voice was kind. The crinkles around her eyes and mouth spoke of a history full of smiles and laughter.

Sierra envied this human. Her time was winding down, but she'd probably lived more joy than Sierra would ever know.

"No." Sierra's gaze landed on the unmarked plot labeled

Jane Doe. Jane wasn't her name. The female had a whole history in another world, but she'd developed feeling for a human who loved another. One murder motivated by jealousy later, "Jane" had lost her wings and wasted away on the street she'd been dumped on.

It wasn't a coincidence that Sierra had located her new headquarters by this church in Vegas. A reminder that, eventually, she'd pay for her crimes.

The woman looked toward the headstone. "Ah. I was here when they brought Jane Doe in." Her face scrunched up briefly. "Forty-two years ago. I was all of twenty-seven. I remember the day like it was yesterday."

"What happened?" Why was she asking? Her fate was in that rectangle of dirt. She didn't need to hear the gruesome details.

"Poor soul. We tried to help her, find out who'd attacked her, but she kept muttering that she deserved it. Refused every ounce of help. Wouldn't even allow us to wipe the blood off her back." The woman shook her head. "We're here to help. We can't force ourselves on someone, but we're here." She bobbed her head. "We're here."

Jane could've had help. This woman and this church would've nursed her back to health and found a place for her. After taking a life, Jane had chosen death.

But there had been people willing to help her without knowing a single bit about her past or what she'd done.

Something to think on.

She turned and followed the path back to the sidewalk. Her rental was only a few blocks away and the sun was beating down. She relished the burn. A small discomfort compared to what Director Richter had gone through—was going through.

A man waited at the junction of the pebbled path and the cement. He was vaguely familiar with greenish-yellow eyes and artfully arranged, sand-colored hair. His suit was light gray and tailored for every inch of his tall frame.

She sensed no demon involvement in or around him, but his presence didn't register like an ordinary human's.

She'd take the long way home.

She was about to turn the other direction when he spoke, his voice rich and the timbre way too pleasing. "Ms. Cormorant."

"Not interested." She should find out who he was and how he knew her name, but she'd had enough of strange males in her life.

"Ah, but you work with my son. Julian."

She didn't know any—oh. Jagger.

She stopped and slowly spun around. "Mr. Haddock."

A grin spread across his face and damn, it was so unfair that a male so vile should be so handsome. Now she saw the resemblance. Jagger didn't have the refined maturity of his father. He didn't wear his power like his father wore that suit. Jameson Haddock's hair was more brown than blond, but his eyes were as unique as Jagger's. They were a sharper green, nearly yellow.

"Call me Jameson, please."

Hot or not, she didn't trust him. "What do you want?"

"Your word that our business doesn't go further than the two of us."

She lifted a brow. "No promises."

He lips quirked. "Wouldn't it be hard to explain me without explaining how you know our mutual friend Stede?"

She winced. Of course Jameson Haddock would know, but she liked pretending the dirty secret didn't go further than a male she still had a chance of killing.

"What do you want?" she asked again.

"Perhaps we could talk somewhere more private."

"Nope." Sweat trickled down her back. It was going to

drip off her hair onto her shirt soon. Jameson looked like the sun was too timid to touch him.

"Very well." He hooked his hands in front of him. He had nice hands. She'd always had a weakness for a guy in a suit and the way they fought with their minds instead of their bodies. A consequence of training around so many sweaty, macho males. "I want you to report to me whenever Stede asks for information regarding my son or that female he's protecting."

"Stede is done with me."

He tilted his head and gave her droll look. "Do you really think he'd let such a good resource go?"

He hadn't found her yet. "Why's he after Jagger? I thought you two worked together."

Even his chuckle was sexy. "Demons haven't cornered the market on wickedness. But I'm a fair partner. Do this for me and tell me what you need in return."

Oh, she needed a lot. A way to turn back time, but he couldn't help with that. A father who was from Numen. Did Jameson know about her secret? Did he know who Harlowe was and that she was related? He had to if Stede did. And since Jameson was standing here on the edge of religious property in a city she'd lived in for all of a month and a half, he could find out easily enough.

"I want to know everything about falling and how you survived."

"I don't think you're ready for the truth, but yes. I can share the whole sordid story." His expression darkened momentarily before his lips curved and he turned the charisma on. His smile was the most charming she'd ever seen. It was unfair. He'd had everything and he'd thrown it away. She'd worked for what little she had and was losing it all.

But that didn't stop her libido—it had been a while since she'd gotten laid.

"Deal." She might have to spare a few hours to swipe right on her dating app. Was it just being around Jameson that set her hormones ablaze?

"Deal. You know how to find me, Sierra." He damn near purred her name before he strode away. A dark sedan with tinted windows that were probably illegal drove down the road and stopped next to him. He climbed in.

She stared at the car as it passed her. He still looked like an angel, but she felt like she'd made a deal with the devil.

JAGGER'S CHEST HEAVED. He'd killed the archmaster and a report to Director Vale was already forming in his head, but Felicia was his first priority.

He spun and rushed to her side, but the sight that greeted him slowed his footsteps like he was trudging through fresh concrete.

In her unconscious state, the morph on her wings had released.

Instead of a glorious unfurling of her wings, there was a misshapen bundle of the softest pewter-gray feathers piled at her back. He'd have to make sense of it after he checked on her.

Kneeling in front of her face, he examined her limp body. He spotted no singe marks from angel fire, and the bruising on her face was purpling but would fade in a day. The head trauma was more significant, but she'd also recover within a day. Vulnerability while unconscious was his kind's biggest concern, but he was her guard after all.

Now, about the wings.

Had they somehow gotten injured even while in the morph?

Maneuvering around to her back, he failed to find any fresh streaks of blood on the feathers. Tenderly shifting their downy weight, he inspected them. Where bone should've arched in elegant lines, it was crooked and bare of all feathers. Each naked expanse of skin was mottled in a too familiar way.

Angel-fire burns.

Working his way to the wing joints in her back made the sourness churning in his belly creep up the back of his throat.

Where creamy, bronzed flesh should've been, the tissue was stretched and scarred, like she'd been carved up by a knife doused in angel fire. He'd seen the injuries before on warriors. Maximal injury, minimal chance at healing properly. And she hadn't healed properly.

Her constant wing morph had to be taxing. The image of her swallowing OTC pain meds jumped to mind.

Who had hurt her like this?

"Fuck." He rested on his heels and stared at her. Guilt waged with rage inside of him. Steadying his breaths, he calmed himself until his emotions no longer clogged his thinking like a sandstorm.

She hid her injuries. From him and everyone else. Did her sister know? Was this why Felicia avoided Numen? His kind were vain, believing that, because they lacked many of the same flaws as humans, they were somehow superior. He wasn't exempt from taking his healing capabilities for granted either. As a warrior, he should be the last of his kind to forget, but he relied on his healing, often taking risks knowing that unblemished skin was a few hours away.

With the heat of battle wearing off, the damp, cool air of the Mist settled in. Felicia needed somewhere to recover.

Going back to her apartment was a no-go. It was nighttime and he could morph his own wings in, but no way could he carry an unconscious woman through the streets of Atlanta with her wings dragging on the sidewalk.

Numen it was then. He could leave the Mist close enough to his place to get into his house without being seen.

He eased her into his arms, cradling her wings to keep them from stretching the scar tissue. Navigating the Mist would be impossible if he didn't know his way around it already. Nothing populated the divide between his realm and the human world but grass, mist, and spirits no one wanted to admit were there. The Mist was all about feeling and intention, and while his kind liked to pretend they knew how it worked, there were mysteries yet unsolved. He'd learned to do his job in the Mist—killing demons—and get home. The demons were dead. It was time to get Felicia home.

Several minutes ticked by. He approached the Mist's edge and treaded along the thinnest portion of its border. His home was several blocks away from the barracks. He'd never crossed the Mist so far from the warrior's living and training area. Was it even possible? Most angels had no reason to go into the Mist. Only warriors required the privacy of the in-between for their battles. Those that weren't granted access to the human world had no business in the Mist.

He exited the Mist at the edge of the barracks, drifting close enough to make out the ordinary rectangular buildings before turning away for home. When he'd been dating Vale-rina, he'd moved into this place. Valerina had found it and while it was inconveniently blocks away from the warrior training ground, he'd wanted her to be happy. Perhaps she'd assumed he'd eventually leave and become the senator she'd thought he was destined for.

She could join Mother in her delusions. He'd grown up in the senator's life and its unfeeling, backstabbing duplicity.

No, thanks. He'd rather get impaled by a demon claw.

Up ahead, his home called to him. A place he hadn't spent much time in lately, thanks to the passed-out female in his arms. Even before Felicia had swooped back into his life, he'd been loath to linger under his own roof. Too many hard feelings. Valerina's accusations. Watching her move out, helpless to stop her. Wondering why she wouldn't believe him over lurid rumors.

He tried not to think about it as he made his way home, looking, listening, and feeling for any prying eyes. No one. His home was dark. Skirting the shadows to his back door, he focused his energy on opening the door. It swung open without a sound. The angels he'd hired to care for the building were earning their keep. Thankfully, they had their own homes to go to after work.

He carried the angel in his arms to the guest bedroom next to his. The room was bare and expressionless, just as he had been when he'd stayed here after Valerina had walked out. The rest of the rooms were in her taste, but like his mother, she hadn't encouraged guests to stay for anything longer than a dinner party, and it showed in the attention this room had gotten.

He laid Felicia down on top of the covers. Though she was a tall female, he hadn't minded carrying her so far. The loss of her heat against him was far too disconcerting. He attempted to summon his anger, remembering how she'd given him a patronizing smile and denied his request to set the record straight about them. She'd had a reputation around the barracks, though he'd grudgingly admit he'd wondered why her behavior was being called out. He'd use up all his fingers and toes naming males who liked to sleep with a multitude of partners.

Why had she started the rumor about them? She'd come on to him and he'd turned her down. Had it angered her that much? He'd kept his distance out of respect for Valerina. He'd had no reason to talk to Felicia, so he hadn't except to say, thanks, but no.

She'd ruined his life. All he'd had was his work to get him through the gossip storm. He'd lost sleep wondering when everyone would remember he was the son of a fallen. But if his kind were good at one thing, it was forgetting those who fell. Their existence was as close to erased as possible, their punishment meant to finish the job without the moral ambiguity of execution.

But he hadn't forgotten.

He wiped a hand over his face and sank into a settee next to the bed. His clothing was crusted with blood and other demon body fluids. The fabric was probably ruined, unless his housekeeper could save it. Worries for another day.

He had an unconscious angel and a lot of questions.

FELICIA WOKE WITH A START. She propped herself on her elbow. A barren wall greeted her. Light filtered in behind hand-sewn drapes. Her mother had once bought a similar set for her and Ode's rooms. They'd been ruined in the fire.

Where was she?

She twisted around. Two things dawned on her and each one increased the pounding in her head. Her wings were out and Jagger was watching her.

The demon fight flared bright in her brain. She hadn't let her wings out and it'd left her vulnerable. She must've been knocked out. Her clothing cracked as she moved into a sitting position onto the comfy bed. Her face felt dried and crusty. Her wound must've bled.

Jagger had fared better. None of the bloody remnants on him were his own. He was an amazing fighter. All that coiled energy and unleashed resentment had been aimed at the demon.

It was dead. She didn't have to ask. And she had more pressing issues.

Jagger clasped his hands across his toned stomach. "Wanna tell me about it?"

He wasn't wasting time.

Her lungs deflated like a month-old party balloon. She held her breath for a beat of three and slowly inhaled. It was time he knew. Protecting her was one thing, but they were going to be in more danger if he didn't know what he was up against—or what her limitations were.

"I was attacked when I was fifteen. They went after both me and Ode one night, in our own house. They tortured me and told me to keep quiet to protect her. And they told her to keep quiet to protect me. She was younger, so they only hurt me."

Shock registered on his face. He hadn't expected her to talk. He might've concluded something atrocious had happened, but not this level of depravity.

"So, yeah. Right before you were ordered to shadow me, my father confessed that he had been ordered to interfere with Bryant's team. At the time, they'd been onto some demons who could be linked to corrupt senators. When Father refused, they sent two thugs to our house in the middle of the night."

"That's…"

"Fucked up? Yeah." The rest of the story spilled out, and telling it was as much of a relief as not having to morph her wings. "Father did the big bad. Bryant was severely injured and members of his team died. My parents tried to do their best for us, then sent me to a boarding school, which I left in no time." She pointed to her back. "It's too painful to hold a morph for that long, especially as tender as they were then.

And you can imagine the questions my classmates had about why I would morph them anyway. Flash forward, and the corrupt senators are making headway with the help of your father, and Ode stumbles onto the plot. She's in danger and I'm in danger and Bryant's team is once again dragged into it." She spread her hands. "There you have it."

His expression hadn't changed, but she could see his mind working. Those eyes of his were sharp as he connected dot after dot. She didn't need to explain why she avoided her home, the realm, and basically all of Numen. She didn't need to rehash Mother's suicide or Father's grisly death.

He still hadn't spoken. She couldn't stand the reason for his silence. Pity. "This your place?"

His mouth quirked. "You have reportedly seen the inside."

Had he quit blaming her? "I never said I had."

"Hmph."

"Still don't believe me? News flash. I really don't care." The lie tasted sour. How could he live with her for so many weeks and still think she would do something like that? How could he hear the most terrible moment of her life and think she was still a liar?

He cut a hand through the air. "It no longer matters, does it? We have a more pressing situation."

What he thought mattered to her. She wouldn't destroy another's life. Lusting after him didn't mean she'd spread horrible lies to get his fiancée to dump him.

He unfolded his body, the power in him so at odds with the delicate grace of the furniture he'd been perched on. "There's a bathroom down the hall. I'll notify Odessa and Director Vale that you're here before I clean up. Perhaps your sister can bring you some clothing."

"Does anyone know that we're here?"

"Not yet."

Her apartment in Atlanta was her safe spot. She knew the

city, her neighbors, and what was out of the ordinary. This was Numen, where she was exposed and vulnerable. Where she was at a disadvantage because of her useless wings.

"You're safe here." Had her expression revealed her insecurity? "If you'd like, I can wait until you're done washing up before I shower."

She liked the sound of that but would never say so. "I might as well wait for Ode and a new set of clothing. Tell her no robes." He dipped his head and was walking out when she made another request. "Don't tell them. About my wings."

He looked at her over his shoulder, his expression unreadable. Argh! She hated being needy around him. "Don't they know?"

"They do, but they haven't seen…" Her wings were tucked as far behind her back as she could get them to keep Jagger from getting a good view, even though he'd already seen. She hid them from everyone.

"We'll wait until they arrive and both clean up at the same time."

"You can go shower."

"I'm waiting."

She crossed one leg over the other. "Seriously. You don't have to."

"It's my job."

His job that he was suddenly performing 100 percent. The thought was catty. He'd always been at the ready, just hating every minute of it. The only thing that had changed was that now he blamed her less, for the demon attack at least. Though he still seemed to think she liked telling everyone that she slept with people she hadn't.

Okay, so she'd done that with her sister's last boyfriend. She'd alluded to sleeping with him, though she hadn't and never argued otherwise. But the male had been a tool, a philanderer. And Ode would've hung on to the bitter end if she hadn't seen him in bed with another with her own eyes. A noble sacrifice, but one that had cost her her sister until their recent reconciliation.

He stepped out to contact Bryant. Grateful he embraced the use of human technology in Numen, she hastily morphed her wings. The pinch of warped muscle and the stretching of ravaged skin made her wince. The gasp couldn't be helped. It was a rush job.

He was in the doorway. Damn. He must've rounded the corner when her eyes were squeezed shut.

"I've already seen them," he said. He was looking down on her but for once waves of superiority weren't rolling off him.

"And you don't have to keep seeing them."

The look he gave her was odd, like she had transformed into another person. But then, as if he sensed her emotional fragility, he did the unexpected and made a joke. "Felicia Montclaire, shy? I never would've thought."

She gave him the middle finger, but his comment coaxed a small smile.

He chuckled. "I'm surprised you don't turn to ash, making that gesture up here."

"The angels here have done worse."

His smile faded. "I know."

"Sorry. Buzzkill. But I think they forget we aren't divine."

The corner of his mouth kicked up. The male had lush lips. "*That* will make you turn to ash."

Her own smile grew. "I can wander around, whispering in the wind. Really mess people up."

A monotone *ding* rang through the house.

"Oh dear God," she muttered. She wasn't ready to face anyone. Jagger was hard enough.

If this was her first conscious hour in Numen, how was she going to tolerate living up here again?

CHAPTER 8

*S*omeone was in her house.

Sierra crept out of her office and down the hallway, wishing she'd thrown on more than shorts and a tank top. She'd done a quick morph of her wings when she'd sensed the presence. Odd how she still abided by the laws of her land in such small things. After the enormity of her betrayal to her kind—even worse, to her team—a human catching sight of her wings would be nothing in comparison.

After all, a male's life had been destroyed because of her deception. Because she was a fucking coward, an outcast who couldn't reveal her heritage to anyone.

Emerging from the short hallway, she clutched the small knife she'd grabbed from her dresser. Her grip didn't loosen when she saw who waited for her.

Stede.

"What do you want?" Jameson had been right. Stede finding her had only been a matter of time. Had she been so naïve to think that he couldn't find her new place in Las Vegas? Director Vale had ordered her to move closer to Jameson once he'd settled into his new position. She was their eyes and ears—and it would end up costing them if both Jameson and Stede could hunt her down this easily. How had they each done it?

The male reclined on her thrift store upholstered chair, looking like any other human businessman wearing black slacks and a red button-up shirt. The mild attire didn't hide the darkness in his gaze or the natural cruelty that stained his brown eyes.

Her sharp words prompted a faint smile. "Since we work so excellently together, I thought I'd stop by. I have another favor to ask." His expression went hard. "Where is he?"

She knew who he was talking about. Dionna had briefed her and ordered her to check on the Washington family, then clear all of Felicia's history in Atlanta. There was no going back for Felicia. At least she had places to go. Sierra was stuck.

"He's back in Numen."

Stede paused as if studying her reaction, so she made sure there wasn't one. He nodded like he'd known all along. "Yes, I thought so. They'd be too afraid of drawing demons to them and hurting humans." He sneered like it was such a weakness. "Where in Numen?"

She gave him a bored look, but a thrill swirled inside. Jameson had known this male would go after his son—and it had upset him. Was that the key to nailing Jameson? "It's not like there's a wealth of safe houses there. Figure it out."

She deliberately stayed loose when she only wanted to go rigid at his reaction. He'd done nothing but lob a few well-targeted threats her way, but danger and volatility emanated off him.

Displeasure rippled across his face, but then he adopted a satisfied look. "Once again, you're a wealth of information. He's at his home."

"I'm not helping you again." Her old director had lost his legs because of her—because of who she was. If she'd known what a liability to her team she'd be, she would've hidden in some remote desert on Earth. Instead, she'd yearned to be by her sister, even if Harlowe had no clue about their relationship and would probably spurn her with the rest of the realm if she did.

He narrowed his eyes. "You will. If I deem it necessary, you will." Rising, he straightened his cuff links.

She stayed where she was. "Jameson Haddock know that you're after his son?"

Despite his placid gaze, the air between them dropped a few degrees. "Julian Hancock is his weakness. I'm just keeping eyes on the boy."

Boy? Julian was older than she was. "And Felicia?"

His left eye twitched. Interesting. "She was a loose end, but Senator Kenton made that a moot point."

Uh-huh. Then Felicia's student's demon issue was a way to get at Jagger through her. "How is the good senator?"

"Ordering whores left and right."

Surprised he'd given her that much, she wanted to ask more. She had a feeling he'd feel no ill will if Kenton were to suddenly lose his head or fall into a vat of angel fire, but Kenton would probably blubber like a three-year-old with a secret—spilling everything with a little pressure.

"Stay in touch, Sierra. I need you accessible to me." His eyes turned cold, all humanity been sucked from them. "And don't even think about finding a way to clue Haddock into my interest with his kid. I'll destroy you with a few well-placed messages. And your sister just for fun." He turned and walked out.

She didn't reply, just glared at his broad back as he left. If there were any way she could get back at the bastard, she'd take it. But good fortune wasn't in her genes and she had a call to make.

~

"I can't *what*?" Felicia couldn't believe what Bryant was telling her. The rest of Jagger's team, with the exception of Harlowe, watched her with varying degrees of sympathy, and that made it worse. She was looked at with derision or superiority, but not pity. Odessa grabbed her hand. It anchored her to the obnoxious backless sofa in the formal sitting area of Jagger's home. "What do you mean I can't go back to Atlanta?"

"Sierra's arranging the sale of your apartment and will move your stuff into storage."

"So strangers are going to go through my things?" She'd rather it be anonymous humans than anyone she knew, but still. Logically, she knew it had to happen. The news was sudden and didn't hurt any less. She'd made a comfortable home in Atlanta. When this mess was done, she'd make a home elsewhere—just not Numen.

"Your work, everything. Taken care of," Bryant said and his tone meant it was final. He turned his gaze on Jagger. "And we have news for you as well."

Jagger leaned against the far wall, where he had a good viewpoint out the window. "I hope it's not a bad as telling me that my existence on Earth has been wiped out."

Odessa tightened her grip on Felicia's hand as Bryant answered. "Your mother was attacked in her home."

"*What?*" He pushed off the wall.

"She wasn't harmed. A sentry was at her house and saved her, injuring the attacker."

Fury played over Jagger's face. "Good, or I'd do it myself." He looked around but didn't meet the gaze of his team until he glanced back at Bryant. "Who was the sentry? Why was he at her house? Was his story checked out?"

Bronx coughed and tried to cover it up. Jagger shot him a glare. Bronx lifted his brows toward Bryant.

"It's our understanding that they're seeing each other. Mateo Armstrong."

Felicia kept her jaw from dropping, but she didn't know how. Mateo was Jagger's age, but that wasn't the surprising part. Chanel Hancock had taken a lover, and then *admitted* it?

The same incomprehension passed through his hard features. Denial lit his eyes and he shook his head, but his look softened. "But you checked his story out?"

Bryant inclined his head. "They've been seeing each other for a while, but he's reportedly staying with her now. I think that if he were a threat, he would've acted on it by now. I believe…" The director sucked in a breath. "I believe he truly cares for her."

"The poor bastard." Jagger went back to his post by the wall. "So now what? She's under protection."

"Since your mother is a target, I have to assume you are as well. We don't know if it's your father or his accomplices trying to double cross him. You'll need extra protection here to be sure." Bryant gestured to Dionna and Bronx on the far side of the room, then to the entry where Harlowe stood post, and to the window where Urban patrolled outside. "Dionna has set up a schedule. You'll have at least one other teammate here at all times."

Felicia bristled. More bodies around her. She'd gone from a relatively solitary lifestyle to having security and a bodyguard. Only now her bodyguard needed a bodyguard.

But she got over herself when she saw the conflict raging in Jagger's eyes. Someone was after his mother and that was bad enough, but it might be his father. What a mind fuck. Even as an adult, it would be hard to take.

She looked around. After two months of doing nothing,

her future was full of more nothing. "We can't just stay here and not help."

Bryant pinned her with his direct stare. "You can and you will. Until we know more, we wait. I have Sierra working on gathering more intel on Earth and the team members that aren't on duty will be doing the same up here."

"How?" Jagger asked, and she could tell it was just because he had to feel like part of the team and not just their duty.

Dionna answered, her rich voice only as loud as it needed to be for them all to hear. "Truthfully, we don't know. Senator Kenton's living quarters and those of Enforcer Stede's were already combed through before we got there."

Which meant there were more up here working with Kenton and Stede. Thus the protection detail and their restricted movement.

She looked at Jagger. His jaw was rigid as he stood with his arms crossed and his feet planted like he was in charge when they all knew he and Felicia were powerless. He lifted his gaze and met hers.

He wasn't happy about being stuck here, he didn't like that it was with her, and he was going to be justifiably moody about his mother.

But for once, he couldn't blame her and she got no satisfaction from that.

A MUFFLED voice came through the other side of the door. "Come on. I need a sparring partner."

Fucking Felicia.

Her restlessness had kept him up half the night. The wall between their bedrooms needed another layer of stone. It was her third night back in the realm and she hadn't settled down. The first night, she'd been unconscious, and he was starting to wonder if it was the only way she'd relax.

During the day, she was surly and short-tempered, and he could match her for every ounce of bad mood. Their rooms were separated by stone, but he felt her in there. Tossing and turning, twisting in his sheets.

He swung his legs down and padded over to the door before questioning whether he should get dressed first. His feathers were ruffled and he wore only a pair of black and orange board shorts.

He yanked the door open. "What the fuck for?"

Her gaze dipped to his chest. He shouldn't want to preen under her appreciation but he stood a little straighter. That pink tongue of hers darted out to wet her lower lip. If she did that again, his board shorts weren't going to hide his reaction.

She lifted her gaze, back to the shrewd angel he'd been guarding. "You don't have a punching bag and Bronx refuses to leave his post. He's startlingly devoted to his work for such a player."

Jealousy swept through him like a spilled vial of angel fire. "You know his reputation as a player how?"

Anger flashed in her eyes but was replaced by wickedness. She leaned close. "Because one time, he and I fucked for *hours*. Days, even. Did you know his dick is—"

A choking noise cut her off. Jagger thought it had come from him, but Bronx's voice quickly followed. "Don't believe her. Unless she says how huge and talented my dick is. Then it's totally the truth but she doesn't know from firsthand experience." A flush spread over Bronx's face as he approached the doorway. It was the first time Jagger had ever seen the other warrior flustered. "I don't need the new director thinking I messed with his mate's sister. He's already irritated that I flirted with Tenley." Bronx adopted Director

Vale's gravelly voice with the light British accent. "'Don't you dare hit on the staff, Bronx. I don't need the drama.' She was the one hitting on me!"

Felicia rolled her lips in like she was holding in a laugh and shot a glare at Bronx. "Bryant will know that his mate's sister can choose whoever she messes around with. Right now, I'm messing with Jagger here." Her gaze went back to him. "Shadow boxing won't cut it. I need a partner."

He raised a brow toward Bronx. The male was up here for a reason.

Bronx lifted a steel-gray wing. "She's been bugging the shit out of me. You might as well spar."

"You came up here to tell me that?" He was not jealous that Bronx was getting Felicia's attention.

"I wanted you to know that we're down a guard, but Harlowe will be here soon."

He was getting babysat by those he'd fought beside for years. The human world was a team short because of him. Was this one of the reasons Felicia had been so cranky when he'd started protecting her? She hated to be a drain on resources. She might not admit it, but it was one of the reasons she'd fled the realm. The feeling of responsibility for another's action. Like her mother's death and how Director Vale's team had suffered because her father had wanted to protect her. Like Jagger was grating his teeth and accepting responsibility for Jameson and other angels who wanted to hurt this realm.

He wanted this over. Then again, it wouldn't be over until Jameson was dead and that...was too hard to think about. Dead-to-me was different that being well and truly gone.

"Fine, I'll spar." He leaned through the doorframe, reveling in her feminine awareness. "But you need to learn to fight with your wings."

"No." She backed away, her gaze darting to where Bronx

had disappeared. He wouldn't have said it if his teammate could've overheard.

"Harlowe and Bronx won't disturb us."

"You've seen them," she hissed. "They'd be useless in a fight."

"They've been tucked away for years. Start strengthening them now." His calm demeanor might irritate her, but he wouldn't budge on this. Hiding them was more than second nature to her. Damaged wings and shame were part of her identity. She'd need more convincing. "Just like I'm Jameson Haddock's weak spot, your wings are yours. The guy who hurt you knows that—and he works for the other side. Don't think he won't exploit that."

Her expression clouded over and he didn't like the way she hunched in on herself. She was listening, though.

"I have a gym in the lower level. We'll lock the door. No one can see in or get in. Harlowe and Bronx are keeping watch."

"It's going to hurt." She didn't say it as a counterpoint. The resignation in her voice was too clear. She'd been vulnerable once and she didn't want to be that way again. "Let me take some meds first."

For a guy who'd hated the idea of her being in his home, he suddenly couldn't wait to spar with her in his gym.

CHAPTER 9

For the eighth time, she checked the bolt on the door.

It didn't make her feel better. The relief at having her wings out couldn't match the trepidation about fighting with them. The scar tissue had adjusted to the weight and while still painful, it still felt better than a long-term morph. Jagger was right.

As much as she hated the thought, she did baby her wings. Her back muscles weren't accustomed to hefting her wings around and the fine muscles in the wings themselves had likely atrophied.

For years she'd assumed that as long as she wasn't in Numen, she didn't need them. But she was in Numen now and the battle in the Mist had shown her how useful they were.

Jagger set his protein shake on a rack of weights. Since metal wasn't in large supply in this realm and was usually requisitioned for warrior weapons, he must've smuggled everything over. Many of their kind did.

The mat they stood on was similar to the rubbery ones in

the gyms she'd trained in. She'd seen warriors practicing on the grass, but Jagger must've felt like he was missing out when he'd moved in here with his fiancée.

There was no way Valerina had stepped foot in here.

"So, are we doing this?" she asked.

Jagger was doing high knee bends and warming up his body. She'd been ready since she'd woken up. Her wings were out and her impatience was just as unfurled.

"Are you warmed up?" he asked.

"I don't need to be."

"Your wings do." He gave her a pointed look. "FYI, we're not sparring."

"What the hell are you talking about?" Why had she woken him up anyway? She'd known the gym was here. She could've tumbled or something.

"I'm talking about starting as slow as we can. Doing some strength training." He shrugged, tilted his head side to side, then flared his wings out. Pointing to her. "Do five of these and see how it feels."

It felt like she wanted to run and hide from the male who was so insulting about her character but cared for her safety and the wings no one knew about.

Her sports bra pulled as she raised her wings a few inches. She'd had to cut out and re-stitch part of the material, but she'd managed a garment that contained her breasts and gave her back freedom.

Lowering her wings, she winced at the pull.

"One." Was he seriously going to count them out?

She repeated two through five. An unfamiliar ache settled into her shoulders.

"Now stretch them out to the side." As he took her through a stretching and strengthening plan only he knew about, she cursed herself for the oversight. She should've been doing this all along.

She was transported back to those first years of learning to fight, when she'd been weak as a lamb. Sweat dotted her forehead, perspiration spread across her body, and she was full of discomfort and then outright pain. She was breathing hard and she'd done nothing more than wing tai chi.

"Good. That should do it." He took another drink from his shake and went to the door.

She put her hands on her waist. "I've got nowhere else to be. Let's fight."

His gaze flicked down to her bare legs, then brushed across the expanse of her bare belly. "I'm good."

"I wouldn't know. You're too chicken to spar." She was antsy, and waiting around that guest room, doing nothing, wasn't an option. After her wing yoga, she needed a confidence booster. The thought of taking her aggression out on him wasn't an idea she was letting go.

He paused.

She concentrated, morphing her wings. After all the warm-up, they ached, but the action wasn't as acutely painful as before. "Come on. I'm bored silly. Make me earn all the sitting around we're going to do later."

He rolled his shoulders and set his drink down. That was her shake recipe—and his favorite, though he'd never admit it. His wings disappeared in their own morph. So seamless, so simple. "One match."

"Best two out of three." She was her father's daughter and wanted things her way.

"Let's see how the first match goes." Was he holding out to see how well she did before agreeing to more?

They faced off. He gave her a dubious once-over. They circled.

"I think you're nervous," she said as she tried to catch him off guard with a left hook.

He blocked her with a simple swat. "I think you're cocky. And it's going to cost you."

He dropped and swung a leg around. She barely jumped and cleared him. She wasn't fast enough after landing. He'd expected her to evade his move. His momentum continued as his other leg came around, sweeping her feet out from under her.

Damn!

She thumped on her back and was mid roll when strong hands closed around her calves and yanked.

Double damn! She'd been so distracted with getting him to spar in the first place, she hadn't put much thought into the actual fight. Rookie moves left and right.

Sliding across the mat, she wriggled and kicked, but his grip was solid. He yanked her right under him and pinned her.

"I guess we could do best two out of three." His wasn't even breathing hard. "Since that was so fast."

"It won't happen again." Even as she said it, she wanted it to happen again. More so, she didn't want it to end. His weight on her was delicious. His bare chest hovered over her face as he pressed her hands to the mat. He was using his legs and feet to keep hers from moving, which was a good thing. Otherwise she might widen them and cradle him against her body.

Raising her head, she snapped her teeth at one of his nipples.

He scrambled back. "What are you doing?"

"Winning the second match." She shoved her feet into his chest and rolled forward to leap on top of him. Their positions had been reversed.

The look he gave her was bored, but his pupils were wide. She was poised just above his waist on his stomach. He could knock her off with little effort.

Could she get him to make a mistake? She leaned down, digging his wrists into the mat, and whispered in her most seductive tone, "If I scoot a couple of inches backward, what am I going to find?"

His eyes narrowed and he bucked her off. They rolled across the mat, attempting to pin one another. When had this become ground warfare?

Grunts of effort pinged off the walls and was it her imagination, or was it getting harder and harder to differentiate them from a porno? She wiggled out of his embrace and the sound that escaped her was straight up triple X.

She rolled to her hands and knees and tried to get up. It didn't make sense. He was down. Maybe she could stomp on his stomach, but the more he touched her the hotter she got. This was no longer fighting. This was foreplay.

His hand caught her ankle and pulled her back to him. She didn't counterattack. Her mind was jumbled and she needed space from his muscles and the way she wanted to sink into them and never leave.

She hobbled, still on one knee, her other foot in his hand. Without looking back, she felt his heat rise up behind her. He was planning to pin her once again.

No, no, no. She couldn't get under him again. She might do something humiliating, like moan. And writhe.

Her body was flushed. Her cheeks hot. Her breasts heavy. And she'd never admit how wet she was. Her shorts weren't going to be enough to hide how turned on she was if she didn't get out now.

One of his arms caught her around the middle and started to spin her. The next motion would be backward as he flattened her on the matt.

No. Nope.

She squeezed her eyes shut. "Stop."

He did. Her leg was dropped. She centered both knees

under her and without opening her eyes, she knew the scuffle on the mat was him getting in front of her.

His warm fingers tipped her chin up. "Did I hurt you?"

Her eyelids fluttered open. His hair was disheveled, a platinum mess on top of his head that made him look like he'd just had a marathon sex session. Concern simmered in his light-green eyes, but his lids were hooded. And he was so close to her.

The longer she took to answer, the more he cupped her face.

"Felicia."

He didn't ask again. Had he hurt her? Yes. A lot. But not today. Right here, all that was forgotten except the panic that he could turn her inside out and toss her away like she was nothing.

"Jagger." She poured all of her helplessness into his name. It was an affirmation. A question. A plea.

His head dipped down.

This was such a bad idea. But for months she'd wondered what it'd be like to kiss him.

Now she knew. Consuming. Heat licked over her and he closed in. They were still kneeling, but that didn't stop them from getting closer.

She was smashed against him. His hands stroked around her bare torso, a ragged groan vibrating his chest as he slid them down to her ass. The solid length pressing into her belly answered so many questions and inspired too many more. Yes, he had a lot to work with, but how? Would he be slow? Rough? Change it up?

His tongue swept into her mouth, shutting out any more questions. His taste. Sweet as the strawberry protein shake, he swamped her senses. The grip on each ass cheek was a punishing caress.

He towered over her and she was leaning back, and the

next second, they were spread out on the floor. The kiss hadn't been broken, like they were so connected that nothing could break them apart.

She gave in to the urge to cradle him. Twining her legs around his waist, his erection was finally where she wanted it. When she rocked up, he broke the kiss, his body shaking.

"Felicia." His body strained, his forearms planted on each side of her head. "We should stop."

"Yeah. We should."

His mouth crashed onto hers, his pelvis grinding against the spot she wanted him the most. Neither of them wore much for clothing, but the shorts were in the worst spot possible.

Like he was thinking the same thing as her, he wedged a hand between them. Cool air brushed over her sex as he tugged the waistband of her shorts down. He took his sweet damn time skating his hand down her lower belly to cup her.

She bucked her hips up.

He pulled back to watch her. "I don't like you. You're too damn cocky."

If he hadn't amended his first sentence, would she have stopped? No idea, and she didn't care. Because with the space he'd put between them to touch her, she could now see how much he shouldn't like her.

Tucking her hand between his board shorts and heated skin, she wrapped her fingers around his thick length. "I think you're an arrogant ass."

A vein bulged in his forehead and his eyelids shuttered. "So does everyone else." Slicking a finger through her wetness, he pressed down on her clit like it was a red button set to detonate.

She cried out. Biting her lips, she glanced at the door. Her guardians would think they were fighting.

He rocked his hips into her grip. She fisted him hard and pumped.

"Fuck, Felicia. Do you have to be good at everything?" He captured her mouth once again.

His fingers played her like a maestro, coaxing whimpers and gasps that he greedily ate up so nobody could hear. She swiped her thumb over the blunt head of his cock and worked him.

Panting into each other, they were primed to blow at the same time when a hard voice pierced the passion.

"Julian, open up. We have much to discuss."

Jagger ripped his mouth off her and rolled away so fast she nearly castrated him.

His horrified gaze was glued to the dead bolt. "Mother?"

JAMESON DRUMMED his fingers on the edge of the weapons cabinet in his closet. This was a special room only Andy knew about. He'd sent Lindy out with a wad of cash and instructions to pamper herself.

He hadn't even slept with her first. The image of downy wings still haunted him.

Wings. Glorious and proud. He'd once had a pair, and he'd stroked many others during the throes of ecstasy. The only times he saw wings now were when he was hunting an angel to kill.

He ran a finger along a Daemon blade. The first one he'd obtained for himself. Cool to the touch, they didn't burn his skin like metal from his own realm now did. At one time, he'd thought the metal was the key to gaining access to Numen, but his experiments with both Daemon and Numen metal had proved that inaccurate. They were good for shedding blood though, and blood seemed to be the key.

He turned away from his weapons display and shed his suit jacket. Next off were his shoes, then his shirt and pants. He selected a maroon UNLV hoodie and blue jeans. He stuffed his feet into athletic shoes and put on a ball cap. It'd help hide his eyes. The Daemon blade that he'd admired earlier was shoved into the pocket of his sweatshirt.

Before he left, he phoned his assistant. "I'll be out for a few hours. If Lindy returns, find something to keep her busy. Send her down to the club or something."

"Yes, sir."

"But report back to me if she talks to anyone." She had a lot of freedom and he made it his business to watch his back.

"As you wish, sir."

What would he do without Andy? He tucked the phone into his pants pocket and took his private elevator down to the main level, but instead of heading out to where his driver waited on call, he went for the private garage.

A plain black sedan got him where he wanted to go when he wanted to go incognito. For funsies, he drove past the front of his club. It was a dark diamond in the rough of the surrounding neighborhood.

He smiled at the line and those who glanced his way, unaware he was the one in the car. Some nights, he stepped outside and mingled with his disciples. They did important work, which for him meant they kept angels distracted doing the good work down here on Earth. He'd gotten some excellent *research* done because his people were the subject of angelic attention. It was how he'd perfected entering the Mist.

And tonight, he was going to do it again.

Tonight, he'd go to one of the older casinos, the type the locals and snowbirds liked to frequent. Hunting was getting harder in Vegas. The angels were growing cautious, working and traveling in pairs.

He smiled. Because of him.

He would've preferred his little self-built empire stayed secret, but that meddlesome watcher from a few months ago had been too astute for her own good. Yet he remained untouchable, thanks to the demons who guarded his place and used the offerings of his disciples. Warriors couldn't get close. Daemon numbers were too great around his club. The force Numen would need to stop him would attract too much attention.

But they had increased their number in the area and what kind of fallen would he be if he didn't turn the change in events to his advantage?

Pulling into the lot of an old casino the size of an entire town under one roof, he parked and strolled to the entrance. Keeping his head down, he studied his surroundings through the smoky din. It'd take an entire load of laundry and at least one shower to get the smell of cigarette smoke off him.

The snowbirds were his target and easy to spot. They were older and wore clothing that looked like they could hit the beach at any moment. Originally from cooler climates, they flocked to Vegas for the weather and cost-effective vacations. Not many angels trailed them. These humans' lives were winding down, and they no longer engaged in any activities that would attract the attention of a watcher.

But...sometimes they had enough emotional turmoil going on in their head to attract a demon. And where there were demons, there would be angels looking to rid the human world of their interference.

Planting his butt on a stool, he fed a few bucks into a slot. Going through the motions, he let his gaze relax as he discreetly scanned the crowd. Watchers were nearly invisible as they did their work. He spotted none.

Had his gamble on this place been all for nothing? Stede suspected him, rightfully so. Jameson had amassed his little devoted army to storm Numen's borders and, more importantly, to fund the whole process, to fund his ability to amass more followers.

But if he could get into Numen on his own? The power alone that he'd have striding through the realm. A fallen. Back in Numen.

Try to forget me after that.

Revenge first. Control would come after, but he wanted revenge. He wanted to look into the face of every senator who had ordered his wings be carved from his back. Then he'd take *theirs*.

Ah, there. Standing behind a man in his sixties was a fresh-faced warrior. Young and inexperienced, she'd wandered away from her pack. She blended as best she could, wearing a baggy sweater and a ball cap with plain blue jeans.

Jameson read her expression. The young warrior thought this was a simple symaster coercing a retiree into dropping his meager fortune into one slot, convincing him it'd end in a big win. Then once the funds were gone, the retiree would spiral into a despair dismal enough to allow the archmaster the symaster served to hijack his soul.

This situation was ideal.

He studied everyone near them. No other warriors that he could see. No watchers. No one was about to die, so no chaperones were waiting to usher them into bright white light.

Perfect.

He put more money in his machine and waited just like the warrior. Waited for the retiree to get up and take a leak— and given his age, it wouldn't take long. Like the warrior, Jameson didn't care to do his business in public. It was bad enough that he'd traded an ounce of his blood for weapons from an archmaster. If he'd known he was chasing down the wrong rabbit hole, he would've told the one called Sandeen to piss off.

But Sandeen had kept coming back for his blood. There was something there. His blood was the key. He could feel it. It was the reason he couldn't stay in the Mist for long and the reason he couldn't go beyond it into Numen. Losing his wings had changed him in more than one way. It was like he was his own kind. No longer an angel, but not human either. Just fallen and all that entailed.

Finally. The retiree stumbled off his stool and lurched toward the restrooms, the warrior following in his wake.

He gave them a head start, then started after them, quickening his pace. He couldn't be late, couldn't let the warrior get the symaster into the Mist before he had a chance to shed her Numen blood.

Pushing through the door, he made it mid incantation. The retiree was bent over the sink, his eyes red and puffy, staring at the female murmuring next to him. The warrior had her hand on the guy's shoulders like she was comforting him, but she was really in contact with the symaster.

Hurrying through the rest, the young warrior should've known to just abandon her attempts. Rushing her work would lead to discovery, but whatever. Either way worked for him.

He jumped next to the warrior and withdrew his blade. Slicing the warrior's side as she was crossing into the Mist, Jameson went along for the ride.

Cool droplets surrounded him. He wiped the blood off the blade onto his hand as the warrior stumbled away, her hand pressed to her wound.

Jameson glanced at the disoriented symaster. It was humanoid, the size of a tall child, and scrawny. Scraggly hair dotted its scalp and its teeth looked like they were in dire need of an orthodontist.

As long as it stayed out of the way, Jameson would deal with it later. He faced the warrior. Not being officially trained, he had to use surprise to his advantage.

Diving for the female, he slashed his blade across her torso. As long as he shed angelic blood, the Mist wouldn't work so hard to expel him. The warrior was fast and trained. Jameson twisted and ducked, grateful she didn't risk the time it took to release her wings from under the sweater.

Fire sliced through his thigh as the warrior spun closer. Damn. Her fist clipped his jaw. Jameson staggered backward. This wasn't going as well as he'd hoped.

Before he righted himself, the warrior jumped him, both of them landing on the ground.

Her young face was twisted, a snarl tearing through the air. Jameson wrestled, the female's bloody blade coming too close to his face.

"Daemon scum," she grunted.

"Wrong realm," Jameson gasped. His strength was failing. As good as he was, he'd taken one risk too many with a trained warrior.

She stiffened, her rage turning to a grimace. His mouth fell open but only a strangled squeak came out. The symaster appeared above her shoulder, its mouth wide, revealing a row of wicked sharp teeth. It chomped into the warrior's neck. And kept going.

Jameson rolled from underneath the dripping mess and gladly let the symaster finish its gleeful decapitation.

Bonus, he was covered in angel blood. The Mist's effect diminished, but didn't erase the urge to return to the human realm.

He watched the symaster as he limped around it. The creature wouldn't be allowed to stay either. Like him, the Mist would repel it, Numen blood or not. And that was a problem.

He couldn't have this creature know that he could cross into the Mist. His contacts in Daemon would find that much too interesting and ruin his plans. And if word got back to Stede... Well, Jameson might just find himself with a knife buried in his chest. Stede liked their partnership unbalanced. The enforcer knew his main advantage was his ability to cross through realms. As long as he didn't get captured and his wings taken, he indeed was a necessary comrade. Kenton lacked the discipline to be of any aid.

The symaster was almost through the spinal cord. Intent on its work, it seemed oblivious to Jameson.

Until it paused to look over its bony shoulder, its fangs dripping blood. "Fallen," it sneered.

"Demon." He ignored the burn in his leg and attacked. Blade in hand, he shoved it between the bony ribs of the symaster.

The symaster shrieked and jabbed him with its claws. Then disappeared.

"Fuck." Jameson spun around. Where had it gone? He couldn't go back now. He was in the Mist, he had to see if he could get farther, or at least stay longer.

"*Fuck*." He let the Mist repel him. Stumbling into the bathroom, he spotted the symaster and stopped as his brain registered what he was seeing.

The symaster. As himself. In the human world. Its scraggly, gory body was here on its own. Jameson wasn't the only one shocked. The creature was poking and prodding at itself, jumping up and down to look into the mirror.

Jameson looked around. The bathroom was now empty and the symaster still needed to die.

He pinned it between himself and the counter. He was too strong for the symaster. Jameson made quick work of the process but as soon as the symaster's head was detached, it dissolved in his hands. The body vanished at the same time.

He rose. His leg throbbed, but the injury was shallow enough. It'd heal and he could hide the limp. But this… He looked at his hands, then to where the symaster had once been.

This was more than intriguing. There was only one reason why a demon would suddenly be able to exist as itself on Earth. Demons and angels had been battling in the Mist for centuries and no demons had ever ended up like this. But the symaster had stabbed him. Gotten his blood on itself.

That explained why Sandeen was so interested in his blood. With it, he could walk the realm as he was, no human host required. One step closer to having the freedom angels had.

Demons freely roaming the world. His blood could do that.

This was *exhilarating*. If he could do this, he would damn well get back to Numen. He just had to figure out how to keep anyone else from discovering this interesting little tidbit.

CHAPTER 10

Mother's attention bored into him. Jagger resisted pulling at the collar of his robe. He'd managed to talk her into waiting in the sitting room as he and Felicia straightened themselves up.

How mortifying. His own mother nearly walking in on him in flagrante with Felicia Montclaire. Mother had merely tolerated Valerina, and his ex had been as well-bred as they came.

Technically, so was Felicia. But it was not only her reputation, but that of her parents Mother wouldn't find so palatable.

He avoided looking at where Felicia reclined on a settee, her long leg bouncing over the edge of the short arm. She'd changed into black leggings, but they didn't hide a thing. He couldn't help but think that they shouldn't. Those legs should be admired. He wanted to worship them with his tongue.

He forced his attention back to the ultimate mood killer. Mother. And her companion.

Mother's—he couldn't say boyfriend. The male had been in his class as a kid, and while his Mother and Mateo were both adults and could do what they wanted, it was a relationship he preferred not to imagine his mother in.

He'd wonder at Mateo's motivation, but the male was so obviously smitten and devoted that Jagger felt sorry for him. Chanel Hancock's heart wasn't a glacier affected by climate change. It was solidly ensconced in an impermeable ice world.

"You didn't contact me when you returned." The undercurrent of reprimand was as familiar as the back of his hand.

The one he'd just had down Felicia's pants. The one that was no longer coated in her scent because he'd had to reluctantly wash up before meeting with Mother. But his fingers still tingled from Felicia's heat. She'd almost exploded in his hands and while he was dismayed to have missed out on it, he should be thanking Mother.

Knowing what Felicia felt like, and how her touch drove him wild, was dangerous to him as a male, especially in this type of environment.

And of course, there was how she'd destroyed his life, saving him from a life with Valerina. No—*ruining* a life with Valerina.

She'd tasted so sweet, though. Like strawberries. They'd had the same breakfast. Would she taste just as sweet if he—

Mother's brow lifted. He hadn't answered her nonquestion. "I did not notify you. I apologize."

Felicia's leg stopped bouncing.

"I heard about the attack on you." *And you didn't tell me that either.* Though he doubted Mother touched mundane human items like a phone. "You are well?"

"Mmm." Mother watched him steadily. "I may as well tell you the good news."

His stomach twisted. Was she syncing with Mateo? He would be happy for her, but he was trying to even himself out emotionally. His erection had run away and hid after

Mother had hollered his name, but it'd roared back in the shower, urging him to take care of it.

He would've if, one, Mother hadn't been waiting for him. He had no wish to have a discussion with her after he'd masturbated. And two, he didn't think it'd help. His hand would never compare to Felicia's touch. It'd be like sating his thirst with stagnant pond water after having a sip from the clearest spring in the world.

He was acutely aware of Felicia's interest in the "good" news.

"Yes, Mother?"

"I've secured a proposal between you and Persephone Nassim. Congratulations."

It took a moment for the words to sink in. He thought he'd heard incorrectly but Felicia's eyes were as wide as saucers.

"She's a lovely choice, yes?" Mother's expression was placid, like she was asking about the weather.

"A p-proposal? What the fuck for?" He'd never spoken to Mother in such a way, but now was the time.

Her back went rigid and she regarded him with the look she'd used to diminish senators over the years. "Julian, watch your tongue. You're not a common vagrant."

"Numen doesn't have vagrants," he said irritably. The sharp look from Mother should've gutted him, but he didn't care. "Mother, I'm an adult. I have a job that I'm in the middle of right now. I don't have time to work around an engagement, much less court a potential mate." He didn't want to court anyone. The thought made stomach acid claw up his throat.

"You're now linked to the daughter of one of the most powerful senators in the realm. It should draw that attention away from you."

"Or center it on her."

Mother's facade cracked. The corner of her mouth turned down for a heartbeat before returning to the flat line he was accustomed to. "She's a coddled angel surrounded by servants. She'll be fine. Meanwhile, I can't allow you to be sequestered here with Ms. Montclaire. Can you imagine the talk?"

Felicia swung her leg down and scooted to the edge of the settee. He sent her a warning glare, but she ignored him. "No, I can't imagine. How would they talk?"

Mother's expression could've frozen hell over. "My dear, don't patronize me. You know exactly what they'll say and why."

"Only fools unable to think for themselves would believe gossip." Felicia rose. "Now if you'll excuse me, I learned a long time ago that I don't need to suffer fools."

Ice crystallized in his blood. No one talked to Mother like that. No one had ever called her a fool. Felicia marched out before Mother could reply. And Mother always had an adequate reply.

Even steeped in shock at Felicia's audacity, he worried that she'd taxed her wings to the point of pain. She'd been walking fine earlier. Did her wings hurt now? Time may be limited, but she needn't be miserable while strengthening them.

"I never cared for her father," Mother muttered.

What difference did that make? "She is my charge."

"No. I've been briefed by Director Vale. You are also a target and don't need to have more danger drawn to you because of your proximity to her."

"Did Director Vale say that, or did you make the decision for him and me?"

Mother arched a brow. Had she seriously not expected his resistance? He wasn't going through with it. Persephone was a gorgeous angel. She was also young and spoiled, and he doubted she'd tolerate his line of work.

This was Mother's way of luring him into a senate seat and away from his calling as a warrior. Two birds with one perfect marble. She'd choose an appropriate mate and get him to quit being a warrior.

"I'm not going through with it."

Mother's features tightened.

He continued. "I'm not, so don't even try to use your authority. And your interference might've endangered yet another person."

Mother rose. Her boyfriend moved to her side, not touching her, but angling his body like a shield around her. "Of course I cannot make you, Julian. But do take a night to think it over. It really is a good match." Her voice dropped low until she sounded almost vulnerable. "I want only what's best for you, and your safety is my highest priority."

She swept out of the room, Mateo dogging her heels.

She was scared for him. The attack had uprooted her world and she'd gone into mama-bear mode. She cared. Surprise shouldn't be the first emotion he felt.

Trudging up the stairs, he passed his room and knocked on Felicia's door. The need to explain hounded him.

She opened the door. Her guarded expression reminded him of when he'd first started his protection detail. When he'd said shitty things just to hurt her.

"I'm sorry for the way she treated you."

As if reading his mind, she asked, "You'll apologize for your mother saying exactly what you've said?"

His mother hadn't lived through the effects of Felicia's *talk*. "She didn't lose her future mate because of it."

Felicia sucked in a breath. "Like I said, I don't have to suffer fools." She stepped back to shut the door.

"I'm not syncing with her. Persephone."

"Why don't you find who spread the rumors about us and ask them to do it again? Then you can blame me again when you don't sync." She slammed the door.

He stared at the fine grains running through the wooden panel. Was she really telling the truth about the rumors? After the way he'd treated her, would he be able to admit that she was?

SIERRA'S FACE was pressed into the couch cushion, her clothes ripped and hanging from her body, and her ass hovered in the air. She strained against the punishing grip holding her down from behind.

"Are you just going to play back there or are you actually going to fuck me?" Lust pounded through her.

Jameson's rough laugh vibrated straight down to her bare sex. He thrust inside. She didn't cry out, just bit into upholstered foam. There'd been no more foreplay than shoving and ripping clothing out of the way.

She'd called. He'd come over, his eyes blazing, but when he saw her wings out the air between them had become charged with an energy she'd never experienced. How he'd gazed at her wings. It made her feel cherished. He was a cheating liar. A philandering commitmentphobe. An untrustworthy opponent.

But he fucked dirty.

She didn't need or want an everlasting promise from him, just hard sex. From a fallen. From a former angel who had already lived through what was destined to be her future. He was virile. Alive. The phantom of her life turned into a booty call.

And the human men she'd hooked up with in the last couple of days had been as lost in the sack as if she'd buried her clit in a haystack.

He buried his face in her feathers as he pounded away. He didn't play with her clit or caress her breasts. His hands were buried wrist deep in her wings. The dude had a serious fetish, and from the way he stared at each shift and movement of her wings, he hadn't acknowledged it.

She grunted as he yanked at the joints in her back until she straightened back into him. Wet slapping sounds filled the room with their grunts.

Her climax hovered at the surface.

"Come all you want," he panted in her ear. "I'm not done until I'm good and ready."

"Or until I morph my wings."

He nipped at her ear. "Do that and I won't tell you my story."

She groaned and not just because he was an admirable size and their position only teased her clit without fulfilling it. Sex was a delay, a way to pretend that she wasn't caught between being a traitor and helping the enemy in order to aid a teammate. For Jameson, her wings reminded him of all he'd lost and how little he wished to relive his past in order to find out what Stede was up to.

She was more than this. More than an angel who got used by males in power. She could go ahead and prove it at any time, but she writhed against him.

"Just get it over with," she hissed, hating the naturally rebellious side of herself that she'd hidden her entire life. Sliding her hand down her belly, she glared over her shoulder.

"No rush, sweetheart. I haven't done someone with wings for decades."

She reached her clit and her eyelids fluttered. *Yes.* "Let me guess—it wasn't your mate."

Instead of getting offended, he just laughed. "Monogamy was never my strength."

"Does your current girlfriend know that?" She set a steady pace, circling her nub. If it weren't for his hands banded like steel around the base of her wings, she'd collapse forward.

He slammed into her. Little guilty?

She certainly felt like shit.

Her orgasm exploded behind her eyes. She cried out. This was all about scratching an itch. Two beings torn over a pair of wings, the symbol of the unattainable in each of their lives.

He released her to grip her hips. "Hold your wings back."

She was still trembling with the aftereffects, but she managed to lift them a few inches.

"More." Thrust. "More."

She flared them wide and he hissed. The shadows that she hoped only she could see clung to her feathers, blocking out the sunlight steaming into the room.

"You can't help yourself, can you?" He brushed one hand around to replace hers. "Naughty little angel tired of hiding her bad side?"

He'd figured it out. Damn him. She should've found a hole no one could locate and stayed there.

He thrummed her like a harp, her gasps and whimpers the notes. "Naughty little angel."

She crashed into her next climax and he came at the same time. After his shudders passed, he hunched over her. Still breathing heavily, she shoved him off her and searched for her top. She found it and her pants flung across the room.

He was mid tuck, his gaze still on her wings, when he paused. "I need to use your shower."

"Afraid what's her name's going to smell me on you?"

His smile was grim. Nope. He didn't like cheating on this mystery human. "Where's your bathroom?"

"Tell me your story first." Her pants were still hanging in her hands.

He straightened, his attention riveted behind her. She twitched her wings just for kicks. He jerked and grew hard—well, harder. "I need to be clean before I delve into those years. But you're welcome to join me and ensure I don't run off."

Say no. Say no. Her body was already firing up for his type of rough and quick. She was sick of being used and tired of getting dragged into another world no matter how hard she fought.

But she'd learned that he had serious feelings for that girlfriend of his. Maybe she'd get him to say her name. All she needed was a name and she could uncover all kinds of info.

She flung her pants aside.

CHAPTER 11

"You're kidding me." Felicia crossed her arms and gave Jagger the most hostile glare possible. "We've been locked up in here, not allowed to help with Mission Stop Your Psycho Dad, but you get a pass so you can break up with a girl?"

Each side of his jaw flexed. She would be less vexed if he hadn't combed his hair back and secured it in a queue. The long white traditional robe he wore was belted with a golden-filigree-lined belt. It was exactly what her father would've worn.

"I'm respectfully withdrawing my sync," he said.

"Tell yourself whatever you want to feel better, killer." She'd kept her distance from him in the week since his mother had visited. Rumor or no, she refused to give Jagger more ammo against her character.

Bryant had convinced him that rushing off to void the contract with Persephone would only insult her. Odessa had thought the female would dig her heels in if she sensed desperation. Apparently, Persephone was the stereotypical bored socialite and liked to stir up trouble.

Not that Felicia cared.

"I'd like to get out of the house too."

Guilt slashed through his handsome face. "I'll talk to him."

"I could talk to Dionna. She hasn't killed a demon in a fortnight and it shows."

His eyes brightened but he didn't crack a smile.

"Harlowe's going with you?" She wanted to keep Harlowe here with her. The warrior talked defensive and offensive moves with her, and in Harlowe's off time, she joined Felicia in the gym. Dionna rigidly adhered to Bryant's orders.

"Bronx. It'd look better if I didn't have a female with me when I went to break my end of the arrangement."

"It's fucked up that it's your duty when you didn't agree to a thing." And until he did, she would stay far away from him. She didn't need the kind of drama she'd gotten last time she'd flirted with him when he was attached to a female. "Kinda messed up that you can be married off"—she snapped her fingers—"just like that. As if the idea of sync mates isn't crazy enough."

"Tell me about it." He turned to go, then stopped. "It feels odd, to go…"

Without her. Yeah, she knew what he meant. "You've gotta cut the cord some time. Go out and fly, little birdie."

And didn't that chafe? She would've gone with—best not to split up the team into so many different parties. Dionna with her. Bronx with him. Sierra on Earth for her intel gathering. Harlowe and Urban getting some much needed rest after the night shift. But without wings, she couldn't fly to the other side of the elite neighborhood where Persephone lived.

His expression sobered. "You're armed?"

She nodded and pointed to her hip where a knife was secured around her waist.

"Just one?"

"We're indoors. Close-quarters fighting and all." If she could consider his sprawling mansion cramped.

"What if you drop it?" He pointed to the weapons room as he walked out of the sitting area. "Grab whatever you want."

Since she tried hard not to be an idiot, she conceded to his expertise. The room he kept his weapons in was small and plain, so unlike the rest of the house. What's-her-name hadn't stepped inside of here either.

There was no need to let Dionna know where she went. The warrior was everywhere and nowhere at once. Her expression was also set on perma-scowl and her answers were as short and sharp as the knives strapped to her legs. The female wasn't meant to be a guard. She was a fighter to the bone.

"Blade, blade, gimme a blade." After the skirmish in the Mist, Felicia had watched a few YouTube videos on knife fighting. Harlowe had given her a few pointers, and if she weren't risking another make-out session on the mats, she'd ask Jagger about using her wings defensively.

Glancing down at her outfit, she considered grabbing more than one. She had plenty of hiding space. Yellow leggings and an oversized white T-shirt. Bronx had gone to her apartment and retrieved her clothing before the movers had gone in. He hadn't made one single crack about her undergarments, but Jagger had stomped out of the room when Bronx had handed them to her. The memory made her smile.

Her hand hovered over a knife in a shoulder harness. No. She wanted to be comfortable. There. Two short blades on an adjustable belt. She swapped her one out for the two. Done.

Blowing out a breath, she left the room. Jagger was right. This was weird. It was the first time they'd been separated by more than the span of the house, which was considerable. Dionna was stalking the perimeter; otherwise she was alone.

And she wandered, steering clear of the gym—she didn't need to remember the last time she'd been in there. She'd stuck to running the stairs and going through her exercise routines in her room. Places where she could focus on the moves and not what Jagger's weight felt like between her legs.

Boredom was setting in. Again.

She missed her old job and the kids, but the hurt didn't penetrate as deeply knowing they were safe. Sierra had checked on Claudia and Mrs. Washington. Both were doing well. The gnomes had been replaced, but Sierra had sent Urban to trash them and leave some ceramic fairies on her front step with a note about how they were good luck. Total bullshit, but gargoyles couldn't stand elegant statues like those.

How easily she'd been wiped out of life. Both times—before and after the attack. Before the attack, she'd been on a level with Persephone. The desired one other angels envied. She'd roam the realm center that was situated around the angel fire fountain with her mother, admiring the beauty of the fire. It burned clean, and when it was pooled together like at the fountain, it was like liquid crystal, opaque with a hint of rainbow, like mother-of-pearl. While they'd lost many of their own to the fire, the fountain was the only source of angel fire in the three realms and it was their pride and joy.

She often wondered why there were no markers of angels' passing, some sort of commemoration to the lives lived. Like her mother's. But if Numen was good at one thing, it was ignoring those who'd died and why.

Guilt sapped her energy and dimmed the shine of the sun streaming through the house. Logically, she knew she had nothing to do with her mother's suicide. But what if they hadn't marveled over the plasma-like substance so many times? What if she had handled the trauma better—or had been able to heal? Then perhaps her mother wouldn't have let the stress and anxiety eat away at her will to live, to stick around and deal with it all—to help her own daughters traverse the hardships caused by the attack.

She could go in circles and drive herself crazy thinking like that. Which was why she kept herself busy.

She entered the sitting area. A puzzle was half assembled on the end table. Two of the four cats sitting around a poker table had been formed. The corner of her mouth lifted as she recalled Jagger's reaction.

What the hell is that? She could've been operating on an alien body the way he'd stared at her.

Why a puzzle had shocked him, she'd never know. He'd taken her wings in better stride.

Sitting on the edge of the couch that had been engineered with looks in mind more than comfort, she found another piece to lock into place. Then another.

A third cat was coming together when a chill raised the hairs on the back of her neck.

She looked up, her hand pausing over a section of a slitted eyeball. It shouldn't have been possible for it to become quieter. She listened for Dionna, for birds, for anything.

Something was up. She rose and crept toward the bathroom. It had a window and was a small space. In the gym, she could take on two opponents. In real life, it was foolish to willingly put herself in that position. The bathroom was her designated panic room. It had a window she could escape through or defend and a door she could lock, plus the space didn't allow for much of a wing span.

She heel-toed toward the hall. Should she pull her knife? Yes. And no. She was comfortable fighting with her body.

This wasn't a smaller sylph. If someone was after her, they'd be her size—or larger.

She was several yards away when she heard a grunt from outside. Dionna?

Another muffled shout caught her attention and she looked over her shoulder. Nothing had changed and she couldn't hear a sound from within the house.

Turning back, icicles crystalized in her veins. A shadow fell across the width of the hall. It originated from an open door. The office.

She let out a whimper. Let him think she was really scared.

She did a shuffle, shuffle of her feet to make it sound like she was panicked too.

A male turned the corner. Her heart nearly froze, but no, he wasn't the faceless one from her nightmares. This male was taller, maybe close to Jagger's age, and had russet-brown hair cropped close to his head. An ordinary male turned sinister by nothing more than the morbidly gleeful look in his eyes. He relished the thought of attacking her.

Widening her eyes, she opened her mouth like she was going to scream, then she charged him. Taking grim satisfaction from his stunned expression, she calculated the distance, then pivoted and kicked. He wasn't expecting to be jumped. The kick took him off guard.

She kept her momentum going as her foot hit his solid belly. He grunted and stumbled back, but she found her footing and advanced. She pounded his gut with her fists, then an uppercut to his face.

His head jerked up and back. A snap of her arm and she smashed his trachea. He fell to the floor. Choking and squirming, the male's hands were at his throat as he tried to get air. He'd pass out before he healed in time.

She raised a leg to stomp on his gut, but he snaked a hand

out. She should've been ready for this bullshit after her sparring with Jagger, but one thing that was hard to fake in the gym was fighting dirty.

Twisting as she fell, she kicked with her other foot, not knowing where she hit, only that she made contact.

He was wheezing, still clutching his throat with one hand while trying to drag her closer with the other. His grip was punishing. She continued to lash out with her free foot and kick his head and shoulder, but he was too close. He'd rolled to his side, protecting his soft areas and damn, she should've neutralized him with a dick shot. Lunging up, she propelled her elbow down on his temple. His head rebounded off the marble floor.

Once he slipped into unconsciousness, she scooted back against the wall. Footsteps pounded across the floor. Dionna rounded the hall, hands at the ready, each holding a sai, looking more badass than Elektra. Blood glistened across both blades. If she'd been wearing a standard robe, it would've been drenched. Parts of her black pants and shirt shone like they were wet.

Dionna looked past her, searching. She was tensed and ready for a battle. "Are you hurt?"

"Nothing that can't heal." She pushed off the ground. "Is that your blood or another's?"

"Another's. He is dead."

Whoa. That had escalated quickly. Warriors killed demons all the time. They protected humans. But killing another angel?

Dionna studied her. "He fought with his pride, not his brain."

"Two males, huh? They underestimated us."

"They underestimated you. If I hadn't set up a small security camera on my phone, I would've been doused with angel fire—thus why he's dead." She nudged the unconscious male with her foot. "Come. We must secure him."

Felicia had major envy of Dionna's toolkit. Ropes, zip ties, and duct tape. The essentials.

Five minutes later, the male was strapped to the office chair and secured from head to toe with no less than three layers of duct tape over his mouth.

"Now what?" Felicia prodded him. Out cold.

"I notified Director Vale and the enforcers. Both shall arrive shortly." Dionna retrieved a small washcloth from her bag of surprises and wiped the blood off her face. Her dark skin was unmarred. Covered in drying blood, with two sais strapped behind her back and more blades tucked into harnesses all the way down to her tactical boots, she looked like a New York Fashion Week model visiting a war zone. Felicia doubted a vat of angel fire would've been enough to keep her down.

Dionna folded her arms across her chest and scowled at her phone. The female had rigged a security system in the middle of Numen. Surely others did too. Maybe? Most thought this realm was as irreproachable as heaven. Or perhaps other horrid events had been hushed up in the name of perceived security.

Dionna was working and Felicia had little more to do than pick her nose. "Can I help?"

"No."

A few moments of tense silence later, Felicia released a sigh. "I'm sorry."

A surprised gaze speared her. "Why? You saved yourself. It is I who failed you."

"We didn't fail, they did. But you're stuck babysitting me instead of doing your true calling."

Dionna studied her for a moment. "The politics of my job are not your problem. Truthfully, the only thing I'd do differently than the director is push for action, to go after the fallen and weed out the corruption in the realm. But up here, there is more than a team leader calling the shots. He has senators and enforcers who have to approve major decisions regarding the warriors. And also, he doesn't know who he can trust. I get it." She went back to her screen. "I don't like it, but I get it."

"Bryant is actually trying to accommodate other branches of Numen society?" She hadn't known him long before he'd taken his new position, but he hadn't struck her as a mediator.

A smile ghosted across Dionna's lips. "He's being a director."

"Then maybe you should be a Bryant. Tell him what you're going to have your team do and let him deal with the mess as it unfolds." As black eyebrows arched higher with each word, Felicia backpedaled. "But of course, you're not Bryant. I mean, there was a reason he was ordered to mate my sister." To tame him. Gotta love her realm. You get a mate, and you get a mate, and *you* get a mate!

"And perhaps the senate could use input from someone with your family legacy and experience. Someone like you could get the senate to realize that angel fire needs a chain of custody, so guys like these don't get their hands on it. And if they did, we could find out how and why. You could do that."

The inclination to be insulted died away. She had a point and her tone was pointed but not negative. "My family legacy isn't anything to be proud of. It'd be nothing but an uphill battle, getting senators to take me seriously."

"Ms. Montclaire, I haven't known you for long, but when have you cared what anyone thought? When have you let it stop you?"

She couldn't answer. That was the very attitude she'd adopted a long time ago.

And Dionna wasn't done. "I often think that's the main problem with our senate. Too much of a disconnect between what we do as warriors and chaperones and any angel deployed to the human realm and what the senate thinks we do. The hereditary aspect of senate seats is taken for granted, and with it the sense of entitlement. More critically, the superior attitude over those of us elbow-deep in Daemon blood. *We* need people like you, who know both sides, to get in there and make them listen."

"Just because my father was a senator doesn't mean I'd be a good one."

"But it means you could try, and that's a lot more of an advantage than other qualified candidates have."

Dionna was stepping on a sensitive button that Felicia didn't want to fiddle with. Her words brought back memories of traipsing into Father's office and following him around. She recalled how he'd tell her about his day or the scrolls he was reading and why.

That time was too long ago. Father was dead. Any good he'd done was marred by the deaths of so many warriors. The open hatred and verbal abuse she'd subject herself to as soon as she announced, "Hey, I think I'm gonna be a senator," would be more than she cared to take. She'd been through enough.

And the sick part? With her lineage, she'd probably get voted in over another more qualified and earnest candidate. She might even get in just because the assholes wanted a chance to ruin her.

Where were Bryant and the enforcers? She lifted her chin. "While I agree with what you're saying, I've already given more for this realm than many angels. Call me selfish, but giving any more is not part of my future plans."

Dionna's gaze was steady. "Yes, you are selfish."

How dare she? Anger ignited in her gut but didn't grow

into a raging inferno. She respected Dionna. When the warrior called her selfish, it made her think she wasn't as impervious to other's opinions as she thought.

~

"WE HAVE TO DO SOMETHING," Jagger growled as he paced the sitting area. Dionna's slight nod made him feel better. All of them were restless while Vale played the politics game. They'd been sitting around for a week and it had done nothing but give the other side time to attack them.

He'd gotten back from his ill-fated meeting with Persephone to find his home filled with his team and the enforcer Tosca, who'd worked with them when Odessa had needed guards.

Tosca was gone now, along with the intruder—who wasn't talking—but Tosca had insisted on doing everything by the book. Jagger was concerned that no matter what the younger enforcer thought, those who employed the attacker would get to him before he talked.

He spun to tread the other direction. "Why aren't we moving on this? Why aren't we burning down my father's club? No meeting place—no cult."

Urban pinched the bridge of his nose. "I can't say I disagree." He and Harlowe had been roused and here by the time he'd returned from a petite, spoiled angel telling him that she was in no way allowing him to withdraw his side of the agreement.

Odessa was right. Persephone sensed how badly he wanted out and had put her dainty little foot down. He'd be irate, but he saw the flash of panic in her eyes, the fear of rejection. She had daddy issues. Or since her mother was a well-respected and well-liked senator, maybe it was mommy issues. He was caught in a power play that he had no business in.

His drama took a back seat to the attack on Felicia and its ramifications.

"This was planned," Dionna said. "They weren't lucky that they caught Felicia with only one guard. They knew where we were, and when only one guard would be here, but they didn't know Felicia's skill level. Or they didn't believe it."

Director Vale's stern expression was leveled on the oriental rug Jagger had purchased and hauled here from the human realm shortly after he'd bought the home. "Just like they knew about all of us gathered at Odessa's."

"And where Felicia lived," Jagger added. "We have a leak."

Everyone in the room eyed everyone else. Finally, Bronx shrugged. "I trust everyone here. I mean, I don't know Felicia well, but it doesn't make sense that she'd set herself up to be attacked."

Jagger nodded. They all felt the same.

"Everyone *here*," Urban said. "Anyone hear from Sierra lately?"

Harlowe scoffed. "It couldn't be Sierra."

Bronx shook his head, but his brow creased.

They all fell quiet.

"We should check on her," Director Vale finally said. "Make sure our hacker hasn't been hacked. Make sure the demons don't have her under surveillance. Hell, make sure fucking Jameson—"

"With all due respect, Director," Dionna cut in, "perhaps what we do next is better done without you knowing. Act first, ask permission later."

Jagger and the rest of his team nodded. Director Vale's amber gaze jumped to hers. "Sometimes the less I know the better, but not with this. You're not going off like renegades and giving those insidious voices in the senate a reason to whisper that we're the treasonous ones."

Dionna's lips thinned but she inclined her head. "We will check on Sierra and go after demons—concentrating on those linked to Jameson Haddock's nightclub. Waiting around is hazardous to our health."

A thought occurred to him and it had nothing to do with the driving need to get Felicia alone and ask her how she was really doing. "Felicia and I need to go off grid." Both his superiors gave him a sharp look, and he didn't miss the optimism in Felicia's face. "They found me at her apartment. They got to her here. The hunted need to become the hunters. I'll report to Dionna using various covert methods and she'll pass on enough to soothe Odessa's worries for her sister."

The more he described his plans, the better they sounded. Move forward, not sit and wait.

The director scrubbed a hand over his face. "No. You need to stay put, at least for a while. Throw them off, wondering what we're doing." Jagger opened his mouth to argue but the director had already moved on to Urban. "We aren't making headway learning where Kenton and Stede scurried to, or who else they're working with here. See if Sierra can help us out, and dammit, if we seem to get farther away instead of closer, then we'll know without asking."

"You got it, boss."

There had to be a good reason for him and Felicia to get the hell out of this prison he called home. He was sick of being around Valerina's style and just…needed space.

He and Felicia alone in the human realm. At one time, he'd cursed his fate. Now, he wished he could pack a bag.

CHAPTER 12

"You haven't mentioned your son lately." Lindy's soft voice brought him back to the comfortable bed he was in. Naked, but unsated. Sleeping with Lindy now was like going through a drive-thru when he'd just left a Michelin-starred restaurant. "How's he doing? You were worried."

Lindy asking after Julian should warm him, but the only question going through his mind was, *Why does she want to know?* When he'd returned to the club, Lindy hadn't been around. Not unusual. He often handed her a wad of money and told her to entertain herself.

But maybe since he'd been thrusting inside another woman, he suddenly wondered what Lindy did with her time. And with whom.

Someone who also wondered about Julian?

Chanel's visit had started this whole mind fuck he was stuck in. Seeing her had reminded him of how much he'd admired her wings. The stormy gray of a summer sky—so at odds with her demeanor. He used to stroke them until his erection was painful. They used to spend whole days in bed, their wings intertwined.

He had a thing for wings. Something he honestly hadn't remembered until he'd seen her. Then again when Sierra had been standing with her darkness-flecked wings open behind her.

"Jameson?" Lindy blinked her big blue eyes at him.

He should move on, send Lindy back to the dance floor and pick up another devoted disciple. But Lindy was here and oh so willing to help him get over lusting after a forbidden angel. Anyone who tangled with Sierra would have two worlds colliding over their heads.

Besides, Lindy had a brain behind those lips that could suck exhaust from a semi's tailpipe. He was starting to wonder how she used it. Lindy was the longest relationship he'd had since the woman who'd turned on him with the help of his mate and cost him everything. He hadn't misplaced his trust again, had he? "It's best if I keep my distance from my son."

Disappointment crossed her face, but she nodded. "I understand. It's not like you dabble in a safe business."

He'd asked her once what had brought her to the club. Why get the black rose tattoo that signaled she was willing to do his demon bidding?

She'd wanted to be useful for more than sex.

He hadn't used her for more than sex.

She traced a finger over his bare chest. "Andy said the club's numbers are better than ever."

Suspicion crept in. He couldn't help it. Ever since his little discovery, his paranoia had leveled up. So what was she talking to Andy about? Was she lonely when he conducted his business?

He trusted Andy more than her—and what the hell would

they have to talk about? "Are you and Andy swapping thoughts on the best nail color?"

She scowled, genuine hurt rolling off her. "No. I got bored when you were in Atlanta."

Bored. She asked about his son and then dropped that she'd hit up his assistant for conversation. His assistant who was his right hand.

What was she up to?

His phone rang. He rolled away, letting the thousand-count, steel-gray Egyptian cotton sheets slip off him. Grabbing the phone, he checked the screen, guessing who it was before he saw the name.

Andy spoke before he answered. The man was good at his job. "Stede is walking through the doors."

What the hell did that male want now? Jameson suppressed a growl and got out of bed. Cool air hit his bare butt cheeks.

"Important meeting?" Lindy followed him until she was on her belly, her ass in the air, her heels swinging.

"A necessary one." Fucking Stede. The male was no longer useful, yet he and Kenton dogged Jameson's heels like needy puppies.

He dressed. No sweats or sweaters for him. He pulled on the red shirt and black suit he'd stripped out of when he'd bent Lindy over the mattress.

As he approached his conference room, he straightened his tie. His loafers barely made a sound on the hardwood floor. He took his time. By the time Stede gained access to the third level of his warehouse-turned-club, he'd have to be ushered to the meeting room by Andy. Jameson didn't want to arrive first, and he'd prefer to keep Stede waiting a good long while.

The male was too comfortable entering his club. Jameson

had watched him before. The male strode past the line of club-goers awaiting entry like he was a VIP. He even had the nerve to demand free drinks.

And the fucking bartenders served him. Jameson's mouth twitched when he recalled the look of awe on the bartenders' faces. A real angel. One that was on their side, not one of the sanctimonious angels who roamed the Earth striving to keep humans in their place—or so Jameson had told those who followed him.

How easy it was to feed people's sense of entitlement, to warp their "fuck the man" attitude until they sold their souls to become part of a special club only a select few knew about. And Stede being in on the secret only supported the blame they pointed toward angels. If this angel disagreed with how his people treated humans, it really must be their fault there wasn't enough money, power, sex, or fill-in-the-blank to go around.

A real angel indeed. Stede had nearly as much blood on his hands as Jameson, only he had earned his the hard way. He'd done a lot of the dirty work himself. Humans were disposable to him.

He approached the meeting room he preferred to do business in. It was as modern and sophisticated as the rest of the floor, with brass accents and a mahogany table. Not one ounce of marble in the entire building.

The low rumble of voices filtered out. Good. Stede had been kept waiting.

Jameson strode in like he owned the place—because he did. "Stede, you must have some interesting developments to grace my club."

He evaluated the room. Andy was in his typical position. A laptop was open in front of him, a pen three inches to the right of his right hand, a notepad one inch from the pen, and he was dressed in a plain gray suit with a black tie. Stede looked like he'd seen better days. Dark circles rimmed his eyes and his thick, dark hair looked like it had been hand combed to the side. Jameson only ever dealt with Stede on Earth, but it was unusual to see the male in plain blue jeans and a blue T-shirt.

Perhaps a little bit of Stede's hubris was squashed now that he was unable to go back home. Jameson rather hoped he tried. If Stede were apprehended by some do-gooder angels, it would relieve a lot of headaches for him.

He selected the chair across from Stede with Andy at his right. Fitting, because Andy was his right-hand man. Once the human had scrambled into his life, looking for a job to support Jameson's cause, his plans had moved ahead at light speed.

Stede glared at him. "Want to tell me what you're up to, fallen?"

Touchy. What had crawled up his cross and died? "I'm not going to pretend to know what you're talking about. Though I do understand that after being kicked out of Numen you're a little cranky."

Stede's expression morphed enough to reveal the cruelty underneath, then it was back to a simple scowl. "Our plans before included all of us, but since I've been stuck in this godforsaken realm, you haven't shared much detail with me. But I doubt you've been stagnant. You're still forging ahead and I want in on the plan."

Jameson spread his hands as if he were helpless against past developments. "I've had to make do without you and Kenton in the realm. How is the good senator?"

"Hookers and blow are occupying his mind. I think we can count Kenton out." Stede leveled him with a dark stare. "But I'm still in this. You and I are still working together. I imagine Gerzon would have something to say if your agenda has changed."

Gerzon was a pain in his ass. But so far the demon was satisfied with staffing the club with extra demons. He thought having more bodies to possess was progress. And that was fine with Jameson. He'd never really planned to bring the demon or his horde into Numen with him—once he figured out how to get in there himself.

"Go ahead and talk to Gerzon. I'd like to see how that goes." Yes, Jameson was utilizing his own blood to try to gain entry into his former realm. But he wasn't about to share that with Stede. If the male caught wind, Jameson would find himself strung up and bled dry.

As far as Stede tattling to the archmaster Gerzon about a topic he only suspected, well, Jameson would call his bluff. Not even a crooked angel was going to approach an archmaster.

He expected Stede to vibrate with anger, but the male's temperament had calmed. Stede flicked a glance at Andy and then back at him. "You're stretching yourself too thin. You can't do it all. Someone's going to suffer, whether it's that pretty little human you keep in your bed or that son who's fending off attacks no matter what realm he's in."

There it was. The reason Stede had drastically reduced his lifespan. He was going after Jameson's kid. "If you don't have news for me, we're done here. Andy, do see him out."

He rose, straightened his tie, and strode out of the meeting room. What Stede had forgotten was that Jameson had been stranded in this realm for a long time. He'd been tossed out and used, and he'd come back stronger than before. No one was going to double cross him.

~

FELICIA EYED the large maroon plastic tote Odessa was holding. Her sister planted herself on the floor of Jagger's office next to her. Since they couldn't go anywhere, Felicia had bugged Bryant for something to do. And he'd turned Odessa on her, to convince her to do a task that she'd been avoiding, one that she'd insisted could be left for a couple of centuries.

Felicia leaned away from the tub like it was going to chomp on her arm as soon as she reached in.

Odessa flipped the lid off the tub. "I made sure to call you when I was ready to go through his items. After the house burned down, I was grateful to have this. He'd taken a lot of mother's stuff with him."

A sharp pain jabbed her heart. At least one of them was a responsible adult. Odessa had packed up Father's place. He'd moved out of their family home after Mother had died, and Felicia hadn't given a thought to what had gone with whom. She hadn't wanted the cold marble mausoleum that was once her home, so it'd gone to Odessa. They were angels and, as such, didn't have many personal belongings. In her apartment on Earth, she probably owned three times what normal angels did. Other than robes and books and maybe an electronic from the human world, angels spent their time in service, whether it was to each other, humans, or the realm in general.

Felicia folded herself down next to Odessa. Her sister sat with her legs to the side to keep her robe from gaping open. Her wings rested on the ground behind her, crossed at the tips like her ankles.

Felicia had none of those worries. She sat crisscross applesauce as her students called it, and as always, her wings were morphed. But as much as her back ached, it helped being among those who understood why she hid them.

Jagger waited outside with Bryant, and that helped too. This raw moment didn't need his brooding judgment.

"Is this all there is?" She frowned at the contents. The bin was a couple of feet tall, but only half full.

Odessa nodded. "I almost bought two or three, but Father lived sparsely."

Another pang hit her chest. Father had been the bad guy for so long. A loving, happy dad turned cold and distant when she'd needed him most. All of her rage over what had happened and the powerlessness it still made her feel was aimed at him. If he hadn't withdrawn, perhaps Mother would've had someone to turn to when she ran out of strength for her children.

A sigh gusted out of her.

Odessa's bright gaze touched on her. "I know. He was suffering in his own way. We all were—are." She glanced at Felicia's back.

"I'm not suffering," she mumbled. She'd survived. She'd adapted. She was still serving the world like her kind did. No one knew it, thinking the worst of her.

"Thank you for helping me with this."

"No reason to thank me. You shouldn't have to do it alone. But Jagger was weird about you coming here with this." Speaking about him was refreshing. He was usually too close for her to talk about, or the only one in the room with her.

"I imagine it's hard. He has nothing left behind." Odessa sifted through a stack of envelopes. Some were pink and—she sniffed—lightly scented? "He has to pretend his father never existed. Did you know they destroy all the personal belongings of a fallen?"

Felicia's gaze drifted until the envelopes were a blur. No wonder he'd been moodier than usual. "Damn." No one talked about Mother or how she'd died, but Felicia's entire existence wasn't threatened just by remembering her. Jagger had been a teen when his father had fallen.

Odessa brought an envelope to her nose and sniffed. "This smells like Mother. Rose and lavender." She opened one. Sprawling calligraphy danced across the page. "A love letter, from when they were courting."

Thinking of her parents young and in love squeezed her chest. She knew how that story ended.

A faint smile lit her sister's face. "They were marked as sync mates, but Father courted her anyway. She was young and scared. He was patient and kind."

And in the end, it hadn't mattered. Felicia pushed off the floor. She didn't want to hear this about the dad who'd been dead to her since he'd given her money and told her she'd be better off if she didn't come back to Numen. He'd let her think he didn't feel for her and that she was only trouble, and he'd run her off. Had it been for her own good?

It hadn't, but he couldn't have known how it would turn out. Only that she'd been endangered because of him and because she was too easy to get to in her own home.

A small gasp had her spinning back around. Odessa covered her mouth with one hand and a piece of paper shook in her other hand.

Felicia rushed over and snatched the stationary. Violets danced around the edges and in the middle Mother's handwriting.

Please forgive me. My love for you and our girls doesn't eclipse my fear. I'm terrified and they are trying to use my fear to get to them. I cannot protect them. Please forgive me.

Mother hadn't addressed the letter to anyone. No other last words, no "love always" or "yours forever," just a desperate plea to understand the feelings that drove her into the fountain of angel fire.

Tears burned the backs of her eyes. Wetness streaked down Odessa's face.

The door banged open and Bryant rushed to his mate's side. Felicia had to look away. He'd sensed his mate's distress, as he should. Hadn't Father felt Mother's anguish, or had their sync bond not mattered? Witnessing Bryant's quick reaction told her enough.

A sync bond alone wasn't enough to make a lasting relationship.

Jagger approached, wary, eying her as if she were the one who'd made Odessa cry. She was about to snarl at his black heart, but his gaze dropped to the bin, and for a heartbeat, heartbreaking loss reflected in his eyes.

Her mean words died on her lips.

He tore his gaze away, his expression carefully blank, and took the paper from her. The muscles in his jaw flexed as he read the words. Without a sound, he handed the sheet to Bryant.

Her new brother spared only enough time to read the message before dropping it back in the bucket and collecting Odessa in his arms.

Jagger stood close enough that the heat wafting off his body was a small balm. As usual, there was no comfort for her. No gathering her up and soothing her own pains. But her sister was cared for and that would have to be enough.

She squatted down and sifted through the rest of the contents. Letters. A phone with a smashed screen. Father's attackers had probably crushed it, or it had been damaged in the fight to his death. Some scrolls that he might've been researching for his job as senator.

She handed two to Jagger. "Here. Read those."

There was likely nothing on them, but going through Father's last days might help determine who else was involved. They only had two names and that wasn't enough. Stede and Kenton might have fled the realm, but there had to be more likeminded and brutally ambitious individuals left behind.

She read one scroll. A sync request for a senator and the much younger daughter of another senator. A power mating. Tossing it aside, she grabbed another. A request for regulating angel fire, which had gotten denied.

There were those in Numen who wanted angel fire regulated? It was so deadly, its burns irreversible, that no one wanted to mess with it. Only warriors had access to the special vials and protective equipment necessary to fill them; otherwise the angel fire was left open to the public. After all, no one wanted to risk even a droplet splashing on them. They all gave it a wide berth—except those like Mother.

This request might be onto something. Most angels couldn't take angel fire away from the city center, but what was stopping those with access from abusing that privilege? The days of thinking there were no bad angels among them were over, and the rest of Numen needed to know that. She should talk to Bryant when this was all over. The senate wouldn't take her seriously if she approached them, but the director would.

Jagger dropped his first scroll into the tub. "A request for information on the blood of the fallen." He frowned. "Why would that be significant?"

"I can search the archives," Odessa offered.

Bryant shook his head. "You're not diving any deeper into this mess."

This was her opening. They couldn't keep twiddling their thumbs at Jagger's or crying over her father's documents. "We should go to the archives. Jagger and I." Bryant was already shaking his head when she charged ahead. "We know what to look for. Those who are after us will think we're still hiding under guard."

"It makes sense." Jagger was going just as stir-crazy. "If we find anything, we'd be the ones with the advantage this time."

Bryant's gaze flicked back and forth. She didn't press him. If he thought they were the best option, he'd send them. But he debated so long she doubted he'd give the order.

"Fine," he bit out. "But be careful or Odessa will make me suffer."

CHAPTER 13

"Those are some tall freaking ceilings," Jagger breathed in Felicia's ear. She shivered. Her heat was like a cozy blanket he wanted to hug against himself. Creeping into one of the most esteemed buildings in Numen shouldn't be titillating, but with Felicia, his heart raced and adrenaline pumped through his veins as they crept through the archives. And none of it had to do with the thrill of getting caught.

"Saves on the cost of additions." They were an old-school society at heart. Parchment was used exclusively for long-term record storage. Though they did process mass data digitally, the most critical information was stored as scrolls. Odessa was right. If there was pertinent information about how completely a fallen had changed, it'd be here.

"I can't believe… The director's suspicions can't be real."

"Can't they, though?" she whispered. "He's not human and there has to be some way to keep a fallen from transcension. I'm just surprised the ramifications hadn't been explored earlier."

"It never felt right, trying to forget him. Maybe we

wouldn't be in this mess if the fallen had been monitored instead of stricken from history." Maybe his relationship with his mother wouldn't be so nonexistent. He thought of Mother's glacial gaze. Or maybe not.

Her expression was sympathetic. "I agree. How we deal with them needs to change."

They approached the end of a long hallway that arched impossibly high into a cathedral ceiling. Jagger scanned each direction they could go.

Felicia gestured to his left. "Odessa advised starting in the west wing, where the most ancient scrolls are. We should split up."

His whole being rejected the idea of getting farther away from her. "Nothing good ever starts with that phrase."

Her lips parted. "Julian Hancock, do you watch Scooby-Doo?"

He scowled at her. "It's been a long few months."

He made sure his tone wasn't insulting. She only smirked. He couldn't imagine admitting to Valerina that he watched cartoons—and enjoyed them—when he needed to kill time in the human realm. She probably would've packed up right then. He was a male who'd chosen not to be a senator. For his ex, that was more than enough dings to his character. Kid shows would've toppled the scale.

Valerina.

He could think about her now without the ball of fury that had Felicia at its center.

He was a warrior who investigated demon possessions. He hunted them. He followed clues. Felicia didn't care about the rules—but she followed them. She was the traumatized daughter of parents who'd been victims of a system that had refused to change since creation, yet she still cared about this realm even when she had no reason to. While she liked to allude to deceit, she never lied.

He believed her. Both he and Felicia had grown up early in their near-immortal culture. In a society where one could live forever if they were careful, maturity had a different meaning than in the human world. Some angels didn't grow the hell up until they left the realm and witnessed real suffering, until they realized that their existence was about more than lounging under pristine white clouds and boundless skies. Others took a century or two.

After what had happened to Father, he'd become a warrior. If watching his father's entire existence be wiped out hadn't made him view his life differently, then his first battle against a yellow-fanged monster had done the trick.

He'd almost lost his first real fight, and it had only made him better, taught him to adhere to his training. It had also fueled his search for a mate. Did he risk getting injured so badly that fate would decide who he was mated with and when? Bryant Vale had been on death's door when his sync brand had appeared. During those moments, angels could ascend or descend to where their future mate was and bond, then use the bond's healing strength. Director Vale had done just that, only the female had been so terrified by his appearance, she'd stopped dead in traffic. Not even a healing bond could rectify a full-body slam by a city bus.

Jagger hadn't wanted that for himself when he'd met Valerina. An esteemed senator's daughter. A respectable member of society. He could engineer his own fate.

Then Felicia had dated a few other warriors and somehow he'd gotten linked to her.

But she wasn't the cause. He'd been spending too much time with her, scrutinizing every move against his will, and being deceptive wasn't her personality. Except for that instance with Odessa's ex. But he'd heard of that male and couldn't help but think Felicia's extreme measures had saved her sister a lot of heartbreak. And saved his boss.

Felicia had hit on him. He'd turned her down. She wasn't a retaliator. She didn't seek revenge. There was no reason for her to spread those rumors.

"I know you didn't do it," he blurted.

Felicia's brow furrowed and she looked down the hall. "Do what? And don't we need to discuss a plan?"

They should've had one before they got this far, but they were winging it at this point. "Just clearing the air. Yes, it'd be better if we split up, but my gut tells me not to. And I don't think you tried to break up my mating arrangement."

She nodded slowly. "Okay. So we stay together and you finally know I'm not a lying d-bag."

"Yes."

"To the left then?"

If she wasn't going to make a big deal out of it, neither was he. He thought they should talk about it more, but her reaction made sense. The rumors had damaged his life, not hers. They had seemed more like a targeted attack than stupid gossip. And that meant they were his problem. "To the left."

He waited for her to move. She was naturally stealthy, sliding against the wall, moving silently. Her long curves were held in check, and her black leggings and long-sleeved shirt didn't highlight a thing, but he noticed anyway. He couldn't quit noticing. Wrong time, wrong place. When had he started pondering the right time and place?

Not until Persephone agreed to break things off. He wasn't mating her. She had to realize it was futile and he didn't have time to convince her that she'd find her one and only.

A tall doorway came into view. Felicia glanced back at him and he dipped his head. It might take two days to search this place. Maybe more, but they had to start somewhere.

The door whispered open. The archives didn't have a

security system. Technically, it was open to the public. History should be accessible to all. Didn't mean that those in charge of the archives weren't nosy. Or that they wouldn't try to deflect searches into subjects they felt were best left forgotten, which might not align with the searchers' goals.

Felicia slipped inside and he followed, quietly closing the door behind him.

"Odessa said the best way to determine what each room contains is to look at a few scrolls," Felicia whispered.

They had yet to pass anyone in the archives, but they weren't alone and they didn't know when an archivist might happen by, or the cleaners who donated their time tending to the routine tasks of dusting and sweeping.

"I'll take this side." Each wall, including the one the door was in, was lined from floor to ceiling with neatly stacked scrolls.

The daunting task loomed over him. He was trained for action. Browsing history records wasn't in his blood.

He yanked off a scroll, his gaze straying to Felicia. She skimmed her first scroll, rolled it back up, and selected another. Her expression captivated him. Interest blanketed her features. She could probably spend hours in here.

Mother had commented on how much she read as a senator. Much like lawyers, senators spent copious amounts of time studying their kind's past to form their decisions for the future, to settle disputes, and to uphold or change laws.

An intrigued "hmph" drifted toward him. Felicia tucked a scroll back in place. "I think this room, or at least this portion, is dedicated to lineage."

He hadn't even peeked at the scroll in his hand. Flipping it open, he read the scrawling script. A lot of "son of" and "daughter of."

"Same," he said. He went to the next wall and Felicia did

the same. This method wasn't the most thorough, but they didn't have days.

After a few minutes, Felicia declared the room a bust and they snuck to the one next door.

Analysts' recordings of fifteenth-century humans. As interesting as those times were, they found nothing of use.

Each room they went through, he looked for any spot with restricted access or scrolls that were more ancient and brittle looking.

Three searches later, Felicia huffed and tossed a scroll back. "The human practice of blood-letting." She anchored her hands on her hips. "The irony being that if you or I were a senator, we'd know exactly where to look."

"I don't think so. I've heard archivists are quite territorial and it's their little way of exerting their power over the senators."

She brushed stray strands of hair that had escaped her braid off her forehead. "Makes sense. Another room?"

"I have all day."

"It's still better than being stuck in my apartment."

It was. More freedom and the illusion that they were being productive.

He stopped to listen before he opened the door. Felicia piled into his back, expecting him to have opened the door by now. Growling, he listened harder, the act increasingly difficult with the lush curves pressed against his backside and the blood roaring between his ears.

A male voice from down the hall carried on the draft. Felicia stilled, a sharp inhale tightening her body.

He didn't spare her a glance as he listened. Were they going to come in here? Walk by? Or bypass them altogether?

"…It's here somewhere."

Jagger concentrated. The voice was vaguely familiar.

"That bastard is up to something…"

The sound was getting stronger. Jagger leaned back and pushed the door as shut as he dared. The sound of a click would be too loud in the nearly silent building, and his intuition begged him to remain undetected. The movement caused him to bump against Felicia.

She stumbled and he shot her a warning stare, mouthing, "Quiet."

Her face was pale, her eyes wide. A slight tremor traveled over her body.

The angels were coming closer. With the door not quite closed, he snaked an arm around Felicia's waist and pulled her to the side, pressing them both against the shelving.

"…best guess is that it'd be in the miscellaneous room, where it can get nice and lost." This from a female.

A reply came that he couldn't make out. Felicia hardly relaxed in his hold. Without using her arms, she managed to cling to him.

"It'd better not be fucking lost," growled the male.

Felicia jerked and turned her face into his shoulder.

This male scared her. Not just scared. She was terrified, her body shaking. And the fact that she was seeking comfort in him rather than stomping away to deal with her feelings in solitude scared him almost as much.

"We must figure out a way to send messages. You cannot risk returning to the realm again, Stede."

"I'll decide what I can and can't do. I can still come here and it's an advantage that manipulative fallen doesn't have."

It was his turn to tense. Stede was the interfering enforcer they'd learned was working with his father, who was obviously the manipulative fallen. He'd fled the realm when Director Vale had announced the conspiracy to the senate a couple of months ago.

And here he was.

Looking for a contract, like they were.

The other male spoke, his words growing fainter as they passed. "It's possible a contract such as the acquisition of metal is stored in a more secure spot."

He missed Stede's reply, but the direction they were going must be to the contract room. He eased away from Felicia, his chest tightening when her arms fell limply by her side. She closed her eyes and leaned against the shelves, her chest rising and falling like she was trying to steady her reaction.

Everything in him demanded he check on her well-being, but they'd been handed an unexpected boon. Stede was back and maybe looking for the same thing they were, but he was also with someone else, another angel who resided in the realm and was aiding Stede.

The door had proved silent earlier. He inched it open far enough to stick his head out. The backs of the two angels were disappearing, but he memorized the image. Stede was the shorter, stockier one, with dark hair and wings the color of an approaching rainstorm. The female was fair, her wings as pale as bleached stone. She was a few inches taller, and the dignified way she carried herself, with a deferential stoop to her posture as if she unconsciously recognized that Stede was her superior, told Jagger a lot. She was not a senator, but more of an academic. Perhaps she worked in the archives or was an analyst. He'd run the description past Odessa.

Before one of them could catch him watching them, he ducked back and eased the door all the way closed, wincing as the faint click echoed much too loud for his liking.

He stood in front of Felicia and set his hands on her shoulders. "What is it?"

Her lower lip trembled as terror rippled across her face. She sucked that lip in, but not before he'd caught her reaction.

"Was it the one called Stede that you recognized? Or the female?"

Her voice was a ragged whisper. "Stede. He sounded just like that night."

In the hallway, he'd been speaking low. Gruff. Angry. Just like he would've been speaking the night he attacked Felicia. The perfect tone to yank a traumatic memory to the forefront. "You didn't get a good look at him that night?"

She shook her head, eyelids shut. "It was so dark."

His interrogation was done. There was nothing he could do for her. If he hunted down the two angels, it'd be two against one, since Felicia was in no shape for a confrontation. The academic with Stede might not put up a huge fight, but Stede would be a formidable opponent. And—he hated himself for it—but knowing Stede returned to the realm occasionally and seeing who he worked with was the leg up they needed to get ahead of his father for once. Did Father—Jameson—know that he was being double-crossed?

Was he concerned about it?

Jagger wouldn't look that deep into what he was feeling.

Gathering Felicia to him, he murmured the same phrase over and over. "You're safe. You're with me, you're safe."

FELICIA PRESSED her fingers to her temples and paced to the other side of the mansion. Urban was outside checking the perimeter and Jagger was perched on the settee, his glorious wings out and draped over the back.

He watched her. Who knew he could be so patient? Not only had he talked her off the panic-attack ledge at the archives, but he'd also cut their search short, gotten them back to the mansion, and waited for her permission to inform Bryant of what they'd overheard.

She chewed on her index nail as she walked. That voice

rang through her head like a church bell striking twelve every minute.

In a second, she'd been transported back to her sixteen-year-old self, trying to hold in all sounds of agony, scared shitless that Odessa would suffer the same fate if she was too weak.

Eleven years had passed, but today it was like not even an hour had gone by. His voice was in her head.

Stede. That was his name. She had that now.

Why hadn't she jumped into action and taken him down? She'd had the element of surprise. This time, she was the one lurking in a dark room and could pin him to the ground like he'd done to her. She even had a knife and Jagger had angel fire. An eye for an eye. In this case, a wing for a wing.

Instead, she'd been useless. Stricken with nausea and trying not to fall to the ground and cry.

But she'd come across Stede before. Why hadn't she known him then, when she could've called him out in front of the entire senate?

The answer came too quickly. To deal with Stede, she'd have to confess to everyone what had happened. Her private horror would be horribly public. And as always, the hidden fear that no one would believe her dogged her desire to tell the world.

But Jagger believed her. He'd held her. Comforted her. Cared for her. She'd worked so hard to be independent and become the opposite of a victim and when her moment had arrived, she'd cowered in Jagger's arm and had a hard time feeling remorseful.

The memory was too clear.

A shudder shook her body.

This sucked.

She hit the end of the hallway and strode back, her

athletic shoes slapping on the marble floor. "I know we have to tell Bryant."

"I'll report that we need to make another trip. As far as Stede…"

He was leaving it up to her. Honor-driven Jagger was willing to follow her lead. But if her lead meant hunting the bastard down and shanking him, would he still be as chill?

"I want to find him, and I want to kill him. But…" She stopped pacing and hugged her arms around herself.

He rose and closed the distance between them. "But what?"

Maybe it was his gentle tone. Or the concern in his eyes. She was getting used to seeing the real Jagger, the one who let his feelings show and die for those he swore to protect. When all that was aimed her way, it uncoiled a tension inside she didn't realize she had. A natural defense she'd built up against his earlier self and everyone else.

"But he also terrifies me and I want to do nothing but hide." She blinked back hot tears. She couldn't cry, not around him. When she cried, she wanted to be held, but she was always alone unless she went out and found company for the night.

That couldn't happen. Not with him. She couldn't take his rejection.

He put his hand on her shoulder and ducked his head to peer into her eyes, like he needed to determine how badly she was hurting on a scale of one to ten. His worry for her overflowed and her tears spilled over. Right now, it was a ten.

His arms came around her and she was pressed into his broad chest. A sob escaped her. He held her tighter.

It all poured out. Holding in her fear at the archives, the resurgence of her past clogging her head, and the helplessness of being two steps behind and not in a place to do a damn thing about it.

She cried and he held her. At some point, he swept her off her feet and took her into the guest room, closing the door behind him, a gesture she was grateful for. Urban or his replacement didn't need to witness this. But aside from lying on the bed in his embrace, nothing else happened. Except something major happened. She had someone during one of her breakdowns. It wasn't just someone, it was the male who'd gone out of his way in the first couple of months to make her feel like gum on his shoe. He'd softened the last couple of weeks, enough to make her wonder, What if?

She'd hit on him that first time because he was hot. Not just sexy, but irresistible in a way that made it difficult to take her eyes off him. That surfer quality he had conflicted with the steely glint in his bedroom eyes. When he brushed his light hair back, she'd expected a casual smile full of flirtation, but his expression had been heavy with caution, reserved. The whole package was catnip.

It still was, but she didn't have the energy to pursue the feeling. His heat surrounded her with his wings acting like a downy duvet. Her cries lessened until she only sniffled once in a while. He was on his back and she was curled into him.

She dozed off. In any other situation, she would've been horrified. Falling asleep with red puffy eyes and crusted tears and snot was more intimate than wandering around with her bra off. Almost as vulnerable as having her wings out around him.

She didn't know how long she napped, but she wasn't surprised when he untangled himself from her and quietly left. Without his warmth, the ache in her back grew stronger. Her wings would have to stay in. She'd been exposed enough the last few…hours?

She rolled over. The chill from a new spot on the bed

highlighted how alone she was. It'd been nice while it lasted, but she'd pull on her big-girl strap-on and forge ahead.

The door whispered open and clicked shut. She'd been around Jagger enough to know his footsteps.

She craned her head around. He had a glass of water in one hand and a wet rag in the other.

He lifted a light brow. "I didn't mean to wake you."

She lifted herself into a sitting position. "I won't be able to sleep tonight if I don't wake up now." Accepting the water, she took a long drink. Next, he handed her the cloth. He'd used warm water. Thoughtful. Pressing the cloth to her face, she relaxed into it. "Ohmigosh, this feels so good."

The bed dipped as he settled on it. She wanted to curl into him. How had he known to do this? His ex? Certainly not his mother.

"My, um…" It wasn't like Jagger to be tongue-tied. She lowered the cloth. His eyes were tortured, his gaze far away. He swallowed and looked down. "My father used to do it for me when I'd get nightmares. He seemed to know when I needed a warm rag or a cool one." His smile was nervous. "I hope I chose correctly."

The father he was supposed to forget about. The one that was enemy number one to the realm. "I'm sorry."

He caught her gaze. "I'm not. Being forced to try not to remember a parent is unrealistic to say the least. I wasn't allowed a grieving process, and Mother…" His chuckle lacked all humor. "Well, you can imagine."

"Her washcloth was always cold?"

A laugh burst out of him. "Ice cold."

She dropped her head onto his shoulder. He didn't comment on the damp cloth seeping through his shirt. Instead, he wrapped an arm around her. His heat seeped into her, soothing. Until it went beyond comfort. A tiny flame ignited in her belly and she was too aware of his muscles under her cheek.

He dipped his head. Was that a soft kiss against her hair?

"Thank you." She didn't want to break the moment but had to express how she felt. Having him with her was better than dealing with it alone. "I just needed a moment."

"I'm glad I could help." His deep voice rumbled next to her ear. She scooted closer. He hugged her tighter.

He stroked her face with his hand and tipped her face to look up at him. "You know what I get jealous of humans about? How easily they can express their emotions. I know many have issues, but even so, compared to us, they're downright hysterical. Up here, well, it's like if we're not farting rainbows, something's wrong with us." His gaze deepened. "But we weren't designed to be like that. We're not faultless beings. We have a higher duty, but we're still living creatures."

"It's why I left."

His attention flicked over her shoulder, like he'd be looking at her wings if they were out. "I understand. This wasn't a good place for you."

"It's a little better now."

She held his gaze, couldn't look away. Then he cupped her face and lowered his mouth to hers. He was twisted to the side, but without breaking contact, he turned until he was coming up onto the bed and she was lying back. His weight settled over her.

As if they had an unspoken understanding that this was going to end with him naked and inside of her, they worked in harmony to strip themselves down. She skimmed her fingers over the feathers. Strong and healthy. She was grateful hers were hidden.

Once he was bared, she took a moment to admire his body and he did the same, his gaze sweeping over her breasts and down to the juncture of her thighs. She couldn't get enough of the view. Defined chest. Hard muscles. Washboard abs even while reclined. Powerful legs. His wings were taut behind him and the only part of him that rivaled their tension was his thick erection.

It would've taken more than a stupid rumor to get her to leave him.

"The next time we do this, your wings are going be out." His gaze brooked no argument.

Her lungs tightened. No, she'd never done that.

But Jagger had already seen them and he'd just demanded they be out—next time.

He didn't dwell on it, pushing her back and spreading her legs. None of his moves were hurried. They were deliberate, as if they had all day. And they did.

Pressing a kiss to her belly, he held her eyes. Somewhere deep in her mind, a warning clanged. Maybe they were going too fast. Maybe she should wait until there was more time between her breakdown and going to bed with someone.

That part of her mind needed to shut up. This was Jagger and he was going down on her.

He used his thumbs to part her folds, and when his soft tongue licked over her clit, she bucked her hips. His wings canopied over him, her legs were on either side of his wide shoulders, and it was the most erotic sight possible.

She went off sinfully fast. Her climax arched her back and she dropped her head until she was staring at the ceiling, trying to silently gasp and moan through the orgasm.

Soon they'd have privacy and she could scream and plead for more. Because for such a fast orgasm, it was the most powerful one she'd ever had.

He prowled up her body and settled his weight over her, but he didn't push inside. Again, like they had all night.

He paused at her breasts, giving each nipple more attention than they'd ever had until she was writhing and arching again. How could she get worked up again so soon?

"Jagger, I want…" Should she have used his real name? It didn't feel right. Had his ex cried out Julian in her passion? If so, Felicia didn't want to remind him of that. This moment was between them. A shared pain that no one else understood.

"I've wanted you for so long," he murmured and nuzzled into her neck. He smelled like her passion.

Finally, he moved his hips until his cock was in position, just teasing her entrance. She rolled her hips, but he didn't advance. His gaze pinned her as he entered. Slowly.

Everything between them was stripped away. In the bright depths of his eyes, she saw how much he desired her. How much her passion turned him on and how he wanted only to get her off over and over until they both passed out. He was stripped bare of more than clothing.

Allowing herself the same, she tried to express without words how much she'd wanted to be with him. Not like the others. They'd been distractions. She'd wanted to learn every nuance of Jagger since the moment she'd laid eyes on him. Unlike many males she'd come across, his honor was more than a temporary show.

And being with him like this was beyond her experience with their kind. And her time with the humans? Their stress over birth control and STDs had consumed the moment. She couldn't get pregnant outside of a sync bond, and her kind didn't get disease. One of the perks of being the guardians of humankind.

Finally, Jagger was seated fully inside, filling her completely. His body shook like he wanted to pump with abandon.

"Let yourself go," she whispered. "For once, just let go."

If he couldn't do that with her, then who?

He took a moment, like he had too much to consider. Her pleasure. The length of the experience. How perfect it should be.

But he did as she asked, just like she'd do with her wings when he asked. Next time.

He thrust. Over and over, his head dropping to hers as the force increased. He hooked his arms under her legs and pumped.

Oh, this wasn't going to take long. Jagger losing his mind was a hell of an aphrodisiac and her clit was still quivering from his tongue.

She exploded over him, and he opened his mouth, a strangled sound escaping. He clenched his jaw, catching himself in time. Neither of them wanted the others to know they were having sex. Another unspoken mutual understanding.

He released, his body going rigid, easing, then rigid again as he emptied inside of her. This was the best sex she'd ever had. Nearly perfect. If she could scream about how good this was, it would be the cherry on top.

He collapsed on top of her, his wings going limp.

She was warm and satisfied.

After a minute, he withdrew and rolled to the side, one wing still over her.

Her smile had to be as dreamy as she felt. "Next time, I want to hear what you cry out during sex."

"Next time, I want to fucking yell. And make you call my name over and over." He dropped a kiss on her nose. The sweetest gesture she'd ever had from him. "But I guess until my mating contract is officially broken, we have to keep this between us."

CHAPTER 14

With one hand still shoved in his pocket, Jagger banged on the door, then stuffed that hand in a pocket too. To say he wasn't looking forward to this was an understatement. But once Felicia had yelled *What?* and shoved him off, it was hard to hide what happened from anyone within listening distance, which, as Felicia's shouting had gotten louder, was quite far. Good thing he had a sizable yard.

Urban had graciously allowed him to be the one to tell Bryant that Felicia had descended to God knows where and ask Odessa where Felicia had likely fled.

The door swung open on soundless hinges and Odessa's curious face peered back at him. Her gaze swept around him before a small frown graced her mouth.

"She's not here. That's what I came to talk to you about. Is Director Vale home as well?" His boss wasn't the workaholic Jagger assumed he'd be, but mating had changed his priorities.

"What do you mean—" Odessa leaned back. "Bryant!" She stepped out of the way.

Crossing the threshold only added a metric ton of weight to his shoulders.

He did not. Want. To do this.

But hindsight made it clear where he'd fucked up. That, or Felicia's justified tirade.

Odessa wrung her hands together, the frown still on her face. "I know Bryant needs to hear this, but is she okay? Because you don't look okay."

He should be better than he'd ever been. Sex with Felicia Montclaire had been off the charts. He'd been humbled and elated at the same time, if only for a brief second before he'd ruined it. "I think she is well, but we had a-a…situation…and she left."

Director Vale's voice cut in. "What do you mean she left? Who went with her?"

Jagger slid his hand out of his pockets and clasped them behind his back. "No one. She was upset."

His boss's amber eyes narrowed on him. "What the bloody hell did you do?"

There was no way to tell the story in a dignified way. He went for succinct. "We were growing closer, then my mom matched me with another angel without my permission. When I went to break things off, the female didn't handle it well. Pushing would've made it worse so I decided to bide my time. But then Felicia and I… And she didn't know that I was still…" Nope. Not dignified, but he refused to hang his head.

Odessa sucked in a breath. "You slept with her while you were promised to another? After how you treated her?"

He didn't need a psychologist to understand that, because of her reputation, he'd laid blame on her that should've been aimed at his father. And while he'd realized that he'd been unjustly unfair about her past, he still treated her like she was as indiscriminate as Father. Of course she would take issue with sleeping with him while he was promised to another, and he should've been honest.

He hadn't meant to be dishonest but his actions had hurt her in the end. Now he had to find her. "I didn't think— I'm not going through with the mating. So no, I didn't make the connection, but I agree. I was wrong. Then and now."

"Did you tell her that?" Odessa's arms were folded and she inspected him the way a scientist must look at a pinned bug.

"It didn't matter at the time." Perhaps if he'd been less of an asshole before.

The director wiped a hand over his brow. "So you came here hoping Odessa would know where she went."

He nodded. Almost three solid months at her side and he didn't know much about her.

Concern infused Odessa's teal irises. "I don't either. Until all this started, I didn't know what she did in the human realm, not where she went or who she did it with."

"I still can't believe she chose Persephone Nassim," the director said. "Why *her*?"

He shrugged, feeling as helpless as he must look. "I think it was her misguided attempt to keep me safe."

"For the healing." The director shook his head. "She should've had faith you'd get a sync mate if things became dire."

"For an angel, my mother lacks faith, unless it's regarding your failings. I'll find her."

Director Vale shook his head. "You can't go alone."

"Being guarded twenty-four seven isn't helping. And we suspect a leak. If my father's people find out she's alone, they will hunt her down."

Director Vale inspected him. "You don't think your father would hurt her?"

Jagger hadn't realized that he hadn't implicated Father—

Jameson. Fuck, why bother? It was clear he couldn't pretend any longer that the fallen and Father weren't one and the same. Why waste the energy calling him Jameson? If anyone could be forgiven for not properly forgetting a fallen, it should be him.

"He'd use her, somehow." His gaze flicked to Odessa. Once upon a time, he'd insinuated that Felicia would get close to his father by sleeping with him, but he no longer believed it. Oh, he'd trust his father to try to get between Felicia's toned legs, but she wouldn't fall for it. And once Father knew that she meant something to his son, he wouldn't physically hurt her.

He shouldn't have so much trust in someone he knew so little. Perhaps he needed a dose of his mother's cynicism to get through this.

"I don't like it," the director said.

"She might be in Vegas." Odessa's sudden announcement made them both spin their heads toward her. Odessa was tapping her chin with a long finger. "Yes, the more I think of it, the more it makes sense. Felicia was never one to run away. It only appears so, but her ear is always to the door. When she found out my ex was cheating on me, she took action. Same with learning to fight. She knew what our father was up to even though she wasn't in this realm."

It made sense in a roundabout way. "And you think she'll be drawn to Vegas, if only to spy on Father?"

"Yes." Her tone was all confidence. "She couldn't go somewhere and do nothing. She wouldn't, knowing what she knows. She won't be overt, but she'll still be in harm's way."

"It's worth a shot." He met his boss's gaze. If he didn't get permission, would he still go?

Yes.

"I don't like it," the director said again. As if that weren't obvious from the man's troubled expression. "Report in often. Sierra's in Vegas. She can pass messages to me."

It was on the tip of his tongue to remind him that Sierra might be the leak, but that was foolish. Sierra was one of them.

She also didn't spend much time with the team and was often aloof and stuck in her own head. But he'd chalked it up to her techy personality.

"Will do." After he found Felicia. His gut warned him to keep his whereabouts, and Felicia's unknown whereabouts, between only them.

He left their place, spread his wings, and took flight. There was one more stop he had to make.

When he landed, he was in front of Persephone's opulent mansion. He rapped on the door, expecting a butler to answer. The Nassims would have a fleet of staff and never run short of angels wanting to work for them.

"I didn't expect to see you again so soon," Persephone said from behind him.

He spun around. Her silky black hair hung over one shoulder. She was ethereally beautiful, and after the Valerina debacle—or before he'd met his ex—he would have been a willing participant in his mother's schemes. But he wasn't that male anymore. Once Felicia had entered his life, his priorities had started to shift.

"Persephone, hi."

She crossed her arms, her naturally manicured nails biting into the skin of her upper arms. She wasn't as relaxed as she appeared. "Hi. Come to try to break up with me again?"

"We can't break up when we weren't seeing each other in the first place."

She regarded him with dark eyes, the rest of her expression guarded. It was impossible to tell what she was thinking.

He decided to go for sincerity. Persephone might have a catty reputation but he was learning the hard way that there was a valid history behind people's actions—and that everything wasn't as it seemed. "I'm sorry you got dragged into this. Truly. The antiquated act of promising children off to strangers should stop."

Her hard expression softened, but not enough to ease his anxiety. If this got ugly, Persephone could cause problems for Felicia and expose that she was MIA. "But it happened and our parents agreed."

He schooled his expression to keep his frustration from showing. "What do you want, Persephone? What do you truly want? An empty sync with me can't be the top of your list."

There it was. That staggering vulnerability and yearning she hid under bitchiness. "What I want is to sync with a mate who isn't using me to get closer to my parents and obtain a senate position. And one who will at least respect me in public."

"Isn't in private also a requirement?"

She lifted her chin. "And now you know why I won't dissolve the contract so easily. I know she's at your place. I've seen Felicia in the realm. You and I go our separate ways and people will think it's because of her."

"I didn't realize you know her." A lie, but he had to understand why Felicia was an issue.

"Oh, I do. My mother still talks about her and Odessa all the time." Bitterness dripped from her tone. "Mother wouldn't try syncing one of *them* off. Their futures are too promising." She lifted a shoulder and looked away, but not before he caught the heavy dose of guilt in her eyes.

What for?

Persephone huffed and shoved her hair out of her face.

"Anyway, I guess this is fate laughing at me for starting that rumor."

He went as still as a marble statue. "What rumor?" he growled.

Moisture misted her eyes and she made a disgusted sound. "All I did was mention to some friends that I saw you two talking and they took off with it. And I let them. But I thought it'd affect her and not you."

All because of childish jealousy? Because "my mother thinks you're better than me?" He wanted to be angry—he *was* pissed—but he had more pressing matters. He had to find Felicia before his father or Stede did.

"You owe me. Release me from this deal. And stand up to your parents," he snapped. He was one to talk. As if he didn't let his own parental baggage affect how he treated people. Like Felicia. Summoning as much compassion as he could muster, he said, "I think... I think you should spend some time in the human realm."

She screwed her face up like he'd suggested she stroll through sewage plants and garbage dumps. "Why would I do that?"

"Because then you can see thousands, millions of lives being lived on their own terms. People who don't have ties to politics other than to tweet their hatred about presidents and prime ministers and congress and parliaments and monarchies and—"

"I get it. But I don't live among humans." She was back to being defensive. Bored even.

His hopes dwindled. "I'm not mating you. My father's a fallen but you can't use that to control me." She blanched at the mention of Father. "And my relationship status with Felicia is none of your business. But she's in danger because of you."

Her eyes shimmered. She was still hanging on to her own

limited dream. She wanted a partnership based on respect. That wasn't the limiting factor. It was that she was convinced it was him.

"Fine. I'll talk to my mother in the morning."

"Or you and I can do it now. Think of how that'll look to the males sniffing around your heels. You break the contract, not your parents."

A fire lit behind her eyes. That got to her. "It's in the office." She pushed past him. As they entered, she spoke loudly. "As I said, it just won't work between us. I trust you understand."

He bit back his smile and adopted a crestfallen look. "As you wish."

The contract was ripped as the eyes of several servants bored into his back. None of them were visible but they were watching.

He left, heaving a sigh of relief as the door clicked behind him. Now, Vegas.

THE CLUB WAS HOPPING. Felicia loitered a block away, peeking at her phone randomly to make it appear like she was waiting for someone. The ruse wouldn't work long but it wasn't like she could go inside. She wasn't that foolish. Staying this far away where the faint smell of piss perfumed the air was a smarter plan.

"Did you really think you could hang around here and I wouldn't notice?"

The cultured, familiar voice scattered goose bumps across her skin. Stupid, stupid, stupid. What had she been thinking, coming to Fall From Grace by herself? Now she was one of those storybook heroines who got herself into danger and just complicated things.

She turned, making the motion casual. She'd assumed that wearing a disguise and loitering a decent distance from the club would keep her from being recognized. She was wrong. Just because she could ascend and they couldn't didn't mean she wasn't risking her wings by doing it in public.

Thankfully, and surprisingly, Jameson was alone. It dawned on her why.

"Did you think Jagger was with me?"

He lifted a shoulder but didn't hide the longing in his uniquely colored eyes. "He is well?"

"Did you show this much concern for him when you were an angel or are the humans getting to you?"

The corner of his mouth ticked. "You remind me of Chanel."

"Solid burn, bro. So, who ratted me out?"

"As if it weren't obvious?" He appraised her red wig and knee-high boots. The black rose tattoo was drawn under her arm thanks to a Sharpie. A good expanse of her stomach was showing above the band of her vinyl shorts, but she was appropriate parts bombshell and grunge.

Not that she'd know it from Jameson. There was no interest radiating off him. From his reputation, it was the last thing she'd expected. Perhaps a thread of honor remained in him. No one had thought it was there in the first place, but they were wrong. He went by his own code and his son was a strong motivator. She could use that.

"Actually, I was looking for you," he said.

"How did you know I was here?" Who all knew she'd left Numen?

A defined brow lifted. "I have my ways and you used credit to buy your baubles. I assumed you'd come looking for me. Care to share why?"

She'd made one large purchase on a prepaid card—that

she'd had to withdraw money to fill. Damn. Who had tracked her that fast? "Tell me about the one you work with called Stede, and I'll tell you how he's backstabbing you."

"Stede?" His reaction was almost believable. "I don't know any Stede."

"I guess we're done here then." She went to walk away, her focus on the alcove she planned to hide in to ascend. She had no bluff to call.

"Why would you think this Stede is trying to double cross me? Or that I wouldn't know already?"

Did he know already? "And I should share that why?"

"I know the name. I admit, I'm curious how you do too. You haven't lived in the realm for years, correct?"

She debated only a few heartbeats before she confessed her past to a man who was an enemy of her people. "He mutilated my wings."

Jameson's mouth curled into a snarl that was gone so fast she doubted what she'd seen. "Indeed. They healed well, I assume." Bitterness dripped from his tone.

"Angel fire."

He sucked in a breath as his shoulders flexed and relaxed, like she did when her back ached. It wasn't a comfort, seeing that, decades later, the trauma of his own experience was still so immediate for him. She only had one decade under her belt. Did it ever get better?

"And his reason?" Jameson asked in a deceptively placid voice.

"To coerce my father into covering for those you were working with. I wasn't even sixteen."

His jaw clenched and released. Jameson didn't seem like a guy who got ruffled easily. His success in this realm, judging by the evidence of the packed club full of his dedicated disciples, was more than he'd probably imagined when his bloody, battered, wingless body had been dumped in Vegas.

But her story bothered him. As if he'd thought that only those who "deserved it" were mowed down to pave the way for his ambitions.

"That is unfortunate." Was that sympathy in his gaze? "However, I stand by my earlier statement."

"Even though he's working on finding out what advantages your blood would give him?"

His gaze cooled until she wondered if Chanel had been the only iceberg in their relationship. Suppressing a shiver, she forced herself to meet his eyes. She'd just handed over her only bargaining chip, but the glimpse into how much it affected him was worth it. He did not like or want his fellow conspirators to know he was gathering Daemon metal.

"And you think you know this why?"

She glanced around. No one was bothering them. Spies were probably stuffed in each corner, but she wasn't concerned about being seen with him. Willing or not, she was part of the investigation. While sometimes she thought losing her wings would save more pain than it'd cause, Bryant would back her up. They were all in this investigation too deep to worry about getting punished for having to talk to a fallen—especially this fallen. "I overheard. He's searching the archives. Looking for a secret about you."

"And what do you think about that?"

"Jagger and I," she said intentionally, studying his reaction, "haven't dwelled on it much. We're more interested in Stede."

His face was a mask of mild interest. "Cut the head off a snake and it'll grow three more, Ms. Montclaire. Are you sure you want to go up against Stede?"

Did that mean he was willing to help her? Why? He must have more contacts, or was he willing to burn one that could come and go from Numen in order to spare his secret? "I want him to suffer like I've been suffering for the last eleven years."

"Then you and I are much more alike than I initially thought."

"And you and Jagger are more alike than I feared."

What had made her say that? Jagger wouldn't cheat on her.

No, but he'd cheated on his contract and dragged her into it. Rumors were easier to ignore when they weren't true.

"My son is nothing like me."

"So he's like his mother?"

The flare of his nostrils was horribly satisfying. Jameson lived in an empire he'd built with people catering to him left and right. While he might have to navigate the intricacies of working with demons and angels alike for a semi-shared goal, he didn't often have to question his own actions. She knew the type. As long as others served his own needs, he had no need to.

His hard gaze swept the street. "Ms. Montclaire, perhaps you should visit any acquaintances you have in Vegas. You never know what might turn up." His intense chartreuse gaze pinned her. "I'm not one to stand in the way of revenge."

"Not when it suits you."

The corner of his mouth hitched up. They would've gotten along in another life.

THEY HAD no idea he was there. More importantly, Felicia had no idea he was there. He'd come to the human realm and bought a wig and club clothes, because if Felicia was hunting down Stede, then she'd have to go to his father for information. She knew no one else who had enough information to get her close to him. He'd have to thank Odessa later for this.

Jagger finished watching the conversation between Father and Felicia. Once Father strode back to the club and mingled with his adoring fans, Jagger veered around the corner, his long legs eating up the distance between him and his target.

Like him, she was in disguise. Two could play the wig game and tonight, he'd brought the wig game hard. Floppy brown hair lay across his brow like he was a teen heartthrob, but nothing about his fitted-to-within-an-inch-of-his-life slacks said boy band. His pants were black and so was the stylishly haphazard suit coat that hung unbuttoned over a white shirt that wasn't tucked in. The overall image was nothing like he usually dressed, topped off with contacts that made his eyes a doe brown. He was pleased with how well the ensemble hid his weapons.

Felicia ducked into a darkened alcove outside the entrance of a vape shop.

"Don't you dare ascend," he growled.

She popped out, her eyes wide. She made a good redhead. Sexy as hell, but he'd love to see her natural locks flow over her sinfully pushed-up cleavage. "What are you doing following me? I was trying to decide whether to gut you or run like hell."

Neither one would've worked. "What am I doing? Why are you at Fall From Grace? Talking to my father?"

She drew back, slamming her hands on her hips. Unfortunately, it drew his eyes to the swath of creamy flesh she'd left exposed. He wanted to lick his tongue across it. "Eyes up here." She pointed to her face.

"The sync contract is shredded."

Hurt flashed through her face but she maintained her strong stance. "And?"

"I'm sorry."

"You've said that."

"I didn't realize that I hadn't told you what exactly had happened, or how the contract would make you feel."

"You said that too."

He lifted his hands. "What can I do?" He wasn't leaving her here to roam Vegas by herself doing God knows what.

"Help me track down Stede. Your father gave me some cryptic advice I can't figure out."

If that was as much as he'd get, he'd take it. "Done, but first I have to get a message to Director Vale and your sister that I found you. He also wants me to update Sierra, but—"

She snapped her fingers. "That's what he meant."

He was obviously missing something.

"Jameson told me to visit any acquaintances or contacts in town. I was like, who the hell do I know in Vegas? But Sierra's set up shop here."

His gut squirmed. Informing Sierra they were in town didn't sit well, and he should feel the opposite. She was one of his team. He'd entrusted his life to her over and over.

Felicia narrowed her eyes. "What's going through your mind?"

"Do you have a room here? Somewhere we can talk in private?"

Her gaze swept down to his Vans and back up. "Do you really think we need to be in private when we look like this?"

"We should leave the neighborhood, though. Did you rent a car?"

"Nope."

He called a car and sent a message to the director. The driver met them a few blocks from where he'd initially made the call and Jagger paid him to weave through Vegas. Confident they'd lost any tails, he and Felicia disembarked at a twenty-four-hour diner, the type of place that was quiet enough he could snag a corner booth and watch all the exits, but busy enough to keep them from standing out. The smell of fried food woke his stomach up. His appetite had vanished with Felicia.

She sat across from him, avoiding his gaze as she perused the menu. Slapping the menu down, she stared at him. "Want to tell me why you're hesitant to report to Sierra? Do you think it was the right call to check into her?"

His gaze flicked to the approaching server. He waited until Felicia ordered a sunrise feast before asking for the same. His mind wasn't in a state to decide and he'd been around her long enough to know that he'd eat whatever she did.

Once they were alone again, he answered. "It was the right call no matter what. I should be confident that nothing will be found, that she's tight and only looking out for the team and the realm. I'm not. It's a gut feeling and I can't explain it and it makes me feel like shit."

"Well, gut feelings come from somewhere, so let's lay it out. I don't know much about her so tell me the basics."

It felt way too natural to sit in this generic diner and discuss his intuition and how it related to his job. After their tension-laden time together, this looseness was nice. He'd have to earn her trust again, and they had bigger issues than them to worry about. There would be no them if Stede or Father followed through on whatever they were planning.

He started in. "Sierra is reserved. Not quiet, though. Once you get her talking, she gets animated, then falls silent almost as if she's afraid of what she might say. But she's killer with tech so she stays on Earth where she can plug into the grid. That many devices would be too hard to power in Numen. She takes care of our phones and any additional comms we might need, and she hacks like a beast."

"She doesn't fight with you?"

He recalled their training days. "She was a couple years behind me in training, but I know she's skilled, like any of us.

It's just that being more adept in technology made her work here critical. I mean, our teams are made up of seven warriors and in the old days that might have been necessary, but with modern advancements, it's getting to be overkill if all any of us can do is fight."

"You don't need the numbers to watch each other's back or run messages back and forth anymore." She pushed her hair out of her face, but all he saw was the curtain of strands parting to reveal ample cleavage.

"Yep." He lifted his gaze. She'd caught him watching and draped the hair back. Since he wasn't usually a lecher, he strove to keep his eyes above her collar line. He'd seen every glorious inch of her, but he'd have to wait until she allowed him to see it again.

"She's isolated in the human realm. Think they got to her?"

He shook his head. "No. I mean, they could try but they couldn't crack her."

"We all have our secrets, Jagger." He didn't want to acknowledge the possibility and she must've sensed it. She pushed. "Think of all the young little angels born twenty years ago. Don't they sigh as you, a big mighty warrior, saunter by? They think you're infallible. They don't know your past."

He knew where she was going with this. "Because they don't know what happened to my father." And they wouldn't understand why Felicia had her wings tucked in. Her story was a secret, and his was supposed to be long forgotten.

"Bingo."

The greasy aroma of their food hit him before the server reached the table. Felicia dug in and gave him an expectant look.

"Who would get to her? And why?" he asked. There had to be another reason.

She stuffed a forkful of pancake into her mouth and held up a finger until she swallowed. "I can see you're still doubt-ful. Let's try the others. Dionna?"

"She's been around most of the time. Her mate is doing relief work in Somalia."

"Someone could've gotten to him, but I have a feeling that Dionna wouldn't let that shit fly. She'd break whoever messed with her—or him."

"Agreed. Urban, Bronx, and Harlowe are all in a similar category. They're all single, they've been on the clock with us since the beginning, and…" He sighed and stabbed a pile of scrambled eggs with his fork. "And I don't get the gut feeling about them."

"Then find out where Sierra is and let's spy on her."

CHAPTER 15

Stakeouts were more boring than they appeared on TV. On shows, they looked dull for no more than five minutes, then boom! Action.

Felicia sighed and dug out another handful of dill-pickle sunflower seeds. This had attained a new level of monotony. "It's a blessing that I can't die of sodium overload."

The muscle in Jagger's jaw jumped. He'd been irritable ever since they'd climbed to the bell tower of the nearby church. Hardly anyone went up here and the bell wasn't in use anymore. Aside from some dust and cobwebs, it was quiet and high enough to see two blocks away to where Sierra's rental was. And bonus, if anyone heard scraping or movements coming from up here, they'd think it was either mice or the spirits of the nearby graveyard.

"But then you drink a lot of water and risk busting us by going to pee all the time."

And grumpy struck again. She'd made him get a separate room at the hotel, but he'd gotten an adjoining room. The front desk clerk had initially said they were full and given Felicia an "are you all right" look.

Keep the damn door between the rooms unlocked, he'd growled.

Truly, she'd been enjoying herself. For once, she had the upper hand between them. Her resolve was strong. He had to prove himself if he wanted more with her. She wasn't in line for a relationship. Certainly not one that would take her back to Numen. They could live apart—

What was she thinking?

Uh, maybe that her no-relationship resolve had crumbled as soon as he'd entered her? Before that even, when his tongue had danced with hers.

But really, had anything changed? She and her broken wings weren't going to live in Numen, where she'd garner pitying looks day after day, reminding her what she'd been through.

No, thank you.

Jagger was dedicated to his job and while she might've wormed her way under his skin, he was still Jagger, the male who wanted to distance himself from his father's reputation. She still had a reputation of her own. He might've forgotten but once the guilt passed he'd remember. And then he'd hold it over her—again—like everyone else did. As if enjoying sex—rather the temporary moments she felt more pleasure than pain—was wrong.

Did she really think that a sync meant happily ever after? She'd pass on that fairy tale. But his momentary temper tantrum and sulking were enjoyable.

She chugged her water and tossed in another handful of seeds. "I went to one of my students' Little League baseball games once. That's where I was introduced to these seeds."

He glanced from the seeds to her, then grabbed the bag. "I never saw the point in these things. Why not just buy them shelled already?" Dumping a small pile into his hands he gave them a brief frown before stuffing them into his mouth. His left cheek pouched out.

"Oral gratification."

He coughed, two seeds spitting from between his lips. His glower was adorable. An invisible string tugged at her heart. If only things were different between them.

That way lie insanity, but it was hard to forget the blast of pleasure that had chased away her constant aches for hours, even after he'd opened his mouth.

The muffled cracking of seeds in their mouths was the only sound. She was rearranging their water bottles next to the notepads they wrote car descriptions and times down on when Jagger shifted.

"What do we have here?" He put the binoculars to his face and she did the same. He hadn't spared any expense, and since she didn't have much money left, she let him pay for everything, including the hotel rooms.

Focusing on Sierra's small, square rental, she watched a male exit a nondescript black sedan. Was it him? A stocky, dark-haired male strode up the door and knocked like he was going to shout, "Police, open up!"

"Is that him?" she breathed, afraid to have confirmation. Then her personal nightmare would finally have a face.

She was afraid Jagger wouldn't answer, but he finally said, "Yes."

Air whooshed out of her lungs. She hadn't realized she was holding her breath. She wanted to run. She wanted to go kill him now. She wanted to tuck herself into Jagger's side and just be held.

"We'll get him, and we'll do it so you don't get taken down with him."

Right. Only two of her three options would let her continue living her normal life. If she killed him in cold blood, revenge or not, she'd be punished. Her realm might only have one punishment, but it was effective at keeping the peace.

Stede disappeared into the house, his hands gesturing. She couldn't make out who opened the door.

"I wish we could listen."

He dropped his binoculars. "It'd help. Too bad Sierra's the one we'd ask to get listening devices."

She chuckled, but it came out too high-pitched. Her nerves were fraying the longer they sat two blocks from her attacker. "The irony."

Jagger twisted to face her. "He won't hurt you again, Felicia."

"I know. But he did."

His hand twitched like he was going to touch her but reconsidered. Gathering their supplies into the tote bags they'd used to haul them up here—much quieter than a wrinkly plastic bag—he said, "At least we know that there's a legitimate reason why I was concerned about Sierra."

"Are you going to report to Bryant? Or to Dionna?" Cavorting with the enemy. What was Sierra up to?

"I'll have to." He finished shoving her bag of seeds away. "But if we get to the car, we can follow the fucker."

JAGGER HAD PICKED up some tailing skills in his time as a warrior. Possessed humans moved freely among other humans, only unlike other humans, they were constantly on the lookout for warriors who planned to exorcize and kill them.

This was a different situation. Stede would be cautious, maybe paranoid. And Jagger couldn't tackle him into the

Mist and kill him. He was an angel. He'd committed a crime and would need to be tried by the senate. Usually, an enforcer would be sent to apprehend Stede, but since Stede used to be an enforcer—and had attacked Felicia—Jagger had no plans to turn him over to anyone else.

He scanned this area of town. Stucco houses and bars on the windows and doors. For Vegas, it wasn't unusual, but for an angel who lived in a pretty moderate part of the realm, it was not expected. He'd thought a male with the connections Stede had would be in higher-end accommodations, where he didn't have to clean up after himself. These were working-class houses.

After Senator Kenton fled the senate hearing, had he set up here? If so, maybe this was more genius than he'd initially thought. No one would look for a senator in this environment. Senators came to this realm for the pampering, if they came at all. Whether or not they visited, they had people who invested and accumulated money for the finer things in human life.

This was a roof over their head. A yard, which to many was a luxury. But for a male like Kenton? It'd be the first rung of hell.

"Now what?" Jagger parked along the busy curb. The neighborhood had enough traffic coming and going that he didn't worry about blending in. The problem was the heat. It was too hot to sit in the car without AC, but they couldn't park here for hours and through the night with the engine running. Eventually it'd draw attention.

"We could keep moving, leapfrog up and down the street while we're watching the place." This information was too important to delay. He sent a message to Bryant.

His phone buzzed seconds later. He answered but didn't get a greeting out.

"What the hell are you doing?" The gravelly voice of his boss radiated with irritation.

"I had a gut feeling. We followed up." He left out the part where Felicia had confronted his father. "Your right. Something's up with Sierra."

"So you followed *Stede* without letting anyone know? What if he has a team of possessed humans surrounding his place? What if they're his neighbors? What if it's a trap? You and Felicia are severely unprepared."

"There wasn't time to wait."

A string of cuss words, some Jagger hadn't heard before, plugged the line. "You really think Sierra is our leak?"

"I think it's too much of a coincidence."

More swearing. "All of us could've been killed that day."

"Like Felicia said, we all have our secrets. Hers must be a doozy."

"Sierra was raised as the child of a warrior."

"Right." He'd heard the story once. Her mother had died in childbirth and her birth father had been killed in the Mist. Nasty battle, but they all were. One of her father's fellow warriors had raised her. "It's time to ask some pertinent questions."

A taxi passed them and stopped in front of the house. Felicia pulled her notebook out, pen poised.

"Wait, there's someone stopping for a visit." Jagger kept the phone to his ear and described what he saw to Director Vale. "A woman. Not possessed. Not dressed any particular way but young and sexy. She has a tote slung around her shoulder. Huh. She walked right in." Were they seriously leaving the place unlocked, or had they expected her and left the door open so they wouldn't be bothered to answer it?

"Stede's getting laid?"

"I don't think it's housekeeping." Unless there were

cleaning services that didn't care if their employees cleaned in cute heels and booty shorts.

"Send me your location. I'll get Dionna to assemble the rest of the team. We can't take the chance. Bring them in."

His warrior spirit rejoiced at the promise of action, the opportunity to be productive and get farther ahead of their enemies instead of chasing their exhaust—literally.

He hung up and relayed the info to Felicia. She scowled at her notepad. "I guess I didn't need this then. Too bad. It made me feel official."

"You should keep it. Anything to support our case to the senators can't hurt."

"As long as the senators are willing to listen and not play putt-putt games."

He arched a brow. "Putt-putt games?"

"You know, when they dick around making a decision because they don't really want to. Because they know it'll be contentious and they might have to answer to the rest of us, so they painfully draw out the process. Father couldn't stand it, but he did the same thing. Like it's ingrained in them to never change."

"They need some new blood."

"They get new blood all the time." Every year a few new senators went into training and some retired, weary after centuries of government. They retired to the human realm, where they could live a pampered life with all their investments.

"You know what I mean. That new blood was raised by the old blood. I wish they chose according to more than birthright. It's a complaint Mother always used to make." Mother would say that while wearing the same superior look that chased senate trainees away.

She snorted. "I dare you to go there and say that."

"You'd be surprised at how many agree."

She narrowed her eyes on the house, like she wanted to quit arguing but couldn't stop. "Still, they do nothing. They're conflict averse because few of them ever had to deal with real conflict."

"You have lots of opinions on senators."

She clicked the pen closed and glared at the house they were watching. "We all do."

"Sure, but not as vehement."

"Like I said, because they haven't had to deal with the bullshit."

He tapped his message out. Did Felicia even realize how much more passionate she was about their government than the average angel? Most of the residents accepted their fate, performed their own duties, and went about their long life. Status quo was critical. No one wanted to live an uncertain life when immortality was on the line. Complacency set in without being noticed.

Until his father was brutally kicked out.

He stared at the screen, but it was several minutes before a message came through.

Dionna shot back *On our way.*

The whole team must be coming. Or what was left. Dionna, Urban, Harlowe, and Bronx. Five. A decent-sized team, but they were hindered without Sierra's specialty.

"They're on their way." He settled into his seat and watched the house.

"I wish it were dark so we could sneak up on them."

"And listen to them have sex?" Listening to their enemies get it on with the female he wanted to do the same with wouldn't help his mood at all.

"We could learn a lot."

"Hard pass. I've had to spy on too many sexcapades to ever do it willingly when I'm confident it won't give me an advantage."

She opened her mouth, closed it again, then her lips parted once more. The way her brow furrowed meant she didn't have a snarky remark.

She normally said what was on her mind. Why the hesitation? "What?"

A faint blush tinged her cheeks. "What happens when a possessed human has sex with another?"

He knew more about this subject than he wanted to. "Demons seek pleasure, usually at the expense of others. It's what gets them off. Often, they'll get violent, even rape. Some prefer to fly under the radar in order to keep the host from attracting law enforcement, or from getting kicked out of the house when a normally docile spouse suddenly develops a harmful kink. But the act won't be loving. It's pure carnal fucking." And he'd witnessed several times when the unsuspected spouse was delighted at the turn of bedroom events. Too bad it never lasted. He and his team moved quickly.

"What happens if the host gets pregnant? Or the partner? Are there lasting effects on the child from the possession?"

A long breath whistled out of him as conflicting thoughts battled in his brain. "There doesn't seem to be. It's something we don't really watch for, the thought being that it's only human biological material exchanged."

"But you're not so sure?"

"It's not as if such children are born with horns and black wings. The DNA is human." No, the problem wasn't as obvious as that. When he ran across a child who'd been conceived when one of the birth parents had been possessed, they were often...troubled. Tormented. Conflicted. As if they'd never come to terms with the very basis of their identity. They were lost, wandering through life, never growing close to another. "But the energy in the genetic material is altered. It has to be."

Like Dionna said, what could they do? The individual was human, neither of Daemon or of Numen. They had to be allowed to live out their life on their terms, subject to human law.

Didn't mean he liked watching people suffer.

"That's another issue I have—that problems need to be as obvious as the wings on our back before anything's done." She dug out a wrap from the cooler.

He punched the car into gear and swung around the block, coming back around to park in a different spot a little farther away. If his team was coming, they risked being too close.

She handed him a grocery-store chicken wrap. "Good thing we can't procreate with humans. Do you think an arch-master and an angel could?"

Their kind didn't reproduce quickly. Some couples were together centuries before they had a child. As for a coupling between the two different winged creatures? "Improbable."

"Improbable isn't the same as impossible."

"We can't exist in the same dimension in our own forms. Except for the Mist. So improbable."

"I wonder if it's ever happened."

That poor child. "The odds are extremely low. And it's why we restrict who gets to travel between realms and why." Except their restrictions were often conveniently lax. "It's not as if any of us would find a demon sexy."

"It only takes once. You said it yourself. Demons will take what they want by force."

He blinked, the idea of the whole process disturbing. "But they're in the Mist to fight—to the death."

"Mm." She picked at her wrap. "Doesn't mean it won't ever happen."

"I guess." He eyed the wrap. His appetite had suddenly vanished. All the terrifying, brutally vicious demon fights he'd had came back. He'd fought all genders because it didn't matter. Once he pulled them into the Mist, it was to kill them. It was because he'd witnessed the demon deconstruct and ruin the life of a human. Those same creatures would love to debase an angel. That's why angels rarely fought alone.

Didn't mean they all did, though.

He should be the one questioning whether it could happen. Warriors should be addressing the possibility. They knew all the ways fights could go wrong in the Mist. When had he trapped himself inside the box? His thinking was restricted to what his superiors told him to think. Not Felicia.

The back door opened and a dark form slid in. He had a dagger in his hand and was twisted around in a second. Felicia had dropped her wrap and her hand was on her own weapon.

Bronx grinned at them, sunlight glinting off his dark hair. He was dressed in athletic shorts with no shirt on, and earbuds were stuffed in his ears. He was outside jogging. In the middle of summer in Vegas.

Crazy.

"Ingenious, am I right?" He took out his earbuds. "Who would think twice about me running in hundred-degree heat?" His expression turned serious. "I can't get any closer than running on the sidewalk. All the yards are fenced and I don't want to test whether that poster about a security system is legit or not. But I heard a few things when I stopped to tie my shoe."

"I didn't see you run by." He'd had his eyes on the place the whole time.

Another flash of white teeth. Bronx was always quick to smile. He'd grin as he buried his dagger to the hilt in a demon's torso. "I was on the opposite side of the block. And the man-groaning coming out of there was loud enough. Someone's having a painfully good time."

Felicia picked up her food and peeled the wrapping back for another bite. "So do we make our move before or after the orgasm?"

CHAPTER 16

"*During the post-coital glow, we strike.*"

Hearing Jagger say those words still stuck with her. It'd been on the tip of her tongue to snidely mention that it was what he did best, waiting until all her defenses were down to strike.

She was past that. It was getting harder to remember why she'd sworn off relationships around him.

It should be easier the more he pointed out that she'd make a good senator. If he'd said that a few months ago, he'd have meant that she was deceptive and arrogant enough for the job. But his attitude had changed and with it came a sincerity she hadn't expected but came to rely on.

He'd been upset and had tracked her down in Las Vegas. He'd approached both Bryant and her sister to find her, regardless of how it might look for him.

And during their stakeout, he hadn't once sneered at her theories or observations. She got the impression he was kicking himself for not pondering the possibilities himself.

Now here she was, dressed in black tactical pants and a form-fitting, long-sleeved shirt that she'd boil alive in out in the sun. It wasn't much more comfortable at midnight. The sweat collecting on her brow wasn't due entirely to the heat. The light pollution of the city didn't cast nearly enough shadows for her liking. The other warriors were in their own car.

She tugged down the sleeve of the shirt Harlowe had loaned her. *"I washed the blood stains out of it. Should be good to go."*

The whole team was here. Felicia not only got to see them in action, but she would join them. It was safer than leaving her alone, and they trusted her abilities enough to include her—with some restrictions. Along with Dionna and Bronx, she'd jump the fence and go through the back. Jagger and Harlowe would take the front door, and Urban had already planned out how to get through the plate-glass window with minimal noise.

No one else knew what a big deal this was. She was part of a group—of angels. Only Jagger knew of her secret and her scars, but the rest had moved beyond the duty of protecting her to absorbing her into their group.

It was a big deal for a girl who'd had her family wiped out one angel at a time. First her mother, then her father. She and Odessa were growing closer, but Felicia wasn't a part of her life. Not really.

Don't fuck this up. She couldn't—wouldn't—get knocked out again. They were on Earth, so using their wings was a no-go. If they stepped outside of the house, then they'd have to cross into the Mist. But her work with Jagger on learning to fight a creature with wings had infused her with confidence. She wouldn't be taken off guard again.

The team hadn't exactly revealed how they'd deal with Sierra. She couldn't blame them. The thought of betrayal by one of their own was hard enough, but there were the consequences to deal with. They wouldn't be good for

Sierra and no one wanted to think about what would happen.

Their priority was to get Stede.

So she'd concentrate on that too.

It'd be over in a heartbeat. There were six of them and only two inside this house. The neighbors would be none the wiser.

Dionna appeared at her window. Felicia's heart leaped into her throat. The female moved as silently as an apparition.

She opened the door and glared past her to Jagger in the driver's seat. "I have a bad feeling about this."

Jagger's gaze flicked to the house and back to Dionna. "Based on?"

"It's too easy."

"They don't even know we're here. Or that we found them," he said.

"We're betting our lives on that. How do we know that your father didn't give Stede a heads-up that Felicia was out for revenge?"

It would be in Jameson's best interest to set each side against the other. It'd solve his Stede issue and keep the warriors off his back.

But it'd endanger his son. Was he willing to cross that line?

Jagger's expression was blank. "Do we abort?"

The lines on Dionna's face hardened. "No, but be alert. There's more to tonight than bagging a traitor."

Nerves fluttered in Felicia's belly and skittered through her body, tightening the scar tissue at her back. A solid reminder that Stede was as cruel as the job necessitated. While Jameson might've fiddled with tonight's events, Stede had already proved himself willing to turn on the fallen.

They were tools to each other, nothing more, and that made all of this unpredictable.

When she took her eyes off the dark house, Dionna was staring at her. "Are you ready?"

She gave the woman a solemn nod. As she'd ever be. They were to capture Stede, and Kenton if he happened to be in the same place.

They fanned out. She went with Bronx and Dionna. The idea was that she and Jagger shouldn't distract each other. The night was dark, and in this neighborhood, the neighbors kept to themselves. It was the best opportunity.

She tried to keep her eyes and ears open for the others but they were undetectable. Turning her concentration to her own movements, she lightened her footsteps and controlled her breathing. She was grateful that Dionna had brought her black athletic shoes instead of boots. It was harder to control how much sound she made than she'd imagined.

Dionna skirted the house, avoiding the motion-sensor light and alarm system. The female defied gravity when she scaled the one-story home to the roof and, with a few flicks of her wrist, disabled the system. Her nod to Bronx was barely detectable.

He leaped the wrought-iron fence and turned to wait. It was her turn and he was her spotter. Dionna crowded close. Felicia planned the move in her head before she rolled into action.

Clearing the top, she landed lightly on the other side. She winced at the crinkle of grass. Stede and whoever was here with him didn't care for watering. Did they even know grass needed water in Vegas?

But it was better than trying to land quietly on gravel.

Following Bronx, they crept to the back door. She wished it were light enough outside so she could see how he broke in. Warriors were more than masters of fighting. They had admirable breaking-and-entering skills too.

The door was opened a crack and they collectively held their breath as they listened inside. Only the tinny sound of an old cop show on TV. The kind where at least one was dirty. So up Stede's alley.

Bronx disappeared inside, holding the door open for her, and she did the same for Dionna.

He motioned for her to fan out to the left. She followed their earlier instructions. Clear all the doorways. Look for sylphs in each corner from floor to ceiling. Communicate all findings using hand gestures.

Dionna took the right. There was no whisper as Bronx slipped a knife from the holster at his thigh. He kept his right hand free. She'd asked about guns since they were after their own, but those attracted too much attention.

Too bad. She'd love to plug one into Stede's forehead and tell him to be quiet as he healed. She'd squeeze the trigger and put the whole scenario on repeat.

Bronx's gaze was stuck on a spot she guessed was the front door. He gave them a signal: one person present, and it was Stede. Jagger and Harlowe would burst in at any second.

Any second.

She waited. Bronx ticked his head to the left, as if he was seeking guidance from Dionna.

Just as Bronx closed his hand into a fist to tell them that the front door was opening, a white blast exploded from the living room.

A cloud of heat shoved her back, a sound so deafening after the near silence it left her ears ringing. She staggered backward, only Dionna keeping her upright. The warrior was shouting at Bronx. The guy had taken the full blast and was on his back.

Good God, it wasn't angel fire, was it?

She blinked, but the finer detail of her vision hadn't come around. He was a dark, writhing form on the floor.

Dionna pointed to Bronx. Her mouth was moving, but she couldn't make out words. She shook her head.

Finally some noise made it past her acute tinnitus.

"Protect. Him."

She nodded. Dionna spun, silver glinting from each hand, and darted into the living room.

Felicia armed herself and stood over Bronx. He'd heal fast, but for now he was still down.

Where were Jagger and Harlowe?

Singing movement behind her. She spun, ready to shove her knife hilt-deep into soft tissue. Urban flicked her blade away with his own. His gaze was all about the *what happened?* but she must still have the wide-eyed gaze of someone still struggling to clear their senses.

She just shook her head in a *I dunno, I think it's a cluster fuck* way.

He gave a curt nod, his gaze flicking past her before he sidled by. She remained on duty protecting Bronx.

The male sat up, his groan cutting through the din. His head was in his hands for only a moment before he popped up.

He exchanged the same silent conversation with her that she'd just had with Urban.

"Fuck," he mouthed and waved his fingers for her to follow him.

The living room wasn't the disaster she'd expected. A few items smoldered, the door hung off its hinges, a couple of chairs were overturned, and the TV was black.

Harlowe staggered to her feet, her hands out and grasping for something to steady herself with. Dionna was crouched on top of a male wearing nothing but green plaid pajama bottoms and a brown robe. His face was ground into the off-white carpet but he was yelling unintelligible obscenities.

Urban emerged from the hallway. "Clear."

Felicia's gaze swept around the room. She spun in a circle, but no, she hadn't missed any hidden corners.

"Where's Jagger?" Her voice was loud to her own ears. She crept closer to Dionna's prisoner. Was that him? Was it Stede?

"Gone." Urban ducked outside and Bronx followed.

Harlowe was still blinking and squinting, her eyes refusing to focus. "They got him."

Fear spiked Felicia's blood, stronger than any cocktail Vegas could serve. "Who? How?"

Dionna kidney punched the male. "Tell us."

He barked out a cry but Dionna eased up enough for him to talk. "I don't know. He just left me here. You've gotta help me."

"Stede?" The name rolled off her lips, leaving behind a sinking, sick sensation in her gut.

"He's a traitor, and-and he's been blackmailing me, and—" He turned his head to blink at them. His face paled when he saw her.

Senator Kenton.

So. He'd been in on what Stede had done to her. And he was trying to play the victim card. She squatted. "Remember me?" she asked sweetly, acting on her gamble. "You can cut the act, we don't believe your bullshit. Tell us what you know or my buddy Bronx here will give me his vial of angel fire to use and I can show you exactly what I went through eleven years ago."

Kenton's lips quivered. Dionna flicked her eyes from Kenton to Harlowe, her brow lifted in question. Harlowe shook her head. Kenton remained oblivious to the exchange, his frightened gaze riveted on her.

Urban and Bronx stepped back inside. The senator's gaze rippled with panic. His beseeching look hit her. "You-you… I was kidnapped."

She dropped her voice to a menacing level, grateful her hearing was coming back and she could control the volume. "Don't forget I was there when you fled the senate hall like the coward you are."

"He had me imprisoned here—"

Urban snorted. "I don't think the chains in the bedroom were for imprisonment. Don't get me wrong, I'm sure you were suspended in them. But released as soon as you orgasmed. Am I right?"

The senator's face flushed, and from the busted look in his eye it wasn't from anger.

"The woman from earlier." Felicia let out a laugh. "A dominatrix."

"She works for Stede." Kenton sounded more annoyed than defensive.

"I bet she does." Bronx lifted his chin at Dionna. "I'll go prep the enforcers for their new prisoner."

"And tell them one of ours will be watching him at all times."

Kenton was sputtering, but Urban talked over him. "They aren't going to like that."

Bronx's grin was menacing. "I look forward to the discussion." He tilted his head back as if beseeching the heavens and disappeared.

Felicia's mind spun. Where could Jagger be? How had they found out?

Sierra?

They'd purposely kept her in the dark. But she knew their procedures and how the team would infiltrate the house. Stede would just need to wait for the opportunity.

Dionna jerked Kenton off the floor. He flopped like a rag

doll. "Bronx and I will take care of this garbage. You three..." She looked from Felicia to Harlowe, and then her gaze settled on Urban. "Keep me informed."

Felicia's hands curled into fists. Good. She wasn't being taken off the hunt. She had no idea what Urban had in mind, but she didn't have to ask what the others had in mind. They were going to rip apart each realm until they found Jagger.

~

"What the hell were you thinking?" Jameson snapped. He'd been soaking in his hot tub when the call came in that he had a visitor. He'd hoped that nudging Ms. Montclaire in Stede's direction would take care of his problem. While he had uses for Stede, the male was too devious for his own good and needed to be killed. "Kenton's going to babble like a four-year-old with a new toy car."

The comment spilled out and yanked him into the past. The woman who'd turned on him had had a little boy. And the kid had loved that damn car. And Jameson had loved hearing about it. It had reminded him of him of Julian when he was young.

Stede ran a finger around the inside of his collar. Chafing. The looser clothing of Numen that allowed for ample wing mobility made human clothing intolerable at first. He assumed that when Stede came to the human realm, it was either for a quick trip or fornication. Days stretching into weeks of human clothing were likely rubbing him raw.

It gave Jameson a wicked sort of pleasure. As did determining the best way to kill him and make his body disappear.

"Mind if I imbibe?" Stede was already pouring himself two fingers of his best scotch.

He should've drugged the alcohol. Then he could have dragged the male to the Mist and decapitated him.

"I wouldn't be a proper club owner if I didn't offer you a drink." He shrugged into his shirt. Stede hadn't waited for him in the meeting room, instead barging past Andy and into his personal suite.

"I was thinking that I managed to bag a warrior without getting caught, without bloodshed, and without enlisting the help of any demons." Smugness radiated off him. "Your son."

Those two words were like a battering ram knocking him off-center.

Julian.

Stede had captured his son? Rage swelled inside of him, ballooning like a nuclear mushroom cloud. How he kept it from showing in his expression, he didn't know. Years of lying to his mate and then getting debased after he'd fallen were coming in handy. He forced himself to sip in a complete lungful of air.

Calm settled over his shoulders and spread through his body. He fastened each button with clear deliberation. Show no emotion. Nothing good ever happened from flying off half-cocked. This was the dangerous part of caring about someone. He was distracted, more concerned about Julian's safety than the plans he'd been toiling over for decades.

Stede had Julian. Was his boy hurt? Julian was a warrior. For fuck's sake, how had this happened?

It was a minor issue compared to Stede's declaration, but the male's tone also suggested that if he'd had his wings cleaved off, he'd have gotten to where Jameson was without bargaining with archmasters and their lessers. *Without enlisting the help of any demons.*

Stede may very well have the chance to find out. If he was ever taken prisoner like Kenton, his wings would be toast. Jameson would do what he could to make it happen, but unfortunately, Stede was cunning, ruthless, and heartless. The male would find a way to screw all of Jameson's plans.

He was already yanking on the tablecloth of a table that had taken years to set.

"Where is he?" Jameson focused on his appearance in the full-length mirror in front of him and snapped his suit coat in place. His mind churned over several options, but the sad reality was that this was Stede. Julian would be in Numen, where Jameson couldn't get to him and where all of his contacts had run through fucking Stede.

Stede tilted his head, his dark, glittering eyes calculating. "You keep things from me, I keep them from you."

What game was this bastard playing at? "And what do you think I'm withholding? How to properly run a successful club in the city of sin? Perhaps all my knowledge of how to recruit human hosts? Maybe I didn't cover Negotiations with Demons 101?"

A half smile lifted the male's lips. "We're both smarter than that or we'd be dead or in enforcer custody." He took a leisurely sip from his glass and settled into the lounger in the corner of the office. "Speaking of which, the warriors have already handed the senator over. Kenton will meet with his own demise soon."

At least there was that.

The clink of the glass hitting the tabletop was the only proof that Stede was coiled tight. He was scared or pissed. Or both. "Tell me about your little side project."

Side project. What Stede was talking about had become his main project once he'd found out what his blood could do to angels. He'd tried to unlock the secrets of getting back to his realm. Was it the weapons? Was it angel blood? Turned out the curse was the answer and was flowing through his veins. His own damn blood made it impossible to fully cross into Numen, but it got him close enough to try.

He just couldn't ignore this.

But at one time, he'd been collecting demon metal to aid

in his experiments. Touching weapons from Numen burned. Literally. He could bluff Stede with that. "I can't take over the realm with a few friends, some challenging words, and my bare hands if I can't even cross the threshold. I've contracted with an archmaster in order to obtain the weapons Gerzon is obstinately refusing to supply."

Stede's eyes narrowed and he tilted his head. "Indeed."

Jameson bit the inside of his cheek. Stede was mocking him. Fury raged inside of him. The male had come here, knowing he was safe because he had Julian. "I will kill you, Stede. Don't doubt it."

"If you had let me in on the secret of your blood, it wouldn't have come to this. You see, sometimes our children pay the price for our incompetence."

Jameson drew his brows together. Stede talked as if he knew this subject personally.

"Now I'll have to see if Julian's blood has the same properties—once he loses his wings."

CHAPTER 17

Felicia charged toward her car. They'd searched the house and come up with nothing.

"You need to let us take the lead." Dionna was catching up to her.

Felicia thinned her lips and kept her gaze laser focused on the car she and Jagger had used. She remembered how to get back to that church and from there, she'd find Sierra's house. And then she'd have a little talk with the warrior.

A talk that included bruises and bloodshed if the bitch didn't lead her to Jagger.

"We are not to do a thing until we contact Director Vale."

"Tell Bryant he'd better hurry." She hit the unlock on her fob and ripped the door open.

Dionna caught up. She was powerful enough to stop Felicia. But Dionna didn't.

Emboldened, Felicia looked the warrior directly in the eye. "You do your job. I'm not as constrained by rules as you are. We both know I can move faster on this and won't have the same hesitation regarding Sierra."

Dionna's nostrils flared as if she'd never heard a deeper insult than the insinuation that she couldn't interrogate and torture her own comrade. "If Sierra is guilty…"

"I don't have time to find out. I've seen enough to know she is. I don't have to prove it before I slam her head against the wall and ask her where Jagger is."

"Sierra's a trained warrior."

"It's a risk I'm willing to take." She dropped into the driver's seat and was off in seconds. Her instinct was correct. Dionna agreed with her. The female would play by the rules but knew waiting on Jagger's whereabouts meant he could get caught between the secondary fight between his father and Stede.

It was all she could do not to speed. Even if she got stopped, she could take off running and ascend. But one, she didn't need to violate her realm's laws and ascend in front of a human. And two, whatever she found out from Sierra might require the use of the car. She couldn't transcend somewhere she'd never been.

When she arrived at Sierra's tidy little home, she didn't bother parking a few blocks away. Killing the engine right out front, she slammed the door and charged inside.

A couple of well-placed kicks took care of the security door. The interior door swung open. Sierra was poised with a gun in one hand and a knife in the other.

"I thought warriors didn't fight with guns," Felicia snarled. She didn't advance. Getting shot would delay her plans too much.

Sierra's eyes flickered with recognition. Her gaze darted behind her to the street. "Get inside before my neighbors call the cops."

The female didn't drop her stance as she backed up. Felicia stepped inside and pushed the door closed. The outside was still hanging off but hopefully any spectators were minding their own business.

Without wasting time, she laid it out. "They've taken Jagger and we know you've been working with them."

The other female's face drained of color. "W-w-what are you—"

"Cut the bullshit. We've seen Stede coming and going, and only an insider could have set up the fire at my sister's place."

Resignation swirled in Sierra's violet eyes but was nearly drowned out by fear. "What happened to Jagger?"

"Stede took him." Felicia narrowed her eyes. How old was Sierra? It was hard to tell. The female looked the same age as her. "How long have you been working with him? Do you know what he did to me?"

Confusion flickered across her expression. "I don't know anything about you other than you're Odessa's sister."

Felicia sidestepped into the living room, trying to build a mental layout of the home. "Oh, but you knew where I lived in Atlanta. That's how Jameson found me there."

Sierra's jaw was set. "What happened to Jagger?"

"Acting like you don't know it was a trap?"

"You come to my house throwing accusations around?" Sierra took a menacing step forward. "Tell. Me."

"You were behind it."

"I didn't do *this*."

Felicia was laying down the truth. But she believed that Sierra didn't know about tonight. "Your whole team went to apprehend Stede, but he was ready and got Jagger. We don't know where either one is."

Sierra's brow furrowed. "There was no raid planned for tonight."

"Like I said, they suspected you were the leak." And Sierra could lower that gun at any time. Felicia's scar tissue didn't heal as fast as the rest of her. "And Jameson knew I was looking for Stede."

The woman bared her teeth. "Then you're an idiot." She took a step closer. Any closer and Felicia could kick that damn gun out of her hand, but Sierra would probably fire first. "Are you fucking Jameson? Is that how he knew?"

Having never met Sierra before, she hadn't known what to expect, but this jealousy concerning Jagger's father was disturbing. "I've been tied to Jagger since this all started." Forget the drama. All she wanted was information. She let her feelings for Jagger bleed into her voice. "I need to find him."

With him missing, it wasn't just terror racing through her. It was regret. She'd had a shot with him and yeah, he'd acted like a dolt, but he'd come around. He realized what he'd done. Holding out on him was needlessly punishing them both. There was no reason not to see where things between them could go.

Sierra's expression wavered. She glanced away, but her weapons didn't lower. She thinned her lips like she'd come to an undesirable conclusion. "Jameson can't get into Numen and he has too many devout followers here with demon help."

"So Stede would take Jagger home? Where? He'd need help up there. Who?"

"I don't know who Stede is fucking friends with," Sierra snapped. "Find someone who's repugnant, arrogant, and greedy, and they'll probably be besties."

"You just described half of Numen."

Sierra blinked, shocked at the blunt statement. But she nodded. "Exactly. But I'd look at fellow enforcers first, or those they work closely with. Think like him."

Stede had been in the archives with someone who knew

their way around. The archivist? That narrowed down her search considerably.

It was time to go find out who Stede had been with that day. Sierra wasn't her problem. She sounded like she detested Stede and whatever she'd been forced into. That didn't make it right, but since Felicia had lost her parents over the same thing, she wasn't going to seek her own personal vengeance. This was the warriors' problem. "Where's the back door? I need to ascend and start searching."

Consciousness came quickly. Jagger snapped his eyes open with a sharp inhale and immediately closed them again.

He wasn't alone.

The last few days reeled through his mind as if on an old movie projector. Stakeouts. Earning Felicia's trust. The raid.

Fuck. The raid.

He'd been taken. In an absurdly easy turnabout, he'd been caught. Stede had been ready and had used a flash-bang grenade to stun him. It had worked too well.

How was Harlowe? She'd caught the brunt of it. What about the rest of the team?

Murmured words caught his attention. Female. "I swear he moved."

He kept his eyes shut. He was lying down on a cool, hard floor with his arms behind him and his ankles aching from some unseen pressure.

"He's out cold," a disbelieving male said.

Wait. He knew that female. She'd been with Stede in the archives. Who was the guy?

"I hope he doesn't wake up until Stede returns," the female muttered. "I don't want to deal with him."

"I'd rather deal with him than a pissed-off Stede." The male sounded disinterested, or distracted. Were they playing cards?

"I'd rather be doing something else."

The male's chuckle made Jagger's stomach turn. Lovers? *Please don't get down and dirty while I'm still in the room.*

How had Stede gotten to them? Or were they willing helpers?

Did Father know Stede had planned this? Was that why he'd pointed Felicia in his direction?

Disappointment coursed through him. Let down by his father again. The brief moments of perceived concern weren't for him, but for Jameson Haddock's carefully laid plans getting interrupted by the son he'd had the misfortune of conceiving. Any fatherly concern was swallowed whole by his ambition and whatever sick sense of revenge he wanted. A teenager was still inside of him, one who wondered why his parents were so wrapped up in their own drama that they forgot about him. A kid who wondered why they'd procreated in the first place.

"Me too, baby. Me too. Anywhere but here or work. I don't want to be around when Senator Hancock finds out her son's been taken."

His mother? The male worked around Mother. He didn't sound like a senator. A guard then. Did he know Mateo? Was Mateo in on this?

"Hancock has no reason to suspect us."

"No, but if I don't show for work... Mateo isn't as dumb as he looks."

She giggled. "He has to be to sleep with her."

He was incensed for both his mother and Mateo. But how did these two know each other? An archivist and a guard. Maybe they were mates.

This little kidnapping business needed to yield more

information or he'd feel even more useless, trussed up like he was a Thanksgiving goose. He was a warrior. He should've expected more from Stede. The male had been abusing his power for years and he'd escaped out from under their noses, even when they'd suspected him.

Jagger was used to humans' actions, and especially demons', but misbehaving angels had caught him off guard. Even after his experience.

Stilling his mind, he surveyed his other senses. His wings were out and bound. He'd been too distracted by the whispers of his captors at first, but the discomfort was making itself known now. Stiff shoulders. Cramped muscles. His arms were cuffed behind him under his wings, and the way his feet were tied together and bent back, he guessed that if he tugged, he'd find his wrists and ankles had been secured by a short length of rope. Hog-tied. He was on his side, with his neck cricked to the floor.

Keeping his inhale steady, he processed as many scents as he could. Stone. Old paper. Not stale air, but not exactly fresh.

The archives?

He was probably sealed in a room that no one ever visited, that no one had any interest in.

The sentries began shit-talking the senators. Nothing notable came from eavesdropping, but he kept pretending he was still out. He had to try.

A door banged open and it was only due to long hours of monitoring possessed humans that he didn't flinch. Chair legs scraped across stone floors. What he wouldn't give to see the panic on his captors' faces. Busted gossiping.

"What are you sitting around for?" Ah. Stede. The male had a distinctive growl.

"You said to notify you when the prisoner woke up," the female said.

"And?" Boots stomped across the floor. The hairs on his arms quivered. This wasn't going to go his way. "He's fucking awake."

A steel toe kicked him in the thigh. Busted. He cracked an eye open. Time for the fun to begin.

CHAPTER 18

*P*ounding on the giant wood door was a nice outlet for the pent-up emotions she was holding in.

Felicia didn't bother waiting for an answer. She balled up her fist and kept hammering away.

The door swung open and Mateo gave her a wary look. "Ms. Montclaire?"

"I need to talk to you and Chanel." She'd purposely dropped the senator title. This wasn't about politics. That's what it looked like on the outside. But all of this was personal. From James Hancock's fall and transition to Jameson Haddock, to Stede's rightfully placed but highly inconvenient distrust of Jameson, to the capture of Jagger. It was all personal.

He didn't budge. "About what?"

"I'm not wasting time repeating myself."

Her tone was hard enough that he stepped back and let her inside.

Chanel came out of the depths of the massive mansion,

fluffing her hair. It was midmorning in Numen and that was part of her issues with the senate. They met a few days at a time to waste their hot air on nothing, and then dismissed themselves for weeks when they "needed a break." Maybe if they were organized and had standards in place for emergencies, they could get some actual decisions made without a bunch of posturing and *harrumph, harrumph.*

But that was just her opinion. And years of hearing her father lament about the same things. Sometimes their longevity was their own worst trait. A lot of the older senators didn't believe that the rapid advances made in the human world affected them, but here they were. A fallen gathering way too much power thanks to smart phones and electronic dance music.

Mild curiosity left Chanel's face, instantly replaced with cool assessment. "Ms. Montclaire."

"Jagger's been taken."

The icy facade cracked. Alarm was rapidly wiped out by pure rage. "That deceitful bastard," Chanel seethed. "I told him. *I told him.*"

She'd actually spoken to her ex-mate? The "him" in question wasn't a mystery. Jameson Haddock was behind this. Somehow the fault originated with him.

"The warriors are tied up in political bullshit. I don't have the same restrictions. But I need your help." She pointed to Mateo. "I actually need his help and he needs your protection."

"And you don't?"

"I have Bryant at my back. But I'm not stupid enough to go charging after Jagger alone."

Chanel watched her a second, but that second was loaded with so many judgments and decisions it weighed on the air between them. Mateo seemed to know his…girlfriend?…well enough not to speak. He was a wall behind her, a way for Chanel to box in what she needed to ruminate over. Like when Chanel had stormed into Jagger's place and mated him off. Chanel and Mateo worked as a team. Did they even realize it?

"Tell me what happened." She glided into an official-looking sitting room where the chairs looked as comfortable as marble. Tapestries managed to soften the ambiance but also added a museum quality. *Look but don't touch and move along quickly, please.*

The female and her matte-silver gray wings draped them-selves over a seat. Mateo positioned himself behind her and crossed his arms. He wasn't her bodyguard. He was her self-appointed protector.

The flare of loss and jealously was unexpected. To distract herself from the internal eruption, she covered the highlights.

Even at their most antagonistic, she and Jagger had worked well together. She could berate herself for not letting him make amends, but what seemed like months ago was really only what, a few days? Almost a week? The days and nights blended together, but she wanted the possibility for more.

So what if she had to live up here? Her kind would stare. Yes, it sucked. But was it better letting them think nothing bad ever happened here? She had no obligation to spill her pain all over the realm, but what if…what if it saved another traumatized teen from losing her mother? Or another mother from losing herself? What if they needed to know that others in this realm went through hell?

As she wrapped up the highlights of what had happened and how she'd broken away from the team to conduct her own search, she couldn't help but think of the future. The worry about whether she'd find him in time tabled every other problem. "Few dare to cross you. What I'm doing can get twisted and used as a distraction from the real problem."

Chanel patted her hair again and glanced away. It was a rich-lady move straight from *Sunset Boulevard*. It made Felicia wonder how often Chanel snuck to the human realm. She probably hid a love for old Hollywood glam.

"You need me to sanction a search for Jagger without enforcer involvement? Done. Mateo, how do you feel about aiding Ms. Montclaire in her search?" Chanel didn't look at Mateo when she addressed him. Her gaze was glued to Felicia.

Mateo's nod was resolute. "We'll do what we need to find him."

"While giving no reason for the enforcers or senate to take your wings." Chanel's expression turned to granite. "I won't risk it. No killing. Keep this mess in the realm, and if it spills over, make damn sure you don't violate the rules."

Killing was never an action to take lightly, and Felicia had never done the deed. But their opponents weren't going to fight with rubber blades. "There might be a little killing involved."

"Then you can go alone. I won't risk Mateo's fate, and I sure as hell won't put Julian any closer to falling than he has been his whole life. A life gets taken during the rescue and our enemies can spin it against me. They've been waiting to for decades."

Mateo's face softened, a subtle shock rippling over his features. If Chanel never showed her emotions, then she damn well never said them aloud. This was probably a declaration of true love in her cold world.

Stede was her business, and since he'd be the type to distance himself from the messy tasks that might get him caught, she might not have to worry about facing him. So technically, she could promise no killing with no mental fingers crossing. "Fine. Grab your weapons."

"I already have them." Mateo's tone wasn't cocky. He was more than a meathead who stood by a doorway. She only saw a knife on his belt, but he spoke with all the confidence of a man loaded for bear.

"We start in the archives."

Chanel cocked her head. "Whatever for?"

"There are apparently some good tidbits there about why Jagger's father can do what he did. I know for sure Stede has a contact there, so that's where we'll start."

The most delicate snort escaped Jagger's mother. "And here I hoped you'd lay a trail of ruin through the senate. Without bloodshed, of course."

"If I had time, I'd use this situation as an excuse. The senate could use a good razing."

Chanel's bright eyes gleamed. "You and I have much in common. You and my son are close, yes?"

"We'd be closer if you hadn't interfered with his mating."

It was the nearest thing to a smile Felicia had seen on the female. "Even I can act rashly. It's only happened twice." A line creased her otherwise smooth brow. "I appreciate that Julian was able to resolve the contract peacefully."

Since they were going there and knowledge was power, Felicia's question seemed both appropriate and inappropriate at the same time. "Do you regret it?"

"Persephone? No. It would've been an ideal match had he not been hung up on you." Chanel fluffed her light hair off her forehead with an elegant hand. "But that's not what you're asking, is it? Do I regret ruining my mate's life? No. I'm at peace with my actions. He's since proved he deserved it." Uncertainty tinted her eyes. "Even if I didn't feel like he had for years afterward. You can understand why I favored a practical pairing."

Take the emotion out, use the brain, and he wouldn't end up where his mother had. "You were the right mate for him. Another might not have had the courage to make him pay for his violations."

Chanel's face iced over so fast Felicia feared it would crack. "Another may have had the fortitude to work it out. But in the end, I'd do it again."

BLINDING pain shot through his body. Jagger clenched his jaw and tensed every major muscle, preparing for one explosive movement to jerk away from the source of agony.

"Hold him tighter," growled Stede.

Hands clamped harder on his shoulders and his calves, but that didn't stop him from jerking left and right, up and down, anything to get away from the blade carving into his back. If only his hands and feet weren't still bound.

"Maybe we should use angel fire." The bright idea came from the female.

Stede's next words were garbled, like he had something in his mouth. Probably the other blade he was using since his free hand was twisting Jagger's wing back. "Are you kidding? The way he's bucking around, we'll be the ones to end up wearing the fire. All I need are his wings off." Stede repositioned, shoving a knee in his kidneys. "Can't get to your father, then I'll make my own fallen."

Fatigue was setting in as Jagger's body frantically tried to heal from the wounds. He was fading fast. Stede wasn't the type of bad guy to offer lengthy exposition, but Jagger had patched together enough. They suspected his father's blood of having special properties, something about not being able to ascend or transcend when stained with it. But since those who fell quickly perished on Earth, they either hadn't been able to track down any survivors or those survivors' blood hadn't had the same effect.

Whatever Father was up to, it was spilling all over Jagger. Literally. He'd lost a lot of blood. Stede wasn't able to dig the blade into his back—too many ribs and bony joints in the way. It prolonged the process but also bought Jagger time. The only other thought going through his head besides escape was that Felicia had survived worse. And she'd done it silently and completely alone.

He didn't want her ever to be alone again. He wouldn't let these bastards take his wings and he couldn't let them target the children of other fallen just because he was uncooperative.

Surging up, he snapped his head back and caught the female in the chin.

An *oomph* preceded the release on his shoulders. He was about to propel himself upward when fire laced his gut.

"It's three against one, warrior." Stede's breath huffed in his ear. "Not even you are that good."

It was just mind games. Stede might know how to fight, but his hired muscle was seriously lacking. The male looked like he spent more time fisting beer than slamming faces. And the female kept looking at her partner, like she was waiting for him to speak against Stede and she'd back him up even as she trembled in fear. And she feared Stede. It was in her eyes, her timidity while carrying out Stede's orders.

"Wanna bet?" he said, using as much false bravado as he could muster. He doubted they understood what he said. It was all jumbled. At some point he'd bitten his tongue and probably cracked a few teeth. Energy was draining out of him more rapidly than he could heal. Getting stabbed in the gut did that to a guy.

He gave himself a few moments, but unfortunately it also gave them a chance to anchor him to the stone floor and

Stede the opening he needed to carve at the joints in his back.

The burn of the knife cut into his ribs. A ragged scream ripped from his throat.

Had this been what had warped his father's mind, made him evil rather than just a little naughty?

The back of his right shoulder blazed like all of the forest fires on Earth were concentrated on that joint. It was now or never. If he didn't get away, he was going to lose his wings.

He gathered all his reserves and focused on a loose tile on the floor instead of his pain. He jerked and wiggled until the half-hearted hold on him loosened, then he rolled. Letting out a roar as his body weight settled on his shredded back, his eyesight crossed. A haze of pain descended over him, but he didn't stop. Stopping meant failing, and failing meant death. He had so much more to give this round, so much more to prove to Felicia.

The bonds at his hands and ankles had loosened from his movements and blood made them slimy. He worked his hands free and rolled up to his feet, ignoring the flares of agony through his body as best he could. It wasn't enough. His captors tried to surround him, but the lack of control over his wings made the movements less predictable. They had the same problem as the ropes at his wrists. Blood made him slippery.

Jagger kept moving, making his way to the door. As soon as one of them came into his line of sight, he threw punches. Nailing the male's throat bought him more distance. The female was hesitant and Stede was screaming at them all. Jagger jabbed his good wing out. Stede's head spun around. Direct hit. He'd smile if he didn't hurt everywhere.

He lurched ahead. His vision was still hazy, whether from blood or trauma he didn't know, but he could make out the dark rectangle of the door. But he couldn't rejoice yet. He was in the archives. His wings were too tattered to fly to the ceiling and bust out one of the skylights. He had to get outside so he could to descend to a safe place and heal—if he could heal from this much trauma on his own.

As soon as that thought drifted through his mind, a tingle flared across his wrist. Like some special sixth sense, he knew that it was his mating mark. There was a female out there gifted with its equal. All he had to do was find her and she could heal him.

Would he allow her to if she weren't Felicia?

A forceful tug on his good wing had him gritting his teeth. He concentrated on whatever muscles were left in his wings and flung the assailant off. A feminine cry echoed off the walls, followed by a sickening thud.

"I'll go after everyone you love," Stede growled, prowling around him but too much of a coward to tackle him. Jagger almost wanted him to try—so he could rip him to pieces with his bare hands. But Stede was cunning. He would run and hide like the dung beetle he was.

Jagger glared over his shoulder. "You've already tried and failed." He staggered out of the room and squinted down the hall. An exit door was to his right. Once he cleared that he could—

"Byron!" Stede snarled. "Byron?"

Jagger laughed and aimed his momentum toward the door, running. Byron was recovering from a throat punch. "Your help sucks, Stede. Your plan failed."

He'd expected an enraged yell, but all he heard was Stede's chilling voice. "Who said that was my plan?"

He should stick around and get more out of Stede, preferably with knives dipped in angel fire. But if he stopped now, he'd drop. Jagger put on one last burst of speed and opened the door, spilling outside.

He couldn't land on Earth looking like he did without

risking revealing his kind. But his mating mark wasn't calling him to that realm. Was Felicia in Numen? But he had to get out of here, or Stede would track him down and recapture him. Would his sync mate find him in the Mist? Felicia would, if she was his mate.

He just had to pray that it was her that arrived.

CHAPTER 19

*M*ateo stopped and held a hand up. "I thought I heard voices."

If they had more time, she would've asked him why he wasn't a warrior, even an enforcer. He had all the instincts and he was really competent. Was it Chanel keeping him planted in front of the senator's door, or just a strong sense of duty? Wondering had kept her mind off what was happening to Jagger.

She cocked her head to listen harder. "The trick is determining whether it's normal daily archivist talk or if it's because there's a prisoner nearby."

Mateo gave a solemn nod.

Their first stop had been Stede's house. The place screamed bachelor angel. It was plain and barren, like it had recently been cleaned out. The male had resided close to the city center, within view of the fountain. But it was clear he hadn't spent much time at home. Doors and windows were sealed, and when she and Mateo had entered, it was probably the first breath of fresh air the house had gotten in months.

The archives had been next on their list. According to Chanel, there were several rooms that normal residents weren't allowed to go in. She only knew of a few but it was a start.

She and Mateo had started at one end of the archives and were working their way toward the other when a yell caught their attention.

Rushing toward the sound, they stayed in the shadows, ensuring they wouldn't be seen.

"That's him, I know it," she hissed. They were hurting him, and she couldn't get all the ways how they could do it out of her mind.

The voices grew clearer, but she still couldn't make out the words. Light flashed from a hallway up ahead, like a door had been opened. She stumbled, nearly falling, but she regained her balance and charged ahead. Mateo matched her step for step.

A sharp pinch squeezed her wrist, and she was filled with the urge to be elsewhere. She slowed and Mateo threw her a confused look.

Glancing down at her wrist, her eyes widened. A mating brand. An injured Jagger. This was absolutely not a coincidence.

Mateo caught a glimpse of the mark and inhaled sharply. "Find him."

They rounded the corner. Stomach acid churned in her belly. Blood dotted and smeared the floor all the way to a door gaping open. But the hallway was empty.

Mateo charged ahead to the opening of another room. He peered inside. "I've got one unconscious female and a male coughing on the floor." He looked at her. "No Stede. I've got this. Find Jagger."

Stede had been here. Was he after Jagger? She kept going.

She had no idea what waited outside that door on the soft green lawn surrounding the archives; she only knew she had to get out there.

As soon as she crossed the threshold, she closed her eyes and concentrated. There was a strong pull toward… Cool droplets of water beaded on her skin. She opened her eyes. The Mist.

He was here and he was waiting for her.

She couldn't process the whole mating aspect of the mark on her wrist. That would all come later. Right now, Jagger needed healing, and every molecule in her body hollered to get to him.

It was almost impossible to see anything but fog and grass in the Mist. She followed her intuition, all the while looking, listening, and feeling for any presence other than her own.

Several directionless steps later, she spotted blood droplets in the grass. "Jagger?"

A faint groan came from the distance.

She sprinted the rest of the way. His crumpled form came into view.

"Those bastards," she seethed. The flesh of his back had been ravaged. Her own back echoed in pain.

Jagger adjusted enough to look at her through bleary green eyes. Somehow, despite his torn wings, blood-soaked clothes, and swollen face, he managed a small smile. "I hoped it was you."

She knelt. "I knew it was you."

How did this go again? She wasn't ready to bond. But this wasn't about a relationship, this was about saving his life.

Laying her hands on him, she concentrated just like she had when she'd searched for him. Her body warmed, but it wasn't enough. He raised his hand, the one with the brand on it, and linked it with hers. Heat swirled through her, into him, and back. Her awareness of him bloomed. They were bonding.

She leaned over him, draping her body across the worst of his wounds and closed her eyes. Healing power flowed through her.

This was the purpose of their people, the purpose of their bond, to be there for one another. Healing would be her duty as a warrior's mate. But as much as she needed to save his life, she couldn't ignore that she was giving hers over to the realm she'd sworn she wanted nothing to do with. Not only that, but healing Jagger linked their souls. Once they were bonded in body, they would be together forever.

And while healing energy flowed through her into him, all she could think about was how well that had turned out for their parents.

Jameson watched Lindy. She didn't know he was here. Truthfully, he'd also expected to be gone longer. He'd made it into the Mist again. Another chaperone dead. Jameson had tracked the oblivious sap, impaled him with demon metal, and ascended into the Mist. With enough of the angel's blood coating him, he'd wandered the Mist, concentrating on his son.

For a few moments, he'd felt a flicker of…something. The harder he'd concentrated on his kid, the stronger it had gotten. But that was all.

Today was supposed to have been the day he went back to Numen—an accomplishment everyone believed impossible. If the motivation was to free Julian, so be it.

He'd gotten close.

Enough to watch his boy bond to an angel, the equivalent of giving his soul away.

But he'd heal. Jameson would concentrate on that.

And make everyone else pay—for threatening his family in the first place, for trying to take Julian's wings, and for making it all possible.

He'd start here. In his own home.

He eyed his target. She didn't know he was here and she was somewhere she wasn't supposed to be.

Lindy ran her finger along the sharp end of one of his blades. She held it close to her face, focused on nothing but the metal. As he watched her search for and find his secret stash, he waited for her to acknowledge his presence. But one of the requirements of being in his bed was that his partners couldn't be inhabited by a creature from Daemon. He wasn't into fucking possessed creatures. It also meant their senses were blissfully human.

She'd found his weapons. How convenient that he'd just bluffed to Stede about them. Had the male thought there was a ring of truth to his words?

Another woman in his life had turned on him. She knew that he'd talked to Felicia that night. She was working with Stede. If she had just twisted the knife in his back, that'd be one thing. The interfering fool had put his son in danger.

He didn't need another woman in his life who was willing to ruin his. And for what? Was she getting paid? Or did she just want the joy of seeing him shredded and bleeding? Did it fulfill some empty hole inside of her to fuck him over?

After this task was taken care of, he'd deal with the traitorous Stede. This problem had to be taken care of first.

He waited. Not even in the shadows anymore. He was behind her, in the entrance of the walk-in closet. She'd located the sizable room at the back. It certainly seemed as if she was looking for something.

She drifted her talented fingers across his unassembled lineup of metal creations. "What are you up to, Jameson?"

"I'm sure you'd find it dreadfully boring."

She jumped and spun, a strangled scream ripping from her. He stepped inside and closed the door. Reaching behind him, he flicked the lock. This space could be secured coming or going. He'd made sure of it.

Her gaze flicked from him to the door. She looked guilty as hell.

Oh yes. He knew that look on a woman. "I don't even have to ask."

"Jameson, it's not like that. I just found this space—"

"Shut up."

She snapped her mouth closed and wrung those hands that had caressed his weapons.

"I no longer tolerate liars." He advanced. She pressed into the counter. "I should've known. An intelligent woman gets through the mass of ignorant youth and spreads her legs whenever I want. Too good to be true?"

She chewed her lower lip and gripped the counter behind her. "I'm not. I was just curious, I swear."

He closed the distance between them and towered over her. Feathering a finger down her face, he soaked up her tension. The mounting terror inside of her. "And just who would you swear to, Lindy Sampson?"

A tremor wracked her body. Once upon a time, he wouldn't have been swayed by such fear.

Today, he drank it in. "They took my son."

Her eyes flared wide. "J-Julian?"

Nodding slowly, he fisted his hand in her blond tresses and tightened until she winced and her head cranked to the side. He'd talked about his boy one night over dinner. His Lindy had offered to listen and he'd opened up to her. "But you already knew that, didn't you?"

A pained gasped squeezed out of her. "Jameson, I swear—"

He yanked her face close to his. "Yes, you swear. You inked that pretty little tat on your tit and swore to me. So who do you swear to, Lindy? Who?"

But she didn't answer. It was hard to when his other hand was clamped over her throat.

CHAPTER 20

Coming to wasn't fun. Only his training saved him from groaning and rolling over. As he took stock of his surroundings, he realized he would've rolled right off the bed.

A delicious body was pressed to his other side, and look at that. Despite the lingering sting and pinching pain in his wings, he could still get achingly erect.

The previous days—hours? How much time had passed? —rushed back to him.

Synced. He was synced to a mate. The bond wasn't complete, not until they came to together in body and not just spirit. But he had a mate. Not just any mate, but Felicia. A strong, proud female that he didn't deserve, but the one he wanted.

"How are you feeling?" she asked.

She knew he was awake. It could mean their bond was strong, but she'd probably been able to tell before.

"Sore." He couldn't help himself. Draping a hand over her waist, he was about to tuck her into his body when she stiffened. "What's wrong?"

She scooted away from him and sat up on the other end of the bed. "We haven't done more than hose off."

"That's not it."

She looked over her shoulder at him. Her eyes were luminous and so full of conflict that his damn heart broke. "How can we make this work?"

"What do you mean?" After what they'd been through, how could they not?

"We come from failed syncs. My wings." Her gaze dropped. "This realm."

"A lot of couples split their time between realms. But... I think you can show your wings off with pride."

She glanced over her shoulder only to roll her eyes at him.

"Seriously, Felicia. Show your wings."

Turning on the bed and propping one leg on it, she faced him. "Say I can get over the whole wing business. Forever is a long time."

"We know what our parents didn't." He rolled up on an elbow. "That we need to talk because we're stronger together."

"I don't *want* to live here." Her lower lip trembled. "I can never fly."

Ah. That hadn't occurred to him.

She swiped at a tear. "But missing flying is superficial."

"No, it's not."

She ignored him. "We were paired during your moment of need. That doesn't make our future a sure thing."

Their parents again. If he could go back in time and talk to her mother—beg her not to walk into the fire—he'd do it. He sat up all the way. His shoulders were tight and he was surprised his wings didn't creak every time he moved. This was only a fraction of what Felicia felt every day.

"I was paired with you because the Almighty knows that I trust you. And I'd only accept *you*."

Instead of melting under his words, her brow creased. She was more dubious.

"Is it my father?" he asked quietly.

"Yours. Mine. They were a mess. Being matched didn't mean anything other than you needed saving."

He maneuvered until he was right next to her. "I would've chosen you."

"You had three months to. Be realistic, Julian."

He put his hand over his heart. "Julian? This is serious."

She gave him a playful shove like this wasn't the most serious subject he'd ever discussed. It was his future. His life. But it was hers too.

"So we what, ignore the mark? Date other people to make sure we don't pair better with another?"

She glared at him.

"Yeah. That's how I feel." He sighed and scrubbed his face. She was right. They hadn't cleaned up and both he and the bed were gross. His own dried blood had flaked all over his pink sheets. He hated those sheets. Valerina had chosen them.

How many years had he wasted with Valerina? What if he'd mated her right away? They hadn't been naturally paired but at the time he'd been convinced they were perfect for each other. Good thing they'd waited.

But not one cell in his body said Felicia wasn't his. He'd be willing to bet she felt the same. Except for that brain of hers. The one he hadn't given her credit for until recently.

"Then we wait. We date."

A fine brow arched. "Date? While we're being hunted and your father is still trying to rule over all of us in this realm."

"Yep. Or I can talk to Persephone."

"Don't you dare."

"I didn't tell you that she spread the rumor about us."

Felicia shrugged like he'd just said it had rained last night. "If it wasn't her, it would've been someone else."

Which brought them back to the realm thing and he didn't want her to explore another reason she didn't think they owned each other.

He didn't pressure her. If she slept with him to complete the sync, he wanted it to be because she was sure of them.

"I guess we could date," she said.

"Our first one can be in the shower."

She grinned like she thought he was joking, but when she saw how serious he was, the smile faded. Her lips parted. "The shower?"

"No penetration. Scout's honor." He lowered his voice. "But I need to be with you."

She waited a few tense seconds before saying, "I'll give you a ten-minute head start."

THIS WAS THE WEIRDEST, most erotic date she'd ever been on.

Jagger refused to move fast. He'd washed off and was painstakingly wiping her down. She was hot, her breasts heavy, and need surfed through her blood.

"Jagger." The whine in her voice was shameful. But he had yet to touch her with more than the cloth or anywhere close to a certain bundle of nerves. "I know what you're doing."

He only laughed, a deep vibration that would curl through her if he got close enough. Instead, he squatted down to stroke down her legs.

As for what he was doing, he was trying to get closer to her. She couldn't speed up this process. Her mind rebelled at the thought. He'd been a giant dick to her because of his parents, and not just his father. She'd been emotionally closed off because of hers. It wasn't an issue they could fuck their way out of.

She wanted to try. Oh, she wanted to.

He was soaping her feet. The water ran at the perfect temperature, like it always did in Numen. An endless supply that was there when they needed it, like the sky or the grass. Effortless, like living in Numen should be. Which wouldn't be the case for her.

He looped the cloth over a shower ledge. "Want me to stop?"

She was plastered against the wall, panting. Did she look ready to stop? His erection jutted up from his squat.

"The date's not over yet," she breathed.

His face went molten and she questioned her no-penetration resolve. Because right now she wanted him inside her. All over her.

Just touch me already!

He rose, his heat lifting with him. Crowding her into the wall, he rested his arm alongside her head.

This was so different than the last time they'd slept together. This was purposeful. Vivid. Light reflected off the stone walls, making the bathroom the brightest place in the house. Or maybe it just felt that way. Like she was bared in every way before him.

Maybe this thing between them was strong enough to weather the years. The decades. The centuries.

He lowered himself in one smooth motion. His knees rested on the floor of the shower and he skimmed his hands up her legs. He held her gaze as he parted her thighs and slowly moved in. When his mouth opened she had to tear her gaze away. It was too much, watching him do this to her.

She cried out when his tongue hit her clit, curling her fingers into his hair. This new connection made anything that had happened between them before seem pale, watered down. Nothing but sensation rolled through her body now. Warm water hitting her skin, cool tile pressing against her back, and ecstasy spreading through her body from where his tongue lapped at her. Her climax didn't have a chance. She exploded against his mouth, crying his name—both of them. She alternated between Julian and Jagger, her mind blending the uptight warrior she'd once offended with the moody male she'd lived with for the past three months. He was one, and he was hers—if she wanted him.

Prowling up her body, he stopped to lick each nipple and nibble his way up her neck.

Her body quivered for him, demanding more. Getting off in the shower with him wasn't enough. She wanted it all, she wanted him.

Why couldn't she have him? The answer her brain summoned sounded faint, like looking down a tunnel at the tiny pinprick of a train coming from miles away. Her reasoning didn't make sense.

She lifted one leg to wrap around his waist, but he anchored a hand on her hip.

"I swore I wouldn't go any farther."

His words had the same effect as a bucket of cold water.

She gave him a shaky nod. "Right. Great."

He twined his arms around her and she dropped her leg. "We'll get there. I have faith in us."

She rested her head on his shoulder and let the water beat down on them both. She had no doubt they would get there. Her real concern was whether or not they could stay there.

"OPEN UP, you worthless piece of shit." The gurgle made it hard to understand Gerzon's words.

Dammit. Sandeen thought he'd had more time, but if

Gerzon was banging on his door, it was too late. Which humans could he possess on the fly? His last host had found God in a major way. The guy barely left church now. Sandeen hadn't been that bad to him, but apparently getting his soul hijacked had been a hell of a wake-up call.

There was the nineteen-year-old. He shuddered. No one could pay him to inhabit a teenager again. The questions. The uncertainty. The bold hubris of knowing just enough to make it dangerous. It didn't help that Sandeen had over-stayed his welcome and experienced a hell of a hangover after the frat party the night before. And he'd been in jail.

He'd just used the kid as a vessel to ride around the human realm and spy on the angels roaming about. Few sensed him. He was that powerful of an archmaster.

But the raging idiot on the other side of the door didn't think so. And that would be his own downfall. Sandeen wasn't going to stick around to watch. He had his own plans and they included walking around the human realm in his own form and experiencing freedom for the first time in his life.

His deal with Jameson Haddock was done and he had several vials of fallen blood to show for it. He just had to get in touch with his informant and see what else he could use the fallen for.

His door rattled. If he hadn't had such a bastard of a father, the door would've shaken off its hinges. But he'd replaced and repaired the wood planks and frame enough that it was now the strongest door in the whole putrid realm.

"Open this hell-forsaken door, you worthless whelp of a sylph whore."

One would think that demons would have more inventive cuss words. He took a fortifying breath. He'd have to get out of the house before he could cross. As sly as he was, he wasn't a coward. He'd plow through Gerzon and leave when he damn well pleased. It wasn't like he was coming back to this realm.

Do or die. Literally.

Between his father and Gerzon, his head wasn't long for his shoulders in Daemon.

Could he make it work again? Exit a human and be in his own body in the human realm? He couldn't morph his wings like those of Numen could, but until he learned, he could hide them. A trench coat or something might work. Then there were his horns.

A trench coat and a hat. He'd be killing it in the human realm.

Time to go.

He gripped the handle, adopted his most fearsome expression, and ripped open the door.

Gerzon's gnarly fist was about to wail on the door. Sandeen caught his hand and flung it to aside like the other male had the strength of a baby.

Two other male demons were with him. Their eyes flared wide and each set of wings twitched, waiting for Gerzon to lose his shit.

And thus his confidence that he was better than Gerzon. The male with crooked black horns and ragged wings as papery as a bat's couldn't control his emotions. So far, he'd ruled his team with brute force, and since he didn't interfere with stronger archmasters, like Sandeen's father, he was left alone.

It was his right-hand female that worried Sandeen. She was cruel, calculating, and, he suspected, just biding her time until she could overthrow Gerzon.

She wasn't around, making this interaction easier.

Gerzon curled a fat lip. "Don't touch me, you—"

"Worthless whelp of sylph whore." He kept his tone

bored. "I heard you the first time. And it explains why I don't know who my mother is."

"She was a—"

Since he didn't need to hear more insults about a female who had left him at the mercy of his heartless-even-for-Daemon father, he cut his hand through the air.

Gerzon swelled, his rage ballooning his chest out. The male's turgid cock engorged. Unlike much of the realm, Sandeen preferred clothing. One, he didn't feel the need to run around impaling unwilling males or females whenever the opportunity arose, and two, it made it harder for others to tackle and rape him.

Home sweet home.

Shoving past Gerzon and letting the door slam behind him, he stepped far enough away from his hovel of a home. The door would automatically seal thanks to a few simple wards.

"Look, G. I'm a busy guy. I don't know what you came here for, but since you don't have an appointment, I've gotta run."

Gerzon narrowed his murky blue eyes. "Whatever deal you have with Jameson Haddock, consider it done. Step on my turf again and I'll kill you."

Shaking in my sylph-skin loafers. "Gotcha." He gave Gerzon a quizzical look. "But who's Jameson Haddock?"

With a wicked smile he crossed into the Gloom and located the older woman he'd been keeping tabs on. She wasn't a God-fearing person and had just lost her beloved nineteen-year-old kitty. She was hating life and everyone in it. It made her soul ripe for the picking.

Gerzon could follow him easily enough in the Gloom. He closed his eyes and targeted the woman. Getting inside of her was as easy as taking a step. One second he was in the dark veil of mist and the next he was drawing a wheezy breath.

"Margaret," he muttered to the host he'd completely blocked from her own body. "Use your goddamn inhaler."

That cat she was mourning was the source of her asthma. She'd probably go out in a week, adopt another cat, and die of an asthma attack.

He gave himself a few moments to adjust to her arthritis-riddled body. Fuck, his knees ached. Going to her medicine cabinet, he sucked a few puffs of her inhaler, then flicked bottles left and right.

Popping an extra dose of her arthritis meds, he passed over the cloudy glass of water on the counter and found an unopened bottle of cranberry juice in the fridge.

His host was a techie, one reason why he'd kept her in mind. Her smart phone was on the table. He punched in Lindy's number and sent a message. *Updates?*

While waiting for a reply, he puttered around the kitchen. He emptied the dishwasher and filled it again. His host was also a takeout junkie, thanks to her nice pension from an insurance agency, so the dishes were minimal. But the fridge was a pit.

He was trashing takeout containers when the phone rang.

Frowning, he peered at the number. Lindy.

Answering, he said, "Did you miss my voice?"

His blood chilled at the response. "Why absolutely I did. *Sandeen.*"

Jameson. Fuck. He was too smart to bullshit and he wouldn't let Lindy get away with a slap on the ass. "Let Lindy go and we'll talk."

"Lindy's gone."

The chill in his veins turned to icicles. "Dammit, Jameson. What did you do? She was just a human pawn."

"Then you shouldn't have sent her to suck my dick and screw me over. She got my son involved."

Shit. He'd heard about the fallen's family, but he'd dismissed the info. It was his understanding that fallen were considered worse than demons to angels. Besides, Jameson and his little games weren't his concern. Means to an end.

But Lindy had paid the price. If he were a proper demon, he wouldn't care. Wasn't that the crux of his problem? He wasn't like the other demons. He wasn't evil, just naughty. That was why Daemon wasn't a suitable home for him, the reason he couldn't stomach smelling the rot and filth of this realm any longer. He didn't rape or pillage and he only killed discreetly, after proper consideration.

"Your son is still alive but Lindy is dead, yes?" Had she suffered? Again, he shouldn't care.

"As a doorstop." A muffled thud sounded over the line. The image was crystal clear: Jameson banging the door into Lindy's still form.

Mix in Gerzon's insults and Sandeen was really fucking tired of these games.

He could take out two problems with one shot.

What about his own plans to find a way to mingle with humans undetected?

That could wait. He had too much of his own father in him to let Gerzon go without some retribution. Same with Jameson. And, well, since those two were working together, then two birds, one stone.

"I'd wish you the best, but come around me and my club again and I'll kill your host."

"Gerzon stopped by today."

The curse Jameson bit off made him smile.

"That's right. He knows about us working together. Think I should tell him why?"

CHAPTER 21

Jagger snapped his shirt into place. Felicia was already dressed and ready and had two protein shakes waiting for them.

He left his bedroom and met her by the door. Grabbing his shake with one hand and pulling her in for a kiss with his other, he prayed for more days like this. Well, not exactly like this. This part, waking up to his mate and getting ready together, he wanted forever. But the part where he was going to meet with his team to talk about hunting down one of their own and possibly his own father? Never again.

Breaking away from him, she peered into his eyes. "Are you ready?"

"As I'll ever be. I'm glad you're with me."

He whipped open the front door and pulled up short. His mother and her boyfriend waited on the other side.

Mother only lifted a finely manicured brow. Mateo recovered quickly, impressing Jagger even more. His type was who they needed guarding their realm, but he'd also make a hell of a warrior.

"Mother."

She waved at the door behind him. "Go ahead and close it, I won't take long." She seemed to gather herself, brushing her hands down her formal robe. Dread swept through Jagger. If something was bothering his mother enough to show this much, it must be bad. "I came by to tell you that I gave the senate my recommendation on how we should move forward with your… With Jameson Haddock."

His stomach could've been filled with lead it sunk so hard. Subconsciously, he'd known this was coming. There were so many reasons to dread this morning, but hearing the final determination of his father's fate topped the list.

Felicia's hand curled into his, and he squeezed it.

The movement didn't go unnoticed; neither did their matching marks. "Well." No mother in the history of Numen had ever looked less pleased that their child was mated. "I won't pretend I don't have concerns."

"So do we," he shot back. "It's not like our role models made this something to be desired."

Mother lifted her chin. "I understand. Just like I understand that your father and I are not the norm." Her gaze shifted to Felicia. "And neither were yours, though dare I say, their fate is a more common occurrence than we possibly know."

"And I dare say," Felicia began, "that both of these circumstances should be discussed and not swept under some rock and rolled up in some attic in the archives. I think that especially my mother would've benefited from open dialogue about what was going on, and what had happened."

Mother inhaled and pressed a hand to her stomach, but her demeanor softened. "While I don't care to think about what it would've been like to have my business spread through the realm even more than it was, I must agree. Ignoring our fallen has only led us to be woefully ignorant about them."

"I extend an offer to discuss it with the senate." Felicia's hand was gripping his like a vise.

Mother dipped her head. When her gaze went back to him, it was filled with regret. "My recommendation was that Jameson Haddock be executed for his crimes."

Mateo dipped his head, and Felicia couldn't hide her sharp intake of breath. Jagger held his mother's gaze. "I understand."

"Yes, well, we all seem to understand. I think perhaps it's time to admit how incredibly awful it is. I also can't ignore how angry I am at him for everything he's put us through." Mother briefly closed her eyes. "I will also admit the problems in our relationship went both ways. To a point."

Classic Mother. But she wasn't wrong.

"It's not just his crimes, is it?" Their kind didn't take executions lightly. "It's what his blood can do to us." Losing the ability to transcend made them vulnerable, as the number of missing and presumed dead angels attested to.

"I'm afraid that is a condition we'll need to research further. But yes, he is a danger to us all."

"Thank you for telling me. We're running late for a meeting with Director Vale."

As he and Felicia stepped around Mother, he wondered for a moment if he shouldn't, like, hug her or something. It so wasn't them, but if there ever was a time, this was the moment.

There was enough regret in his life.

He closed the space between them and engulfed his mother in a strong embrace. She stiffened for a heartbeat and then clung to him more fiercely than he'd ever thought possible. She was a strong female; he had never doubted that.

When he stepped back, he looked at Mateo. "This thing between you two, I'm happy for you and wherever you to decide it should go."

"As far as she'll let it."

~

IT FELT like she was intruding on a private family moment.

Sierra's house loomed in front of them. When Felicia had been here last time, it had seemed like a small, cramped rental. Right now, it could rival the size of the archives.

Jagger's team surrounded the home. Even Bryant was here.

Odessa was under the protection of Enforcer Tosca. There were few people Bryant trusted anymore. Felicia was honored to be one of them.

Grim faces surrounded her. There was no hiding what they were here to do. She had told them about her confrontation with Sierra, and honestly, she didn't expect the female to be around.

Bryant did the deed. He marched into the house, and the rest filed in. There was no subterfuge, there was no chase. If Sierra was here they would take her into custody.

Felicia was the last one in, save Jagger behind her.

She almost bumped into Bronx's back. Everyone had stopped in the entryway.

Sierra sat on the threadbare living room couch. She was pale, her short blond hair tucked behind her ears, her hands clenched in the leggings covering her thighs.

"Sierra, why?" Bryant's voice was soft. This was hard on all of them. It had to be like arresting a sister.

She glanced at Jagger. Or hunting down yet another family member.

The team faced Sierra like a wall. A somber, resolute wall.

Sierra took her time looking at each one of them. Had to give the girl points for a hefty set of lady balls.

"I was protecting myself." She sounded strong, even

though she looked like a stiff wind could topple her. "And I should've known that, in the end, I was destroyed anyway."

Dionna spoke, a thread of anger releasing each word. "Any chance you'll give us the specifics, or are you just going to wait and see how those will be used against us too?"

Felicia almost winced. The guilt swamping Sierra was obvious. She looked like she bore the weight of all the realms on her shoulders.

"I'll help you track down Stede and then you can take me in."

Everyone went quiet, considering her proposal. Stede was in the wind. Neither the male or female that had been with Stede was talking other than to say it was all Stede's fault and he was forcing them. They refused to say how.

The only dirt Bryant had found was that they were having an affair with each other, but neither one was officially synced to their current partners, though that didn't make the affair right. It only proved that Stede could find the weaknesses in others and exploit them. How had he found them when he'd been in the human realm the majority of the time?

What did he have on Sierra?

"How can we trust a damn thing you say?" Bryant asked.

"You can't. I deserve my punishment, but before I lose my wings, I need to make sure Stede loses his head." The warrior in Sierra was visible. Her violet eyes glittered with menace and her hands were now curled into fists.

"We need to deal with Stede," Jagger said quietly. "And I'm not only saying that to delay going after my father. None of this will make a difference if we don't get Stede. He has some connection in Numen that we don't know about."

Bryant gave Sierra a hard stare. He broke it only to glance at Dionna.

"What did Stede know about you?" Dionna asked. It was

like she needed to know how badly Sierra's back was against the wall before she agreed to work with her again. "What are you hiding?"

Sierra lifted her chin. "The circumstances of my birth are…shameful. And I have—I have a sibling who knows nothing about it, or about me. Stede threatened to use me against her, and that's all you're going to get."

"Stede knows but we can't?" Bryant's perplexed expression matched how they all felt.

"I prefer my secret die with him."

"How did he find out?" Bryant asked.

"I've come to the conclusion that he must know my father. My *real* father."

Infidelity seemed to be an epidemic in Numen. Felicia stole a glance at Jagger. She slid her gaze over his slicked-back platinum hair, down his strong jaw line, and to his eyes. It was clear he was fighting his sympathy for Sierra. Her resistance to completing their sync wasn't about whether or not she trusted him.

"Is your father a concern in this case?" Bryant regarded Sierra warily.

Her gaze dropped. "I don't even know who he is. I only know he's not good."

Felicia could readily interpret that confession. Sierra's mother had been forced. And she'd hidden it, like everyone else did in the realm. Another tragedy, and Sierra was going to pay for it.

Fury roiled under Felicia's skin. There had to be a way to change this thought process, this "we don't talk about the bad stuff" mentality.

There had to be a way, and maybe, just maybe it started with her.

She spoke, risking the others' irritation. "I say we let her help, and then we speak for her during her trial."

Urban shook his head. "Her actions caused serious injuries."

Harlowe had been quiet the whole time, but she said, "I agree with Felicia. She should've been able to trust us enough to come to us."

Sierra was shaking her head as she rose. "No. I will help you hunt down Stede, and then I will pay for my crimes. There will be no talk, no revelation, no argument. My history stays secret."

"Why is it so important?" Harlowe snapped. "We're trying to help you."

All the fight drained out of Sierra as she gazed at Harlowe. "I'll only be losing my wings. I guess one thing Jameson has taught us is that there is life after falling. Once I recover, I can still use it for good." Her eyes misted over as a tremble shook her strong body.

Bronx cut a hand through his hair. "This sucks. This all just sucks."

Bryant considered Sierra. Then he pivoted to look at all of them. Felicia wanted to sidle closer to Jagger, to comfort him, but this wasn't the time.

"We hunt down Stede as a team," Bryant declared, "and then we support Sierra's fall as a team. And if the senate thinks we'll all fucking forget this one, they can stuff it."

The subject was too serious for Felicia to smile at Bryant's bold statement. Despite how tragic this law was, she was sure of one thing: things were going to change in Numen, and she was going to be part of the process.

CHAPTER 22

"You think he's doing what?" Jagger had heard Sierra clearly the first time. But her statement was insane. And if true, appalling that it had gone unnoticed. "How do you know this?"

"He's stockpiling angel fire," Sierra said as if that weren't terrifying. "I checked our database and there was a missing order of vials."

He was standing next to Felicia in Sierra's spare room—her office. Two large screens loomed over her. She glowed under the light, her eyes intent. Focused. She was going to make Stede pay. Jagger only wished she had come to them earlier.

Bryant pinched the bridge of his nose. "Those bloody missing vials. I thought it was some noob clerk."

The fountain didn't have protection. Angels were free to walk into the fire, and warriors refilled their stock when needed. Everyone else wanted to keep their distance.

Sierra didn't spare them a glance. "Nope. That clerk was the angel the female was seeing, the one who helped imprison Jagger."

"What's he planning?" Felicia asked. All of the others but Harlowe had left on Bryant's command. He wanted them out and mobilized. "Besides an attack, obviously."

Jagger wouldn't admit what a relief it was to switch the focus away from hunting his father. He doubted Jameson knew of this new development with Stede. If he did know, what would he do about it?

Sierra didn't take her eyes off her laptop. "The fire. Fallen blood. He can take control of any place in Numen. Ping 'em with the blood. Hit 'em with angel fire. He could mow down a sizable population fairly quickly. Use panic to his advantage and no one would know where it was coming from." Her fingers flew over the keys.

"Where's the stash?" Harlowe peered at the screens. Who were they going to get to replace Sierra?

He couldn't help but think of Father around her. The two were completely different. Father hurt others irreverently.

This time Sierra spun around from her computers. "I had been working under the assumption that he moved it all to the earthly realm. Felicia said Stede's home was barren, like he'd recently cleaned much of his stuff out. Or that's what he wanted us to think if we ever caught on. But having his stash of angel fire in this realm wouldn't do him any good. He doesn't understand security, or why would he blackmail me to do his dirty work?"

"But where would he store it in Numen?" Jagger didn't want to get impatient. He could see Sierra's line of reasoning, but she needed to get to the point.

"If I knew, I'd tell you," she snapped.

"Would you?" Felicia countered and Sierra winced.

"I want Stede worse than the rest of you. Don't doubt that." She swiveled back to her computer.

They all fell quiet and let Sierra do her thing. When Sierra slumped in her chair with a "huh," they all stared.

Her gaze was glued to the screen. "That's weird. I'm running through all the watchers' notes trying to link anyone to Stede."

"Smart," Bryant replied. "Odessa said they're never deleted, but they're not official records that make it into the archives."

"Well, there's mention of a Stede dying on Earth in a revolution. Decapitation." She grimaced. "A female. Nora Stede. The watcher made a side note of informing the husband and child."

"Stede has a kid?"

Sierra frowned, her fingers a flurry of clicks over the keyboard. "There is no other Stede in the realm, believe me. I've checked. Lemme look at this Nora." A few minutes dragged by. Felicia didn't think any of them dared to breathe. "Hoven. Her birth name was Hoven before she mated Stede."

The name was sort of familiar.

"Hoven?" Bryant barked. "Like Tenley Hoven? My new fucking assistant?"

"What the hell is going on now?" Jameson strode into his place. Fucking Stede was reclining on the couch. "Who let you in?"

He hadn't tasked Andy with the undesirable chore of disposing of Ms. Lindy Sampson. What was the man so preoccupied with that he'd let Stede sneak in?

"Disappointed that Lindy is no longer around to feed you information?"

Stede's brow furrowed. "Who?"

He seemed genuinely confused. But Lindy had—what? Asked about his son and then wandered into his closet. Not exactly insider information.

Had he acted rashly? No, of course not. He'd had reason. She'd been playing him. He knew it. She had to have been playing him.

That didn't stop doubt filtering through his mind.

Stede crossed his legs. He was dressed like he usually was as an enforcer, dark pants and a dark shirt. Official in Numen. Sinister in his living area. And his wings were hanging out, as if he was taunting Jameson with them. They were a murky gray, like the shade Lindy had turned after death.

"Know why I agreed to work with you in the first place?"

Jameson should've killed Stede when he fled with Kenton. There'd been no reason to keep either one around after that and they'd only brought trouble to his doorstep since then. "Enlighten me."

"I knew you were different. Something about you was different."

"Maybe because I didn't deserve to fall."

"You've earned it since."

Touché. "What are you doing here?"

"I'm tired of messing around. Your son was less than cooperative, so now I'm here."

Rage boiled in his blood, but he adopted a snide smile. "I take it my boy got away from you. I'd like to say I'm surprised."

Stede's expression didn't crack like he'd expected it to. The male was up to something. "Your blood is more desirable anyway."

Jameson snorted. "And what? You think you can march in here and take me on? If you were so confident, you would've done it months ago."

Stede uncrossed his legs but didn't move to rise. "I was letting you do all the heavy lifting. I knew eventually you'd find out that you were different and learn how to use it to your advantage."

Stede's calm demeanor set off all kinds of alarms. Awareness prickled along his skin. Something was wrong.

"And you didn't disappoint." Stede shot him an ironic glare. "You also didn't share your knowledge. That's the problem with all you senators. Your arrogance is your crutch."

"If I didn't know better, I'd say you were jealous." What was Stede up to? Jameson tallied all the weapons within reach. The room hidden in his closet he'd busted Lindy in was all locked up, but he had a regular old gun in his end-table drawer. The one Stede was sitting by.

Angels didn't carry guns. Stede would only have a knife or two. But Stede could heal much faster than him. Unfortunately, he wasn't that special. He'd lost his rapid healing abilities with his wings.

"Jealous? Perhaps at one time. I've since learned that there's only one way to fix our senate. Total destruction."

Once upon a time, their ambition had included taking over the senate and ruling via brute force. Jameson had only planned on killing the really avid opponents. Stede's bright idea sounded a lot like mass murder.

He wasn't on board with that plan.

And there was his true weakness. His conscience. He still cared about his son and he gave a damn about the amount of death he doled out. Some of those senators didn't deserve to die. He'd even argue his ex-mate's right to live, depending on his mood. And he was becoming more and more guilt laden about Lindy's death.

Stede was watching him, his fingers tapping on the arm of his chair. Jameson had another gun in his shoe drawer. To distract Stede, he snapped an arm straight and fiddled with the cuff as he spun toward his closet. "How do you plan to run the realm when you've destroyed its ruling body?"

Movement caught his eye. Something heavy, swinging toward his head. He wasn't fast enough. The object smashed into his temple. He reeled and toppled, his world going dark.

Who else was in his apartment? The last thing he heard was, "That's for me and my daughter to worry about."

CHAPTER 23

"Do you think they would've hidden all the vials here?" Felicia shrugged her shoulders. Her wings were morphed. She planned to keep training and strengthening them, but during a fight, they were still a liability.

"It's only obvious if you know Tenley is Stede's daughter," Jagger murmured. "But they've been planning this for decades, waiting. She made herself forgettable. And no one liked Stede enough to get close to him."

Half the team was with Sierra—to make sure she didn't run. They couldn't turn Sierra in yet. If they ran into a dead end at Tenley's place, they'd need her skills.

Tenley's home was small. Quaint. A cute little brick cottage in an unremarkable part of the realm. Many of her neighbors were in charge of Numen's upkeep. The realm's curb appeal was due to the angels that lived here, those who didn't fit into the ranks of governing, record keeping, or protection. Some were archivists like Tenley. Others cleaned the archives. The biggest difference in living arrangements, other than size, was that the houses were built with brick instead of marble.

A perfect place for a viper to lay low and appear as docile as a garter snake.

As much as she was grateful to be going after the real and most immediate threat to the realm, it didn't erase the fact that Jameson was next. That it'd be hard for Jagger to deal with losing his dad for good.

Her heart swelled with emotion even as she swept along the quiet lot, prepared to do whatever it took to stop Tenley. She would be there for Jagger. Always. If they were lucky, life would be long. Why not enjoy every moment possible with him?

Would Father have let Mother go if he'd known how it would end? Would Chanel have given up on—okay, that wasn't the best example. Chanel might've ditched Jameson and never looked back if she'd had an inkling he'd hurt her so.

But Jagger wasn't his father. That was obvious.

She glanced at his stark profile. The sun was setting. Same time every day. Jagger's gaze was focused. His expression grim.

He caught her eye. "Ready?" he mouthed.

Her nod answered his question, but also her own. She *was* ready.

They darted over the lawn. Her and Jagger in back. Bryant and Harlowe in front. This wouldn't be like the Vegas debacle all over again.

Waiting felt like the eternity it was, second by second ticking by as they looked, listened, and felt for anyone inside. Her and Jagger's job was to make sure no one escaped out the back while the others cleared the interior of the place.

Nothing.

The back door clicked and was pushed open. Harlowe scanned the property as if anyone would be lurking after she and Jagger had hung out here. But Felicia wasn't offended.

Not when her own personal boogeyman could be lurking nearby.

Jagger gestured for her to go inside first. She eased around him.

The place was quiet. Neat and tidy, but with very little personality. That wasn't unusual in a realm not known for its knickknacks or clutter, but somehow this seemed more sinister.

The kitchen was to the left. Harlowe started opening cupboards and drawers. "Jagger, take watch. Felicia and I can search the place."

She made quick work of the main area. As she entered the bedroom, it was like all sound had been wiped out. Frowning, she turned in a circle.

Sensing Harlowe at the door, she said, "This room seem small?"

Harlowe treaded inside and did the same move. "Super small." She brushed her hand along the wall by the door. "Dammit. Even the interior walls are made of brick."

In the fading light, it was hard to inspect the interior, but one wall appeared darker than the others. Felicia ran her hand along the wall Harlowe had just touched, then down the interior wall. "It feels different. Soft."

Jagger stepped next to her and pressed his fingers to the surface. "Spongy. A faux finish."

Harlowe snickered. "I can't tell if that's genius or lazy."

They all poked and prodded. There was give under Felicia's palm and a panel clicked open. She looked at Harlowe, her eyes wide, her body tense. "Should I open it the rest of the way?"

Harlowe glanced at the opening and nodded. "Carefully."

She held her breath as she tugged it toward her. Nothing but darkness greeted her. She poked her head inside, found a cheap light she recognized from TV. The thing stuck to a surface and, once touched, flickered on. She tapped it. The area brightened more than expected as the lamp's rays bounced off of row after row of crystal.

"Oh! Oh no." She stepped back so Harlowe could see.

The warrior peered in, her eyes going wide. "That's a lot of angel fire."

The crystal vials were stacked floor to ceiling, but these weren't the one-ounce containers that warriors typically carried. Those were here too. But so were crystal flasks that had to hold as much as twenty ounces. Enough to line the ten-foot-long wall that spanned the length of the bedroom. Instead of a closet, they'd just built an extra wall.

"This took a while to collect. Filling that large of a bottle would attract attention even for a warrior." Harlowe eased inside and withdrew her phone. She photographed the display. Then she ran a finger down the bigger containers. "These are thinner. More fragile and easily shattered." She shuddered like she was trying to shake off the thought of a Molotov cocktail made with angel fire. "Be right back. The director isn't going to like this, but at least we found it."

Harlowe disappeared and it was only minutes later that Jagger appeared.

He let out a low whistle when he looked in the closet. "Bryant went to wake up a few senators and make a report. Harlowe's recruiting another team of warriors to clean this up. You and I are on guard."

"Do you think Stede and his daughter know we found all this?"

"No. I hope we can get it removed before they find out. I just wish I could see the look on their faces when they walk in and find this empty."

She chuckled. During times like this, it was the small things. "Why don't you guys have crystal armor or something? If it can contain angel fire, why can't it be used for protection?"

"The weight of it would interfere with movement too much. Then there's the question of where we would wear it. A helmet? Chest plate? Either place would make it hard to fight. Our opponents aren't as encumbered."

And they would be faster. "Still, I think with a little research and brainstorming, something could come of it."

A smile played over his lips. "And again you have a lot of ideas for an angel who wants nothing to do with the realm."

"I'm sure I'm not the only one with these thoughts."

"No. But you have the family name to back them up." He gave her a knowing look and sauntered out of the room.

"Point taken." And ignored. "Want me to take the front or back door?"

"Your pick. But we should watch from the outside in."

She split for the back door. Not much light filtered into the place. It made it easy to come and go without being seen.

She opened the back door and came face-to-face with Stede.

His head was turned back, talking to someone she couldn't see. "…anchored in the Mist for now, but I couldn't cross with him—" He faced her.

Felicia's lungs seized until drawing in a breath was as hard as breathing through a soaked washcloth. Seeing him, in the dark like this, transported her back in time. She couldn't make a sound.

"She'll suffer for you."

Her mind couldn't tell her that it wasn't true. That it wasn't eleven years ago.

Stede's upper lip curled and he charged her. She wasn't prepared and toppled back. Her back hit the floor with his snarling face looming over her. As soon as the pain in her back flared, her brain came online. Her training kicked in.

She elbowed him in the face. Shoving him off, she rolled, coming to her feet faster than him. Another form flew through the door with a roar.

Tenley tried to tackle her but Felicia wasn't going to make the same mistake twice. The other female wasn't an experienced fighter. She was a liar. A manipulator. But not a trained, skilled, or experienced fighter. And she had no idea how fast Felicia could move.

A sharp punch to the face followed by one to the gut and Tenley dropped.

Her skin prickled. Stede was going to jump her, but footsteps pounded. Jagger.

Stede ducked out of Jagger's reach. "You touch me and your father's dead."

Jagger pulled up short.

Stede swiped a hand across his nose. "That's right. I have him."

"He's in the Mist. I don't think they can get him out, but they can't keep him there long." Felicia circled Tenley. She was starting to cough and struggling to get to her feet. Felicia kicked her in the stomach. "But lookit here. We have his daughter."

Stede's sinister grin faltered. He lunged for the door, knocking Jagger out of the way. Felicia kicked at him, knocking him off-balance. But he made it outside and disappeared.

"Stay with her." Jagger sprinted after him, vanishing into the Mist.

Felicia took stock of what was around her to keep Tenley subdued. Knocking her out would be best, but then she couldn't answer questions. The female didn't seem to be one to have spare rope and duct tape stored away. Loads of angel fire, yes. Actually useful items, no.

She sank into a squat, glaring at a groaning Tenley. Harlowe had better get here soon with backup.

Cool droplets surrounded him. Jagger squinted through the Mist. Had he gone in at the same spot Stede had entered?

He stalked through the damp grass, hunting Stede. And his father. Nothing stayed long in the Mist. Did Stede think he could keep Father here and bleed him whenever he wanted? Did Stede think he could get Father into Numen?

He hoped not. For Father's sake. And for the rest of the realm. Jameson Haddock might be in danger now, but after Stede was taken care of, Jameson would become the danger.

"Dammit." He couldn't hear a thing. But he wasn't giving up.

Maybe he couldn't track Stede, but he could zero in on Father.

Where are you?

He drifted to his left.

Are those voices?

"Wake up, you fool." Stede.

Jagger slowed. It was better to preserve the element of surprise as long as possible.

A moan. Father? "Stede. The Mist?" A grunt and a weak laugh. "I won't be here long. You can't keep me here."

"You're coming to Numen with me. Now concentrate."

The laughter was stronger this time. "I strongly suspected you were an idiot. I can't cross over. Don't you think I've tried?"

Jagger hovered far enough away to keep from being seen.

"Now you have help. Concentrate." Impatience dripped from Stede's tone.

"I've used Daemon steel, the blood of warriors, chaperones, watchers. Nothing has worked."

"Numen steel." The whisper of a blade being released from a sheath resonated through the Mist.

A yell ripped from Father. "It burns, jackass. Don't you think I would've tried it if I could have held on to it?"

Jagger kept low and inched closer. Stede was towering over a sprawled Jameson, holding on to his collar.

Stede snarled and shoved Father to the ground. "I'll have to keep you in the human realm." He stalked a few feet away. "Fuck!" The rage was coming straight from a male watching years of planning crumbling around him.

"Tell me, Stede." Father sat up. His hands and legs were bound like Jagger's had been. For all of his planning, Stede was a one-trick pony. "Did you pick me to fall or capitalize on it like the parasite you are?"

Stede stalked back to him. "I get sick of hearing your arrogant voice. It's time to go."

Father jerked away, his suit wet and wrinkled. "Listen. We can still work together. You find a way to get me into Numen and I'll give you all the blood you want."

The other male paused. "You can't be serious."

"As a hit on the head." The wry note was unmistakable. "We're both out for number one, I get that. But you want my blood and I want back home."

Was Stede actually considering it? Father had lost everything but his charm. It was what had gotten him the farthest.

"Or"—Stede flipped the knife in his hand to sheathe it—"I could be over making deals."

Jagger stalked toward Stede on silent feet. The fucker was going to descend out of the Mist, then he'd be back in the wind and nearly impossible to find.

Stede didn't sense him until Jagger was plowing into him. Stede's blade tumbled to the ground.

"Julian!"

He had to ignore Father. Getting Stede into custody was his priority.

But the male rallied. He spread his wings, making it difficult for Jagger to get close. Air buffeted around him as Stede whipped and snapped his feathers, creating a disorienting chaos. It was an unusual, but effective move. Demons were too intent on the kill to use their wings as anything more than weapons.

When Stede got enough distance between them, Jagger knew he'd lost his chance. "I'm going to bathe you in angel fire and take my time with your mate." Then he was gone.

"No!" Felicia was alone with Tenley, and Stede was going back. Fuck! He looked back at his father. Chartreuse eyes regarded him. Father was using the end of his sleeve to hold on to Stede's knife and cut himself free.

But Jagger's decision was made. Felicia's safety was more important to him. He'd deal with Father later.

Crossing back into Numen, he was a hundred yards from the house. The back door was broken down and the thumps of fighting from inside rang into the night.

He ran, knives in his hands.

When he dove through the opening, the sight that greeted him filled him with nothing but panic.

The kitchen, where he'd left Felicia and Stede's daughter, was empty. Stede had herded Felicia back to the bedroom. He was trying to get to the angel fire.

"Felicia!" he yelled, more to let her know he was there than to garner a response.

As he sprinted down the hall, a grappling Stede and Felicia disappeared into the room. When he rounded the entry, Tenley was slipping behind the fighting pair and into the closet. Felicia had been trying to keep her from getting to the room, but Stede was too much of a distraction.

Stede was faltering. Felicia was better.

Tenley emerged from the closet, a large vial poised and ready to throw. Felicia's back was turned. She made a perfect target.

"Felicia, behind you."

She didn't glance at him, but she ducked and shoved her shoulder into Stede's gut. By the time he let out an oomph, Felicia had turned and used him as a battering ram.

As he fell back into his daughter, Felicia freed herself. But Stede's unsteadiness impacted her and she cartwheeled, about to fall forward.

Jagger leaped to grab her arms and pulled her into his. Stede toppled. A shattering sound preceded a burst of light and Tenley's scream.

Angel fire wicked up their feet. Stede's cry mixed with his daughter's. Jagger squeezed Felicia. She was frozen, watching the horror unfold.

Stede's wide, frantic gaze met theirs. The regrets rampaging through his mind played out on his face. It was over. It was over for both him and his daughter. He let out a scream, his face mottling with rage as he lurched to his feet and wavered, barely able to stand as angel fire claimed first his skin, then his muscle.

He flung his arms out. The whole scene seemed to be in slow motion, but it lasted seconds. Stede grabbed a bottle. As he was falling to the floor, he lobbed it toward them. Then he fell backward, toward the rack of bottles.

Instinctively, Jagger spun, an "I'm sorry" escaping him. The bottle would shatter against his wings and if it stopped at just those, he'd be lucky. But he'd likely die. The amount of fire that would explode over him would see to it. But he could buy Felicia enough time to escape before the closet full of fire claimed the entire house.

"Jagger!" A figure burst into the room with a roar and dove between him and the bottle.

Glass broke as Jagger twisted, his body covering Felicia's. Her hands dug into him as she craned to see what had happened.

"Father!" Searing heat swamped the room. Light bloomed from the closet. They only had seconds before the pool of fire spread out, seeking any substance to expend its blistering energy on.

Father was on the ground, angel fire already blazing through his clothing and into his body. The look of peace on Father's face made Jagger pause. The male was burning alive, but wonder filled his expression. When his bright gaze landed on Jagger, his words were hard to hear.

"I could only think of helping you. And then I was here. Home." He reached a hand out.

Ignoring the danger they were in, barely aware of Felicia's steadying hold, he released her to briefly clasp Father's hand.

All the years they lost melted away and they were nothing but father and son again.

"Go." Father's voice was a pained whisper. "Let me save you. Let me do one good thing in my life." Father's hand went limp, dropping away before the angel fire could touch Jagger.

If tears streaked down his cheeks, they evaporated too quickly to see. Felicia was tugging at him and he didn't have the energy to fight her. His feet moved of their own accord, but his gaze never left Father's until the life wicked out of them and Jagger was gone from the room.

CHAPTER 24

*H*e was too cheerful. Showered and dressed in a short white robe, his damp hair hanging in his face, he didn't look like someone grieving.

"Jagger. Do you need to talk or something?" She'd found him in the kitchen after waking up. The bed had been empty and she'd tossed on a white T-shirt and black shorts. Not her usual colorful style. If he were feeling like himself, he would've commented on it.

But he couldn't be feeling like himself. Not after last night. Bryant had banned him from lingering after the dust had settled. Angel fire left little to clean up, so there was that.

When they'd returned after the fight, they'd done little more than change into clean clothes and crawl into bed. She had drifted off, but she doubted he'd gotten a wink of sleep.

"I'm fine." He was assembling a charcuterie board. Grapes, cheese, crackers. He must've made a regular Piggly Wiggly stop at some point to get the crackers.

She edged next to him, pressing her butt on the counter and scooting closer. A playful gesture, but one that should tell him that she wasn't letting up. He was facing the other way, artfully arranging the freaking cheese stack.

"I don't want to nag, but last night seems too monumental to ignore. You may not need to talk now, but just know that I'm here."

He pressed his hands on the top of the counter and looked at her, his gaze deceptively serious. The lighthearted breakfast-making guy hadn't been an act, but deliberate.

"I did a lot of thinking last night." He paused so long she wasn't sure he'd continue. "For years, I was obligated to forget my father existed. That didn't happen. Then when I knew more about him, I didn't like him. But I loved him. In the end, he chose me over everything else. Over everyone else. It was more than I ever thought I'd have from him. He's gone, and I hate to say, it's probably better that way. He would never be a good guy."

"But he was your father."

Jagger nodded, his eyes dimming. She didn't have to ask—and she wouldn't—what he was thinking about. Jameson Haddock's sacrifice. It didn't matter what name the male had gone by, he would've been the same conflicted angel he'd always been. And then there was the horrible things he'd done, the beings he'd killed in cold blood.

He tucked a grape between her lips and said, "I'm done being caught with one foot in the past. We're moving forward."

She flicked out her tongue, licking the tips of his fingers. His pupils dilated. Oh yeah, they could complete their bond right here on the counter. She finished chewing. "I'm ready."

"Yeah?" He crowded her against the cool marble and lowered his head so his lips hovered over hers. "For what?"

"To finish the sync."

He drew back. "Are you sure?"

"Yes. You and I are in this together. I have faith we'll stick with it. Together."

He twined his hands around her waist and pulled her close, but he didn't kiss her. "You can have all the time you need."

"We're overdue."

A slow grin spread across his lush lips. "Let your wings out."

Her sexy sync moment didn't include her wings. But her future did, and that started now. She peeled off her shirt and unfurled them, shifting her shoulders to ease the stretch and pull of them straightening.

They hung behind her. Was it stupid to hope her boobs would distract him from looking at them?

The heat in his eyes didn't diminish. It grew stronger. His gaze traced over each wing. "That's better." This time, he didn't hesitate to capture her mouth.

She'd expected a frenzied coupling, but she didn't get it.

Languid. Relaxed. He left her breasts alone as he slid his hands around her rib cage, massaging his fingers into her back.

She moaned and released the tension she'd held in her shoulders. He obviously found her sexy. That hard-on couldn't lie.

He brushed his hands along her wings, kissing the worry out of her before turning his attention to her shorts. He hooked his fingers over her waistband to roll them down.

Growing impatient, she buried her hands in his loose hair.

"Hands onto the counter," he growled.

Her breath hitched. Was he making her pay for waiting?

"We only get this one time to complete the sync. I want to take you here with the sun shining on your golden skin and your cries echoing off the walls."

She licked her bottom lip. Yeah. That sounded excellent. She pressed her hands into the cool stone. Once he took her shorts off, he kissed his way up her thighs until his hot breath wafted over her sensitive flesh. He slid his hands between her thighs and draped one leg over his shoulder.

Gazing up at her, he leaned in and licked through her seam.

She bucked against his face. That was all the warm-up she needed. She was ready to implode, explode, it didn't matter as long as the coiling energy inside of her had a place to go.

But he went frustratingly slow. Lapping steadily, then changing his rhythm. She buried her hands in his hair and rocked against him. Whenever she was about to crest, and he changed his pace—to her audible whimper—she could feel his smile against her skin.

"You're so bad," she panted.

With that, he nipped at her clit. The shock sent her over the edge. She gripped the edge of the counter, clinging to keep from collapsing against his face as her orgasm rocked her.

He rose, kissing and nipping up her belly, over her breasts, and nibbling his way up her neck.

She wrapped her hand around his hard length. The heat of him nearly seared her hand. "It's my turn."

He touched his forehead to hers and shook his head. "Next time. I can't wait."

"I thought we were taking it slow."

"I can't." His tone was ragged, pained. He shrugged out of his robe, letting it slip off his wings and hit the floor. "We'll have forever to take it slow." He gripped her ass and lifted her in one smooth motion to keep from jerking on her wings. She automatically wrapped her legs around him.

He impaled her with a hard thrust. She had no idea what she said as he jacked in and out of her, but it was a mixture of his name and how much she loved him. She thought it'd be a bigger declaration, or even an offhand "You know I do" confession, but like Jagger, she didn't want to wait anymore. She loved him. He should know.

His body tensed, but he didn't close his eyes and let his climax take him. He cupped her face and breathed, "I love you too. I always will."

The minor details could come later—where they'd live. What she'd do for a living. How she'd deal with his work. Right now, it was just about the two of them. They'd figure out the rest later.

~

"THIS IS FOOLISH. ALL OF IT." Chanel swept her arm around the room. Her bedroom. But where her robes normally hung, now there was a pair of pants and dark shirts. Weapons lined her vanity and large pairs of boots rested at the base. Mateo had moved too many of his items in. They slept together almost every night and last night that was all they'd done. Slept.

It was over and she was exhausted even though she hadn't lifted a finger. The mental stress. The...remorse. Her mate was dead. The realm might dictate that their sync had been over when James had lost his wings, but it hadn't changed her mind, or her heart. He'd still been alive and a part of her soul had felt like she was still synced. Now he was dead.

And she'd cried. Mateo had held her and she'd cried like she hadn't done since she'd been a child. Not even when she'd witnessed for herself the tenderness with which James had treated his mistress and her child had she sobbed. Her heart had frosted in glacial proportions that day.

"It's not foolish, Chanel. I'll quit my job if that makes it better."

Quitting his job wouldn't age him a few centuries. Mateo had gone to school with her son! It was one thing to know it when he'd just been a convenient lover, but it was quite another when he'd managed to thaw his way into a part of her. She cared for him. Unacceptable.

But to think that he'd quit over what others would say? "I'd never have you quit. Anyone who dares say a thing can look me in the eye and speak it. I'll gut them with words sharper than obsidian knives."

Mateo's lips twitched. "Our age gap doesn't bother me. It doesn't bother Jagger. Fuck everyone else."

She fanned herself, more for a distraction than to cool off. He was naked and so was she. She'd just woken up and seen Mateo and decided that this had reached an unacceptable point between them. All these pesky emotions. He couldn't have said anything more perfect. To have a partner who was proud of the way she was?

No. He was too good to be true.

"Come here," Mateo said softly. He held his arms out and like a sap she went to him.

He dropped kisses at her temples. Then worked his way down. All the way down. She writhed under his expert touch until she cried out. And then he did it again. And then he crawled over her and brought her to climax again.

Her throat was raw by the time he reared over her. His smile was so radiant that she had to cock her head and ask, "What?"

"You called out my name every time."

She swallowed hard. It was like she hadn't been able to heal completely until her mate was gone. "I don't know if I can do this again."

He kissed the tip of her nose. "You can. You're the strongest person I know, and I don't need a sync bond. Just you."

He was young. He might change his mind.

And she might be ready by then.

~

SANDEEN APPROACHED the skinny man standing in front of the window overlooking the dance floor. Andrew Petrovsky. Andy. He and Lindy had been rooked into this mess by the same man. Lindy was his inside source to get close to Jameson. Now she was dead. Jameson was gone. Yet this club was still going as strong as before. The drinks had more of a kick and the humans had fewer inhibitions. Archmasters weren't as stringent about hiding themselves, and judging from the partying going on, the humans didn't care that they were not only surrounded by demons, but being used by them.

He was disturbed by the scene much more than he thought he'd be.

Andy turned. He'd changed. Instead of a geeky little accountant, he was suave. Tailored suit, slicked-back hair, and an air of utter competence now lined with cruelty.

This human was as dangerous as any archmaster Sandeen could name, and considering his own father, that was disturbing.

"You called?" Sandeen asked lightly, but inside he was reeling. Jameson was gone and with it his arrangement with the fallen. As his fallen blood supply dwindled, so would his ability to walk in this realm as himself. He'd only tried it a few extra times. The biggest rush he'd ever experienced, but it was over.

So he'd been in his cat-lady host, surfing Netflix, when her phone had rung. Andy had found him. Andy knew things. Like how much fallen blood he had and exactly what it could do.

Even more of a surprise? Andy knew his father.

Andy straightened his tie. "Yes." The way he stared back was disconcerting. Andy could do what his own kind couldn't: wield technology like a weapon. He had eyes and ears everywhere. Not even that angel Jameson had blackmailed was as good as Andy. "That angel who lost her wings. I need you to find her."

His gaze swept the dance floor. "Why not one of your crew?" Because they were now Andy's. These disciples had probably been Andy's in the first place. The human had given Jameson the illusion of control.

Andy's mouth quirked. "Demons can't be trusted."

Sandeen cocked his head. "Exactly." Why him?

The smile on Andy's face made his stomach churn. "I always wondered if you knew. Interesting."

"Knew what?"

Andy shrugged. "It's not important right now. Sierra. Find her. Jameson said that with the exception of himself, the fallen are dumped on Earth where they have no contacts, but I can track her down. Await my direction."

That was it. He didn't have a say. "And you'll make me do this how?" Because Andy wouldn't be so cocky if he weren't holding something over him.

"I'm not one to tattle, but I'm sure Zadren would find your whereabouts interesting."

His sire. He ground his teeth together. Yes, he'd get dragged back to Daemon and imprisoned. Keep the bloodline going. Sandeen was the only surviving child, and he hadn't yet procreated. A lifetime of imprisonment and rape wasn't appealing.

"Interesting." He said it like he was hiding an ace up his sleeve even though he didn't have a damn thing on Andy. "You're a unique man."

"I was taught by the best even if he didn't know it at the time." Andy dug a quarter out of his pocket and flicked it over the backs of his fingers. A power move or a distraction? "I was raised by a single mother. She was a hell of a con artist, but there were a few short years she dated a guy she'd met at the gentlemen's club she worked at." The ghostly smile was back. "His name was James Hancock, and he told her a lot about another world."

James Hancock. Why was that familiar?

The connection dawned on him like a brilliant sunrise. Jameson Haddock had fallen decades ago. And Andy was, what, fifty-ish? He'd managed to worm his way into Jameson's inner circle and fucking take it over. He'd known everything since he was a kid. A genius psychopath who had learned about their world, and it had made him more dangerous than any of them.

Numen might be safe now, but the human world had never been in more danger. With the empire Jameson had started, Andy could continue—with the aid of all Daemon. They wouldn't touch him. They needed him to continue recruiting human hosts. And the more humans they possessed, the more power they had. Jameson had made the snowball and started it rolling, even if it had been for a different reason. Andy was going to grow it and bury Earth in an avalanche of nightmare proportions.

A human. A being whose neck would snap so easily if he weren't still in cat lady's arthritic body. If he weren't wearing orthotics, standing here would be excruciating.

This assignment had just gotten a whole lot more interesting. "Sierra, you say?"

Andy's eyes glittered. He liked the idea of Sandeen going after this female. Why?

"She's the half sister of one of her warrior teammates, only that one doesn't know it."

The only two females were the one called Harlowe and the other. Dianna? Dana?

But Harlowe, he remembered. Tall, blond Harlowe. If Sierra looked anything like her half sister, this might not be so bad. He did have use for a fallen, after all.

"All right." He yawned for effect. He'd find Sierra. Then he'd use her skills to get ahead of Andy and kill him. "Tell me where to start."

ne month later...

JAGGER STEPPED INTO HIS HOUSE. He hoped he never got tired of the pleasure that rippled through him each time he crossed the threshold.

Instead of furnishings that lacked identity and comfort, he was surrounded by bursts of color. Pictures of Felicia's students dotted the walls. She didn't teach at the gym anymore, or anywhere on Earth, but she'd visited one last time to check on her pupils. Claudia had lost the haunted look and was a radiant, normal kid.

He also enjoyed coming home to find Felicia in her shorts and either a sports bra or a tight T-shirt, or a combo of both. Since he had no clue how much longer he'd get to come home to her, he soaked up what he could.

Making his way into the kitchen, he smiled at the view. Felicia—with her wings out.

"Getting better?" He went behind her and pressed a kiss to her neck, careful not to hang on to her wings.

She smiled and leaned back against him. "Yes. I even took a walk. Some kids stared, one asked a ton of questions, but surprisingly his mom didn't rush him off."

"As long as you didn't seem like you minded, she didn't mind?"

"Right. And I think word's gotten out." She turned around and took a drink of her strawberry protein shake. "I haven't even taken any meds today."

"Nice." She offered him a sip, but he shook his head. "Mother had breakfast."

"Did she hug you or give you a fist bump?"

He chuckled. "We half hugged." They'd kept the momentum of their initial hug going, however awkward. Mother had taken to straightening his collar and patting his shoulders before giving him a peck on each cheek. It was nice. "If I'd known Mateo was going to be there, we could've made it a double-date breakfast."

Mateo was good for his mom. And Jagger was becoming accustomed to the male's presence. He couldn't talk his mother's beau into joining the warrior ranks, but Mateo had gotten a promotion as a trainer for the senate guards.

"I had a meeting with Senator Nassim," she said. "I start training next week."

"The realm's newest senator." Right after they'd fully synced, he'd broached the idea of keeping his place here and then they'd get a place in the human realm wherever she wanted. And she'd said that would work—if she wasn't accepted as a senator. The senate vote approving her application had gone through last week. "You're going to do great."

She snorted. "The Stede thing really spooked them. Otherwise I wouldn't be allowed through the doors."

"They would've come around." More in the senate than just Persephone's mom were ready for a change.

"Oh, and Senator Nassim said no hard feelings about Persephone. She thinks you would've been a fine addition to the family, but she hopes Persephone finds someone who won't let her get away with being"—Felicia lifted her wings instead of shrugging—"well, being Persephone."

He stroked her wings and massaged the muscles around her joints. "I found someone who didn't let me get away with being Jagger."

She groaned and sank back into him. "No, I didn't let you get away with being Julian. *Jagger* is hot as hell."

"Hey now." He nipped at her neck.

"Julian was pretty fine too. But he was a dick." She spun in his arms and smiled. "What are you planning that might get me all pissy?"

"Oh, yeah." He had to adjust himself. An occurrence whenever he touched his mate. Taking the shake from her hand, he led her outside and into the middle of his expansive lawn. "Put your arms around my neck."

Her lips formed a troubled line. "What?" But she did as he asked.

"Hang on," he said as he spread his wings out behind him and launched into the air.

She let out a yelp and tightened her hold. "Jagger—what the hell are you—" Her gaze caught on the ground growing smaller under them. "I forgot how beautiful it was."

"Wrap your legs around me."

When she did, he tucked her into his side so she had a better view.

It was the middle of the day, but the sky wasn't full of commuting angels. He snuck a peek at her. Her eyelids fluttered, a look he often saw when he stroked through her wet flesh.

"The wind in my feathers." She pinned him with her bright gaze. "It feels so good. Doesn't hurt at all."

Her back muscles had gotten stronger, no longer putting strain on her scar tissue. It was why he'd waited so long to try this. "I was afraid you'd… I know you can't fly anymore, but I hoped you'd enjoy flying with me." Her wings would never be able to hold her body weight, but he wanted her to experience what she could.

She exhaled and looked down at the manicured lawns and square buildings passing beneath them. "I'll always miss being able to fly myself, but I'd rather spend life finding out what I can still do instead of running from what I can't. My wings can be out all the time now. I can fly with you. I can be a senator and help our people move forward instead of being in a stasis that does us no good. And I can be mated happily ever after."

He held her close and continued their flight. A couple soared past and waved at them, their gazes only lingering on Felicia's wings for a second.

To think he'd been afraid that Felicia would cost him everything he'd worked so hard to maintain. But she'd given him more than he'd ever had before. A mate. A new family. A real relationship with his mother. And in a way, his father. "You and me. Living and fighting happily ever after."

———————

DID you catch Bryant and Odessa's story in the first book Angel Fire?

ARE you a fan of paranormal romance and can't wait for

Demon Fire to come out? Check out my very first paranormal romance available for FREE on all retailers, Fever Claim.

THANK you so much for reading. I'd love to know what you thought. Please consider leaving a review of Angel Fire.

FOR NEW RELEASE UPDATES, chapter sneak peeks, and exclusive quarterly short stories, sign up for Marie's newsletter and receive a download link for three short stories of characters from the series.

ABOUT THE AUTHOR

Marie Johnston lives in the upper-Midwest with her husband, four kids, and an old cat. Deciding to trade in her lab coat for a laptop, she's writing down all the tales she's been making up in her head for years. An avid reader of paranormal romance, these are the stories hanging out and waiting to be told between the demands of work, home, and the endless chauffeuring that comes with children.